## PRAISE FOR THE AUTHOR

'Robert Newton tackles big themes – overcoming loss,
being comfortable in your own skin and not judging others based
on their appearance – with humour and a light touch …'
*Books and Publishing*

'Newton's writing teems with bright, engaging dialogue,
a compelling historical setting and fully developed characters …'
*Publisher's Weekly (US)*

'*Mr Romanov's Garden* is not only striking for its
unexpected tangents, layered, sensory writing and contrasting
images and colours, but also for its tender portrayal of the
transformation of Lexie and her young friends.'
*The Australian*

'Finding yourself, finding your path, not pre-judging people,
multicultural and multi-generational friendship, resilience:
all themes in this novel. This book feels important from
the moment you start reading.'
*Magpies*

# PROMISE ME HAPPY

Robert Newton works as a full-time firefighter with the Metropolitan Fire Brigade. His first novel, *My Name is Will Thompson*, was published in 2001. His acclaimed and much-loved novels include *Runner, The Black Dog Gang, Mr Romanov's Garden in the Sky* and *When We Were Two*, which won the 2012 Prime Minister's Literary Award for Young Adult Fiction. He lives on the Mornington Peninsula with his wife and three daughters.

# PROMISE ME HAPPY

## ROBERT NEWTON

PENGUIN BOOKS

UK | USA | Canada | Ireland | Australia
India | New Zealand | South Africa | China

Penguin Books is part of the Penguin Random House group of companies
whose addresses can be found at global.penguinrandomhouse.com.

Penguin
Random House
Australia

First published by Penguin Books, an imprint of Penguin Random House Australia Pty Ltd,
2019

Design and cover artwork by Marina Messiha © Penguin Random House Australia Pty Ltd
Printed and bound in Australia by Griffin Press, part of Ovato, an accredited ISO AS/NZS
14001 Environmental Management Systems printer.

 A catalogue record for this
book is available from the
National Library of Australia

ISBN: 978 0 1437 9644 2 (paperback)

Penguin Random House Australia uses papers that are natural and recyclable products,
made from wood grown in sustainable forests. The logging and manufacture processes are
expected to conform to the environmental regulations of the country of origin.

penguin.com.au

FOR ALANNAH, MOLLY, POPPY AND TESS — MY OWN KIND OF HAPPY.

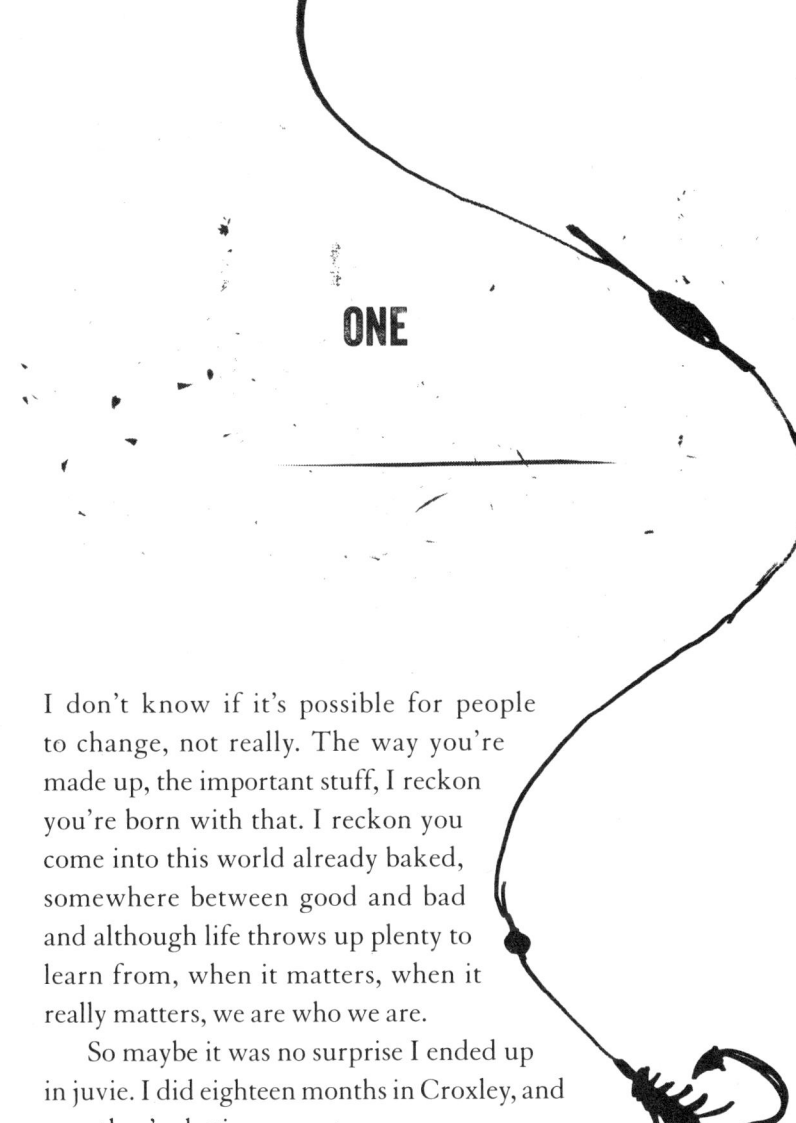

# ONE

I don't know if it's possible for people to change, not really. The way you're made up, the important stuff, I reckon you're born with that. I reckon you come into this world already baked, somewhere between good and bad and although life throws up plenty to learn from, when it matters, when it really matters, we are who we are.

So maybe it was no surprise I ended up in juvie. I did eighteen months in Croxley, and now they're letting me out.

I've already said my goodbyes, the important ones anyway. Now all that's left is this interview, this waste-of-time chit-chat session with some ponytailed

1

counsellor they've just hired. It's his first placement after graduating, and he's got that misguided enthusiastic look about him.

When he calls my name, I haul myself up from my chair and walk through the door on my right. I close it behind me and head towards the square table in the centre of the room. He doesn't acknowledge me at first. He waits until I'm almost there, then he gets to his feet and throws me a smile.

'Hello, Nate,' he says. 'Can I call you, Nate?'

I shrug my shoulders and consider his outstretched hand and the tangle of plaited leather bands around his wrist. It's been a long time since I had the need to touch another human being and all of a sudden the idea of shaking hands with someone I've only just met seems kind of ridiculous. I decline the offer and see something register in his face.

'My name's Marcus,' he says, withdrawing his hand awkwardly. 'Why don't you take a seat, Nate, and we can get started?'

The plastic chairs are set for a chat, uncomfortably close, so I drag mine back a little, then nudge it sideways with my knee. Once it's at the opposite end of the table, I push it forward, then sit. Marcus does the same at the other end. He drops his gangly frame into the chair and smiles. Again.

'I suppose the first thing I should say is congratulations,' he says.

Counsellors hate it when you don't engage. As he starts to bang on, I keep my mouth shut and give him the silent treatment whenever there's a pause I'm expected to fill. Basically, I'm not interested. I'm not interested in anything he has to say. He catches on after a bit, and decides to read aloud some of the things I need to keep in mind when I'm paroled. No alcohol. No drugs . . .

I don't even know what he's saying after a bit. His words roll into each other and lose their beginnings and their ends. His voice becomes a meaningless drone and starts up a duet with the humming air conditioner on the wall nearby. I tune out and start to pick at the plastic trim around the edge of the table in front of me.

I don't have much luck at first. I scratch at rough bits and try to tear them free. Most of them break under my nail, but then I find one, a chunk of plastic that peels sideways and keeps going like a strip on one of those tri-coloured sour straps I used to buy when I was a kid.

'So, how are you feeling, Nate?' he asks.

The question catches me off guard. It makes me look up, and just for a moment I find his eyes.

'Feeling?' I say.

'Yeah,' he says, 'about getting out?'

'Orright, I guess.'

'Just orright?'

Marcus raises a finger and taps my file on the table in front of him.

'You're seventeen,' he says. 'You're well known to police and you've got an eighteen-month term already under your belt . . . You've been busy, Nate.'

He pauses for a moment and lets the silence do its thing, but even in the quiet, something seems to pass between us. It's nothing you can hear or anything. It's a gentle prodding, a back-and-forth, chess-vibe kind of thing.

I turn my head and see a buzzing blowfly to my left,

butting its head against the window pane, over and over again. Marcus looks as well and the two of us watch it slam into the glass.

'You'd think it'd work it out after a bit,' I say.

But Marcus doesn't get it. 'Come on, Nate,' he says. 'Let's talk, hey? Let's talk . . . about him.'

Chess-wise, it's a big mistake. He's moved too early, exposed his King.

'Talk about who?' I ask.

'Your dad, Nate.'

I shoot some air from my nose and half snort. 'You already know what he was like,' I say.

'I know a little,' says Marcus, 'but why don't you tell me? He was violent, yeah?'

'Yeah,' I say. 'He was violent. But it's not happening.'

'What's not happening?'

'I'm not talking about him.'

'Why not?'

'Because I've been through this a hundred times before,' I say. 'I'm about to get out of here and I'm not talking about my father.'

Marcus takes a moment, lets a few seconds grind by.

'Don't you think talking can help?' he asks.

He's getting on my nerves now so I focus on the little tuft of hair below his bottom lip. He's a vegan for sure.

'Look, it's all in there,' I say, pointing to the file. 'The last bozo was into highlighting. He marked the good bits in fluoro green.'

Marcus dips his eyes to the file, then looks up.

'There are lots of good bits in here, Nate,' he says. 'Drugs, alcohol and a list of priors as long as my arm. But let's go with the reason you're in here, hey? The break and enter and the aggravated assault. Nasty business that. Something you'd like to take back, I bet?'

If there's one thing you get a lot of in juvie, it's time. You can tell the boys who've been in Croxley a while. They learn how to slow things down and make the little things last. They learn how to walk slow, talk slow, even clean their teeth slow. But no matter how long you've been in, slow doesn't work at night. When the screws lock the cell doors, when they shut down the lights and they trip off down the corridor, a ghostly black creeps into the cells and swallows everything up. You get to thinking then, about all sorts of stuff. There's nothing else to do.

So, yeah. I wish I could take it back.

'He wasn't supposed to be there,' I say.

'But he was there,' says Marcus. 'The poor old bloke came back while you were robbing the place and you put him in the hospital.'

Marcus sits back in his chair and makes a clicking noise with his tongue. He fixes his eyes on me and tilts his head like I'm a puzzle he's trying to solve.

'I'll tell you what's interesting though, Nate. No one seems to think you're the violent type.'

I stare back at him. 'So, what type am I, then?'

'Not sure yet,' says Marcus. 'You've been pretty well-behaved here in Croxley. A few punch-ons, self-defence mostly, but nothing you've instigated, nothing . . . malicious.'

He holds his gaze, and I feel his eyes on my face.

'So why, Nate?' he says. 'Why did you put an old man in hospital?'

I look down at the strip of black missing from the edge of the table in front of me.

'Nate?'

'I never meant to hurt him,' I say.

I reach a hand out and pick at the plastic trim again. 'It's not something I'm proud of.'

Marcus picks up the pen, tucks it behind an ear and flicks through the pages in the file.

'According to the police statement, there were three intruders that night. Not just you, like you claimed.'

I breathe in and let out a giant sigh.

'Do you think your friends would have done the same for you?' asks Marcus. 'Do you think they would have lied? You got an extra six months for that, you know?'

I shrug.

'I'd like to help, Nate,' he says. 'I'm not the enemy.'

'So, you're my friend, are you?' I ask.

'I could be. Why not?'

'You've got a ponytail.'

Marcus isn't sure what to say about that. He plucks the pen from behind his ear and finds a space on the page in front of him.

'Doesn't . . . like . . . ponytails,' he says, as he writes. 'I'll highlight that later, by the way, in fluoro green.'

He's really starting to annoy me now so I sit up straight in my chair. 'Listen, Marcus . . . can I call you Marcus?

'Sure.'

'I know you think you might be onto something, right? You think you're about to unlock something all the other counsellors failed to see. But the truth is, Marcus, you don't know shit. Neither did the last bloke or the lady before him.'

'I see.'

'No, you don't see, not yet, but you will. Do you want me to tell you how it'll go?'

Marcus sighs. 'Knock yourself out, Nate.'

'Okay, so you'll do this for a bit, you'll have your little sessions with your table and chairs. You'll ask your stupid questions and the boys out there, they're going to answer. And they'll tell you their stories, their sad little stories one after the other. Oh, it'll be great at first. You'll think you're special. You'll think you're actually making a difference when no one else could. But then slowly things'll begin to change. The days'll become weeks and weeks'll become months and before you know it all those sad little stories, they start to sound the same. And one day that smile on your face will turn into a sneer, and you'll decide that life's too short to be banging your head against a brick wall so you'll pack it all in and take up mowing lawns.'

Marcus cocks his head. 'Wow. That's mighty insightful of you, Nate.'

I raise myself up from my chair and as I get to my feet I hear a familiar voice booming in the hallway outside the door. It's the only voice that scares me in Croxley. I catch Marcus's eye and throw him a smile.

'Something funny?' he asks.

'Not funny,' I say.

'Really? Why are you smiling, then?'

I crane my head to the door.

'You've got Jackson next,' I say.

# TWO

I don't know what I was expecting. I suppose part of me hoped my father had
changed. Every now and then, when
it got closer and I let myself think
about getting out, I imagined it like
a movie. I imagined walking through
Croxley's huge metal gates, standing
on the footpath outside as the cars and
trucks darted left and right along the
busy road in front of me. Then, just as I'm
about to give up and look for a bus, there'd be
a break in the traffic and that's when I'd see him,
my father, leaning against his battered Toyota,
smoking a cigarette.

But he's not coming. He never was.

Turns out someone else has come instead.

I make my way down to admin with Marcus, and there's a man standing at the desk filling in forms. He's mid-forties, wiry and weathered, like he's someone accustomed to working outdoors. He's dressed casually in a pair of jeans, a t-shirt and thongs, and he's calling himself Uncle Mick.

From a distance he seems agitated, even annoyed. It's probably got something to do with the last time I saw him.

When I walk towards him, he glances briefly my way then dips his head and continues writing. Soon enough he drops the pen, straightens up and stands in front of me, staring. He searches for something in my face, then his blue eyes stop moving and just for a moment they lock on mine. It feels like a test so I hold his gaze. I've been in Croxley too long to look away.

Despite his stroppy attitude and cold exterior, I see something familiar in his eyes. It's something I used to see in my mum's eyes. There's hurt beneath the blue. A whole lot of hurt.

'You got any gear?' he asks.

Sanjay, one of the better screws, throws me a wink from behind the admin desk.

'Here you go, Nate,' he says.

I walk over and he slides a large zip-lock plastic bag across the counter. Inside are my belongings and clothes, the ones I came in wearing eighteen months ago. I touch the cover of *The Old Man and the Sea*. It was in my bag when I came in – the only thing of my mum's I have. I toss it with my mobile into the backpack, and after signing some more forms I head for a cubicle to change out of my green overalls and white runners.

It feels weird when I step back out in my old clothes. I even smell weird. The nylon pants feel coarse against my thighs and the pale-blue shirt clings to my torso and arms.

I've grown.

The clothes seem so foreign now, the colours so bright and out of place. I'm suddenly all out of whack. It was easy, being green. For eighteen months I was green – green like everyone else – but now . . . I don't feel right. It's like I'm someone else.

Marcus wants a word. He's stepped away from the desk and is standing against the wall holding what looks like a canvas shopping bag.

Walking feels strange too. My feet no longer fit the mould I'd left in my boots, and their soles make a squeaking noise as I walk across the polished lino floor.

'A show bag?' I say.

'Apparently it's a new thing,' says Marcus, handing it over. 'A bit like me, I suppose. They call it a Parole Pack. A few brochures, contact numbers, that sort of thing.'

I don't even look at what's inside. I'm focused on something else. I nod my head and turn and stare at the man who's come to collect me. I know he's my uncle, but he doesn't feel like one.

Marcus glances over his shoulder and follows my eyes.

'Uncle Mick, hey?' he says.

I nod. 'My mum's brother,' I say. 'I was only little when I first met him. Some family thing, I reckon it was. Might have been Christmas. I remember red-and-green party hats and swimming in a river.'

Uncle Mick heads over to the water cooler and pours

himself a drink. The plastic cup looks tiny in his hand.

'Mum never talked about him, though. Like, *never* talked about him – her own brother. Then out of the blue he turns up at her funeral wearing a suit. And he fucking smiles – smiles right at me when I was walking out. I guess I lost my shit.'

Marcus shifts a little my way. 'Well, it's better than a group home, Nate, and you did sign the consent forms.'

'Yeah, yeah, I know. It's just . . . weird.'

Uncle Mick pours another cup and downs it quickly. He tosses the empty cup into the bin then turns my way.

'Righto, then,' he says. 'You good to go?'

I nod and stand there, not sure what to do. Marcus puts his hand out and this time I shake it.

'It was nice to meet you, Nate,' he says. 'You know, I reckon we might have got on, you and me.'

I look at Marcus, at the tuft of hair below his bottom lip and half smile. 'I doubt it,' I say.

Jangles, one of the newer screws appears behind us, jangling a nest of keys. He stands next to Marcus, who gives him a nod, then he heads off down a corridor with me and Uncle Mick trailing behind. After a few more corridors and doors, Jangles turns a key in a lock and we walk outside.

When I step out from under the awning, I angle my face to the afternoon sun and feel it warm against my skin. Accustomed to the outside world, the others are a lot faster than me. I walk slowly, following the concrete path, bordered by yellow lines, until there's nowhere left to go. When I catch up, Jangles brushes a plastic card against a small black box and the last metal gate clicks open. Uncle Mick goes first. He walks through the giant frame and, as

I follow him, Jangles mumbles something I don't catch.

Getting out is nothing like I imagined. I thought everything would be over when I walked through the last of the gates. I thought there'd be this moment, a lightning bolt of freedom and release. But it doesn't feel over at all. Croxley was hard, harder than I ever imagined it would be. There were times when I wasn't sure if I'd be able to see it through, but at the same time it's been home for eighteen months. Eighteen long months. I'm not saying I'll miss it, not one bit, but I suppose in a way it's a part of me now. Maybe forever.

Uncle Mick's ride is a battered F100, one of those American-style gas guzzlers with the big tray at the back and a bench seat across the front that fits three. The tray is filled with fishing gear – nets and baskets and buoys. I toss my backpack in there too, open the passenger-side door and climb in.

Uncle Mick dons a pair of cheap sunglasses and starts the engine. It rumbles to life.

The cabin's a mess. As we move off into the traffic, I make a space for my feet amongst the pile of junk that's been tossed there. I scan the empty junk-food wrappers that litter the dash.

'You on a health kick?' I say.

It's like he doesn't hear me. He keeps his eyes on the road and as we take a left turn I spot something beneath the wrappers, something grey and hard. I reach forward and pick it up.

Uncle Mick glances sideways. 'Do you know what that is?' he asks.

I turn it over in my hand. 'A scallop?' I say.

'It's an oyster shell.'

For some reason I lift it to my nose and sniff.

'You don't remember?' he says.

'Should I?'

'Maybe not. You were young.'

Everything outside seems to be moving so fast. Through the window, I see a blur of colours and shapes. I try to hold on to one thing at a time, to a building, a car and a tree, but nothing seems to stay still for long enough. I shift my eyes back to the cabin and try to take stock of where I am, of who I'm with.

I'm not sure how to feel about the man sitting next to me. Maybe if we had a history, I'd know. Maybe if the two of us had done some uncle-and-nephew stuff, if we'd actually shared something memorable and meaningful, I'd be able to slot back in and pick up where we left off. But there's nothing familiar about this man, nothing except his eyes and the hurt beneath the blue.

'So, what do I call you, then?' I ask.

'Mick'll do,' he says.

I feel like a chore, and it makes me wonder why he even bothered to pick me up.

'You don't like me much, do you?' I say.

'I don't even know you, son,' he says. 'And what I know, I read in a file.'

'So, why did you bother coming?' I ask.

'It wasn't my idea.'

I'm not sure what he means so I turn my head slightly his way.

'Me and you,' he says, 'this custody thing . . . it was your mother's idea.'

I get the feeling there's going to be more so I sit there and wait.

'It was a few years ago,' continues Mick, 'around the time she took out the restraining order against your old man. She wrote me a letter, just in case.'

He doesn't need to explain the 'just in case' part. I know what he means. He means my father and all the shitty stuff that comes with him.

'Hadn't heard from her in years,' says Mick. 'Then this letter turns up, just like that.'

I can't remember a time when my mum and I didn't live in fear of my father. Of course, there were moments that were bearable. There were times here and there when things seemed as if they might get better. Maybe it was the hope that kept my mum there, kept her hanging on and coming back. But my father was an unpredictable man, and that was the thing that scared me the most. He was blue skies and storm clouds, a man of opposites who never made sense.

I haul myself back from the past, from my father and a long-ago slanging match in our kitchen. Mick's staring at the road.

'As far as I'm concerned there are no excuses for the things you've done,' he says. 'And, to be honest, I'm not asking you to give me any. But there's something we need to get straight, right from the start. You get one chance with me, and one chance only. You stuff up again – you're on your own.'

I was expecting an ultimatum early, a laying down of the law. I've got no comeback for that so I swallow it down and we rumble along the highway in silence. I don't mind not talking. Before Croxley, I wouldn't have been able to just sit there in silence after a spray, but I've learnt a thing or two about when to talk and when not to talk, and now it doesn't worry me at all.

We drive for about ten minutes and neither of us says a word. We hardly even move. On a straight stretch of highway, a few kilometres further on, Mick reaches up and flips the sun visor down. There's a solitary CD in the plastic sleeve. He plucks it out and pushes it gently into the stereo. I'm expecting something heavy, AC/DC maybe.

I'm wrong. It's cheesy disco and high-pitched voices, the type of stuff they play in supermarkets and elevators.

'You've got to be kidding.' The tone in my voice is a little harsher than I expected.

'What?' he says.

'The Bee Gees?' I ask.

'What's wrong with the Bee Gees?' says Mick.

'Nothing, if you're sixty years old. You got a seniors card as well?'

Mick whips his sunglasses off and looks at me hard. 'You know, you might want to show some bloody gratitude,' he says. 'In case you haven't realised, looking after you wasn't something I had factored into my life plan.'

'Obviously.'

'And what's that supposed to mean?'

'It means you're seventeen years too late, that's what it means. And anyway, I never asked you to look after me in the first place.'

'Well, you're stuck with me for now, but you can get out and walk if you like.'

'Okay, I will.'

Without a word, Mick veers left and brings the pick-up

to a stop by the side of the road. I reach for my seatbelt, unclick the buckle and open my door.

'It's not hard to find,' says Mick. 'This is the Mitchell Highway. Keep walking until you get to the Glamorgan River sign. You can't miss it. Once you're there, you turn right and head for the General Store.'

'How far is it?' I ask.

'Two hundred k's,' says Mick.

'Two hundred kilometres?'

'Give or take.'

I've been played. I'm sideways in my seat with my feet resting on the running board. I'd love to get out of the pick-up. I'd love to grab my backpack and hitchhike back to the city, but my parole comes with conditions and unfortunately my uncle is one of them. I turn around so that I'm straight in my seat, and the song fades out on the stereo.

Mick's voice sounds different when he speaks again. 'His name was Morry.'

I glance sideways, and he's staring at nothing through the front window.

'What?' I say.

'The old man you robbed,' says Mick, 'the old man you put in the hospital. His name was Morry.'

I've had a long time to think about what I did. I've gone back to that night, to the darkened house in Cullen Street, more times than I can remember. I've tried to make sense of it all. I've tried to work out what happened and why. But I never could.

And now I'm back there again.

'His wife died two years ago,' he says. 'A few months

before you lot broke in as a matter of fact. Been married sixty-two years, they had. Morry's got dementia. And he's pretty much on his own now, so he spends most of his time pottering around in his shed and making wooden toys.'

I raise my head up and snatch a look at Mick. I know exactly what he's doing. He's grabbing the moral high ground, getting in early and letting me know where he stands.

'You've done some research,' I say.

'Yep.'

'Why?'

'Because he's not just a police report,' he says. 'He's a person. He has a name. And that's something you might want to remember.'

I feel Mick's eyes on me, but I can't bring myself to look at him.

# THREE

After about forty minutes of driving, the
world outside the car starts to feel bigger.
We've left the city behind and we're
heading north, following the signs
towards the Glamorgan River.

The driving seems easy now. It's
mostly two wide lanes on either side,
cut through rolling sandstone hills. As
we go further, the buildings are replaced
by trees, by a lush expanse of green. I grind
the window down and breathe in. The air
smells earthy and fresh and strangely familiar.

Neither of us says much for the next leg of
the trip, I'm too busy taking in the surroundings
and watching things change. We drive downhill for a

while and leave the sandstone hills and the double high-way behind. The road tapers into single lanes and I start to see buildings again but they're buildings of a different kind. Peeling weatherboards and dodgy fibro shacks hide amongst the foliage as if they're embarrassed about the way they look. Every now and then I pick up a glimpse of water through the trees.

Soon enough, Mick slows the pick-up and steers left at a turn off. We drive for a few minutes, then pull up out the front of a lonely cream-coloured weatherboard shop. The sign says *Molly's Pies and Cakes*. Mick leaves the engine running and sits back in his seat. He doesn't look at me when he talks.

'Coffee?'

'Yeah,' I say. 'Thanks.'

It's strange not knowing where I am. When Mick disappears into the shop, I look out through the open window into the leafy green hush.

It's so different to where I grew up. The concrete apartment blocks in Surrey Heights were always noisy and buzzing with life. There was always someone around and something going on. Kids hung around and chatted after school. They sat on fences and leaned against walls. In the evenings when everyone came home from work, they'd turn their music up loud. Twanging sitars competed with doofing drum beats. People chatted and laughed and sang.

And then later, after I left Surrey Heights, after my mum died, when I headed for the city and slept rough in laneways and under bridges, there was always something to see, something to hear, something to smell.

I suppose I got used to that – all those years of something.

A few minutes later, Mick walks through the shop door with two medium-sized coffees. Without making it look obvious, I watch him as he ambles over, balancing something on one of the cups. He isn't built like my mum. He's fuller, bigger-boned with tanned skin and medium-length, sun-bleached hair. His face is set in a way that suggests he doesn't smile all that much.

He catches me looking as he approaches.

'Where are we?' I say. 'Shitsville?'

But Mick doesn't bother answering. He passes my coffee through the window, and when he gets back into the pick-up, he empties two sugars into his cup and stirs it with a plastic spoon. He replaces the lid and has a healthy sip, then he drops his cup into a drink holder in the console between us and drives off.

'Didn't you get me any sugar?' I say.

Mick glances briefly my way. 'You didn't say you wanted sugar.'

'You didn't ask. A normal person would have just grabbed a few extras, just in case.'

'A normal person?'

'Yeah.'

'Why didn't you just say you wanted sugar in the first place?'

'Because I thought you'd get some.'

'I'm not a mind reader. If you wanted sugar, you should have specified that before I went in. You should have said, "Mick, can you grab me some sugar because I like to have sugar in my coffee?"'

'Well, most people grab a few extras when they don't know someone. That's all I'm saying.'

'Don't drink it, then.'

Mick reaches for the dash. He turns the stereo up, and the two of us settle in for the rest of the drive.

There's not much to see through the window, but looking at something other than a brick wall is a lot more satisfying than I thought it would be. I start to appreciate the things around me, things I once took for granted, like the road itself. I think about the people who carved out the earth and laid the bitumen, the people who painted the white lines down the middle of the road. I think about how tyres are made. I look at the oyster shell and wonder who the first person was to eat an oyster and say it was good. All of a sudden those things seem to be important and I wonder why I never thought about them before.

The Glamorgan River sign appears just as I start to cramp up. Mick turns left and takes a few bends. Ten minutes later he slows the pick-up. He indicates left then steers us into a gravel parking lot opposite a row of shops. The biggest shop, a double-fronted building with big windows, catches my eye. I look up and read the words painted across the shop's awning – *Chester's General Store, Oyster Bay*.

'Pit stop,' says Mick.

I climb out of the pick-up, and when I'm steady on my feet, I arch my back and stretch. It's a strange feeling to be out in the open without the fences and gates, without the yellow lines to tell me where to walk. They said it'd be like this. They said that eighteen months of learned habits would be hard to unlearn.

Mick's made a beeline for the store, but instead of following directly after him I walk in a zig-zag pattern just for the hell of it, just because I can. When I get to the store, there's an old bloke sitting in a chair to the left of the door. He's wearing a pair of old footy shorts, a blue singlet and a green cap with *Jimmy's Bait and Tackle* written in gold letters across its front. I hear him talking to Mick as I approach.

'Snapper are on, they reckon,' says the old bloke. 'Coming in to feed. One of Hendo's boys landed a five kilo off Wisemans.'

'Bank or boat?' asks Mick.

'Boat,' says the old bloke.

'What bait?'

'They're not saying.'

It's like they're speaking another language.

Mick nods his head and the old bloke turns his attention to me.

'This the troublemaker you were telling me about?' he says. 'Katie's boy?'

It's been a long time since I heard anyone speak my mum's name, and an even longer time since I heard anyone call her Katie. Something explodes inside me and I see her in my head wearing a pretty red dress. I try to cling to that, to the red dress and her beautiful brown hair, but that rainy day comes rushing back – the phone call, the hospital and the cold of her hand when I touched her for the very last time.

'That's him,' says Mick, his gruff voice pulling me back. 'Singlets, this is Nate. Nate, Singlets.'

And just like that, Mick leaves me stranded. He heads into the store and I look at Singlets, not sure what to say. My mum never talked much about her teenage years in

Oyster Bay so I've got nothing to go on. Whenever I asked her to tell me stories, she was always guarded. She gave me snippets and bits and pieces. She told me stuff about swimming and jumping off a jetty, and she told me how beautiful the river was. But she never said anything about the people.

'So, you knew my mum?' I ask.

'A long time ago,' says Singlets. 'When she was a girl.'

He looks out across the gravel, as if there's something out there actually worth looking at.

'She was different,' he says.

'What do you mean, different?' I ask.

'A real dreamer, she was.'

Singlets smiles, then raises a hand up and points to something behind me. 'You see that lamp post over there?'

I turn my head and follow his finger to a single wooden pole that's seen better days.

'What do you reckon?' he says. 'Got to be, what, twenty metres of clear space around it?'

'Yeah,' I say. 'I s'pose so.'

'Well, one day, I was sitting right here, and I see this young girl, your mum, walking along, singing a song. She must have been nine or ten, I reckon. Like always, she's got her head in the clouds, daydreaming about something or another. Anyway, she's walking along, like I said, singing her song and blow me down if she doesn't walk straight into that pole.'

I'm not sure what to make of Singlets' story. I'm not even sure why he's telling me, but I try to picture the scene in front of me. I stare at the pole for a bit then turn back to Singlets in his chair.

'Are you a dreamer, Nate?' he asks.

'Nah,' I say. 'Not really.'

'Can you cook?' he says.

I don't know what's weirder, the question itself or the fact that I have to think about the answer.

'Ah, no,' I say. 'I can't.'

'Then you'd better learn,' says Singlets. 'Fast.'

I've got no idea what he's talking about, and I don't stay to find out.

I say goodbye then push through the plastic fly strips and walk through the door of Chester's General Store. It's cold inside. There's an ancient air-conditioner vibrating against the side wall, its white vanes sweeping slowly left and right.

When my eyes adjust from the glare outside, I see a girl unloading packets of bait into a waist-high ice chest. She turns around when she hears me, and it's like someone's knocked the wind out of me.

She's all wrong for Oyster Bay, but there's something about her that says she doesn't care. And there's something about her not caring that makes her interesting straight off. I snatch subtle glimpses without making it look creepy. But she's onto me.

'Are you right?' she says.

I drop my eyes down to my shoes then look back up. 'Who? Me?'

'Yeah you,' she says, glancing over her shoulder. 'What, your mum never tell you it's rude to stare?'

She looks me up and down for a bit then goes back to work. But I can't get enough of her.

She's roughly my age, I reckon, with smooth olive skin,

and although I'm a newcomer to wherever the hell we are, she seems beautifully out of place. She's wearing a dark-green knee-length tartan skirt and a black leather jacket with red Doc Marten boots. Her hair is black and buzzed short, except for a wisp of purple that hangs down the left side of her face.

Thankfully, Mick's busy gathering supplies so I've still got some time to think of something interesting to say.

I shuffle off to the magazine rack in my itchy nylon pants, grab a magazine and pretend to flick through it.

After off-loading the last of the bait, the girl returns to the counter a few metres from where I'm standing. She ditches the box, and Mick calls out from the fridge down the back.

'Where are those chicken thingies, Gem?'

'Where they always are, Mick,' she replies. 'They're next to the mince. Dig around a bit. Don't make me come down there.'

She rolls her eyes and slides a knife blade along the tape line on a new box of bait.

I can't drag my eyes from her face.

'I take it you're the nephew, then?' she says.

'Yeah,' I say. 'I suppose I am.'

It's been a while since I spoke properly with a girl. Before Croxley I had a thing with Amy Medcalf, but I knew all along she wouldn't be there when I got out. We were company, mostly – warmth. She was someone to lie next to, someone to talk to at night.

I'm not usually shy or anything, but this girl in front of me is different. I'm not really sure what to say, so I stare at the small oven behind her filled with pies and sausage rolls.

'So, you got a name?' she asks.

'It's Nate.'

It's not what you'd call a stare exactly. She looks at me just long enough to make me feel uncomfortable, then she nods her head to Mick at the back of the store.

'You want some advice?' she says.

I shrug my shoulders. 'Sure,' I say.

'Your expectations,' she says. 'I'm not sure where they're at exactly, but now might be a good time to lower them. Like, *really* lower them.'

I sneak a quick look over my shoulder. 'That bad, huh?'

'Yep, that bad. Of course, he does have . . .'

Her voice trails off as Mick makes his way back to the front of the shop. He's carrying some chicken fillets, a loaf of bread and a couple of bags of bait.

'I think that's everything,' he says, dumping them onto the counter.

The girl looks up at me again.

'And the *Woman's Day*?' she asks.

I look down at the magazine in my hands and feel my cheeks burn. 'Ah, no . . . not today, thanks.'

It only takes a minute to ring things up. When it's all done and paid for, Mick and I take a bag each. I follow him and stop for a moment at the door. I turn around but the girl has gone.

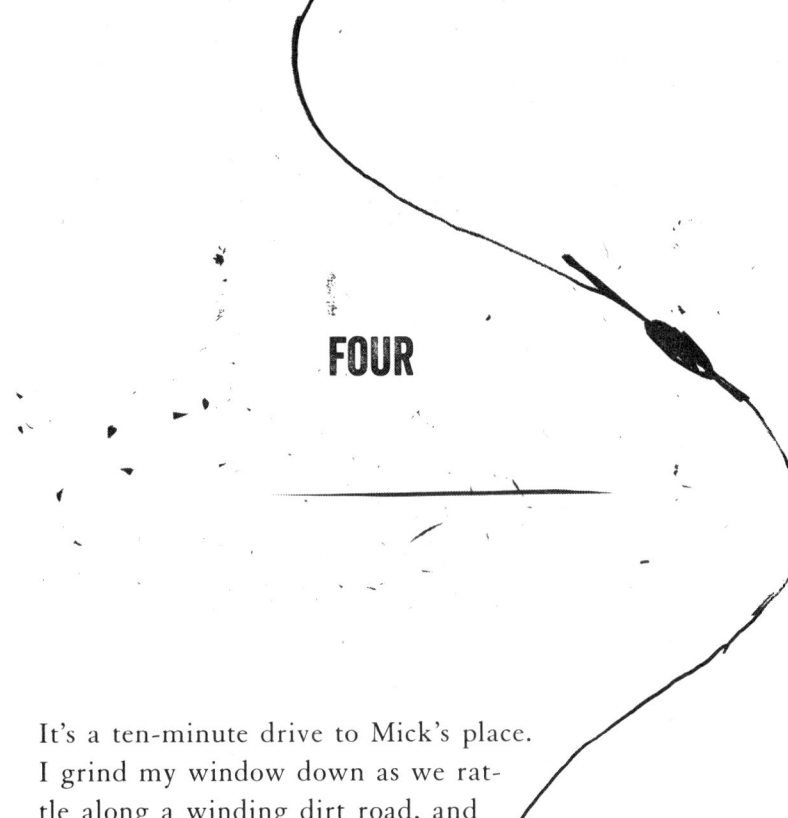

# FOUR

It's a ten-minute drive to Mick's place.
I grind my window down as we rat-
tle along a winding dirt road, and
although I can't actually see the water
I know it's there beyond the trees.
I can feel it. I can feel its shifting presence, and I can taste the muddy cool
of it in my mouth. I take a deep breath
and fill my lungs with it.

All of a sudden Mick pulls down on
the steering wheel and we head left down a
smaller dirt road.

The pick-up seems too big for the new road.
I hold on to the dash as we crash through branches
and bounce over potholes and ruts. It's rough going

for a few minutes, but soon enough I spot an opening up ahead.

Mick keeps the pick-up straight and when we burst into a clearing I see a mass of water stretched out in front of me. I'm not sure where to focus at first. I start at the wooden jetty and run my eyes across the sparkling water to the bank on the other side.

I don't even notice the wooden shack to our right. I only become aware of it when I see movement in the purple bougainvillea that runs the length of its verandah. An ugly white dog with a black patch around one eye leaps through the foliage. It barrels towards us, all head and chest.

'What the hell is that?' I say.

'That's Barry,' says Mick.

'Barry?'

'After Barry Gibb,' explains Mick. 'The only surviving Bee Gee.'

I don't need to look at Mick to know he's serious.

'It's a dog, right?' I say.

Mick doesn't answer. After stopping the pick-up, he opens his door and leaps out. Barry jumps up and starts snorting with excitement.

I'm a little nervous getting out myself so I crack open the passenger-side door and ease myself quietly down. Unfortunately Barry hears me close the door. He pricks his ears then charges around the pick-up. He sniffs my leg for a bit, then gazes up at me with that face. It looks as if he's got a thing for running into brick walls.

'You know what they say about owners and their dogs,' I say.

Strangely enough, Mick seems pleased with that. He looks proudly at Barry and smiles.

'What's with his eyes?' I say. 'Are they always like that?'

'Like what?' asks Mick.

'They're all red. Is he sick, or something?'

'No,' says Mick. 'He's a bull terrier. The white ones tend to have red eyes.'

'Right.'

Barry looks like an alien. Reluctantly, I reach my hand down and let him sniff my fingers.

'They used to breed 'em for bull fights in Europe,' says Mick, making his way over to my side of the pick-up. 'They've got jaws like a vice. Once they lock onto something, they don't let go.'

I'm tempted to pull back after the history lesson, but Barry starts to lick my fingers and his tongue feels rough, like sandpaper against my skin.

'That's odd,' says Mick.

I glance up.

'What do you mean?'

'He likes you.'

'You seem surprised.'

'I am. Barry's an excellent judge of character, as it happens. Never known him to get someone wrong. Still, there's always a first time.'

I head for the rear of the pick-up and grab my backpack and a shopping bag from the tray. I follow Mick towards the house, but I can't take my eyes off the water, off the two fibro buildings and the white boat tied to the jetty.

It's spooky. In Croxley, when it was cold and things got too much, I'd put my head down to sleep and I'd imagine myself lying on a jetty in the sun, my back all sticky with salt. I'd peer down between the wooden boards and listen to the *slish-slosh* sound the water made against the pylons. Lying in my cell in the dark, I'd wait patiently for the gentle puffs of wind that shot up through the gaps in the wood and brushed against my face. I'd see schools of tiny fish, darting left and right in formation and speckled toadfish cruising through reedy river plants.

I'd imagined it over and over, but it never once occurred to me that those things were memories. It never occurred to me that the place I'd dreamt about was real.

I hear Mick's voice. I must have stopped walking.

'Come on,' he says. 'Dump your stuff inside. You can go for a wander while I start on dinner.'

After seeing the run-down exterior, I'm surprised when I step inside the house. It's small and basic and simply furnished, but at the same time there's an easy kind of warmth to it.

I walk to the fridge to put the chicken away. On the door is a purple card sprinkled with silver glitter. It's trapped under a large pineapple fridge magnet and says, *LET'S GET READY TO RHUMBA*. Next to it is a strip of three photos, like the ones that come out of those novelty photo booths they used to have at shopping centres. It's Mick and a woman with dark hair. They're hamming it up with zany wigs and big plastic glasses. They look like they're at a party and they're happy, ridiculously happy.

I take a step back. It never said anything about family on the custody forms I signed at Croxley. The idea that Mick might have a wife or partner, even kids, never actually crossed my mind.

It doesn't matter, anyway. They're clearly not here now and I'm not ready to ask so I off-load the shopping bag and dump my backpack onto the couch. After a quick toilet stop, I take off my shoes and socks, then push through the flywire door with Barry at my heels.

He takes the lead and I follow him down the gently sloping path towards the river.

The grass tickles my toes and when we get to the jetty Barry walks me through some things of interest as if it's his job to show me around. A pile of oyster shells is his first stop. He trots over to the silver-coloured shells, then cocks his leg and sprays. He gives me a few moments then stares up at me with those eyes. For some reason, I feel compelled to respond.

'I'm good thanks, Barry. I pissed inside.'

He moves to the boathouse next and barges in through the half-open door. Everything inside has seen better days.

At the rear of the boathouse, against the patchy wall to the left, is an old white-framed bed with a worn-out mattress and pillow. Up in the ceiling, the cobwebbed rafters store a canoe, a dinged-up paddle board and paddles. Life vests, fishing rods and other gear hangs from metal hooks on the wall opposite the bed.

Barry's looking at me again.

'It needs a good clean, Barry,' I say.

Next stop on the tour is a shed-type building, a workshop about three times bigger than the boathouse. Barry trots over and stands patiently in front of the double doors. I head over, slide one open, and when I peer inside I can hardly believe my eyes. In the middle of the shed, propped up on a series of padded supports is a work in progress, a half-done wooden boat hull.

Long sections of golden-coloured wood, just under a metre wide, curve over a frame and run from one end to the other like the rib cage of some magnificent beast.

I've never seen anything like it. I take a few steps forward and let my eyes adjust to the dappled light inside. I reach a hand out and press it against the grainy wood, and when I run my palm slowly along its length the hull feels alive, feels as if it's breathing and pulsing with life.

I look down at Barry and I swear to God . . . he smiles. As if talking to a dog isn't bad enough, I actually smile back. It's only a half-smile, mind you.

When my eyes leave Barry's face, I notice there are wood shavings on the floor. There are hundreds of them, maybe thousands – thousands of golden-brown ringlets scattered beneath the hull. I don't know where it comes from, but all of a sudden I feel this strange urge to step on them. I can't help it so I start walking towards a table on the other side of the room and the ringlets crunch under my bare feet like leaves in a park.

The table is covered with jars of nails and screws and littered with various woodworking tools. Some of them I've never seen before but there are standard tools amongst them, ones I remember from school – screwdrivers, hammers, planes, chisels and sanders.

A coil of butcher's paper sits off to the side so I find its end and unroll it. Drawn in lead pencil is a rough sketch of what I'm guessing is the boat behind me. The plans seem basic enough. In fact, a lot of the measurements have been crossed out and there are question marks attached to some of the comments below them.

Barry seems keen to keep moving so I let go of the paper and it springs back to the way I found it.

I follow him and he trots his way onto the jetty towards the fishing boat tied up at the landing. It's an impressive-looking thing. Towards the front, under a faded canvas canopy are two bucket seats covered in white-and-blue leather – they look like they belong in a sports car.

Except for a few storage containers and bench seats, the stern of the boat is all deck. I assume the wide-open space is designed for fishing, for the hauling in of baskets and nets. On the side of the boat, painted in a cursive black, are two words: *Forever One*.

I'm keen to walk out further along the jetty, but a whistling noise pricks Barry's ears and he swings his head towards the house. He whines to tell me it's time to go back.

I gaze out across the river one last time and take it all in. I know it sounds funny but after eighteen months of bars and walls and routines I feel hopelessly lost in the real world. When I was in Croxley, I would have given anything to get out, but now that I am, without the walls, without people telling me what to do . . . I don't know what to do.

I shiver. The temperature has dropped and the dying sun casts a crimson haze through the trees.

A small fish breaks through the water, then another and another and they skitter across the glassy surface about twenty metres out. A black-and-white bird launches itself from a gum tree on the opposite bank. It works its wings and gets some height, then tucks itself up and dive bombs the unsuspecting school of fish.

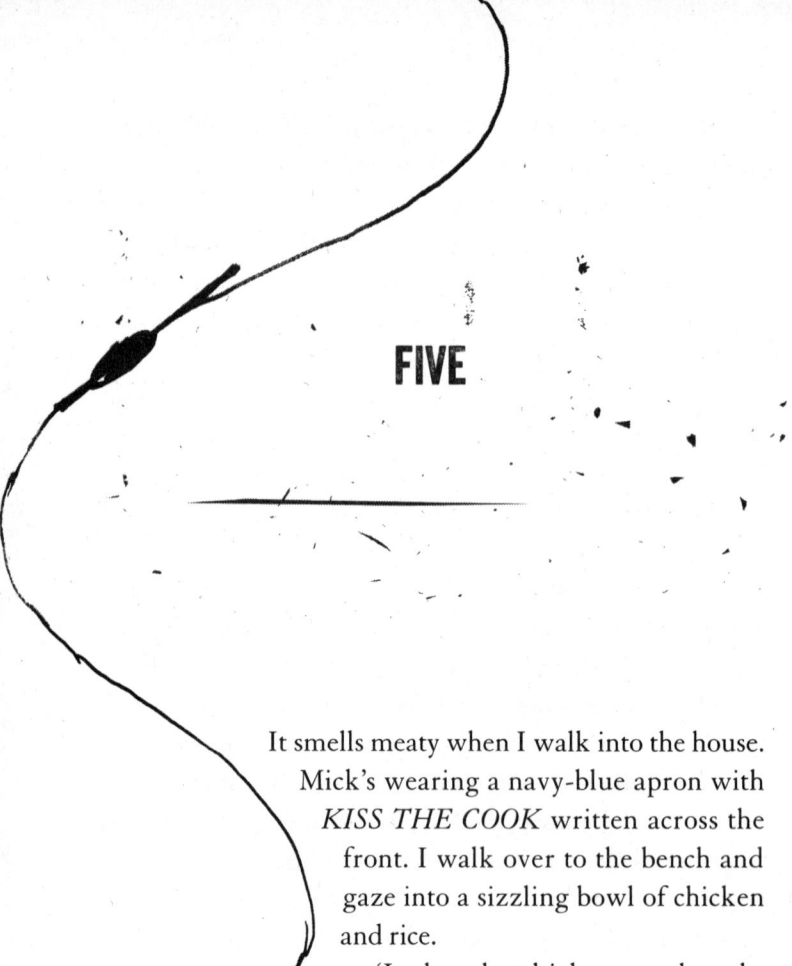

# FIVE

It smells meaty when I walk into the house. Mick's wearing a navy-blue apron with *KISS THE COOK* written across the front. I walk over to the bench and gaze into a sizzling bowl of chicken and rice.

'Is that the chicken you bought from the store?' I say.

'Yep,' says Mick. 'Thighs are best, I reckon. Tastier.'

'So, you can cook.' I pick up a fork. 'Yum.'

'Hold your horses,' he says. 'The chicken's for Barry. This is us over here.'

Mick nods at the microwave and, as if on cue, a tiny bell sounds. He opens the door and pulls out a black tray, one of those pre-made dinners in a plastic container divided into sections. I can't believe it. My first meal out and, although it's a much smaller, throw-away version, the plastic container looks just like the meal plates we had in Croxley.

Mick grabs it with his fingertips and places it beside another one on the bench.

'Let's see, now,' he says. 'We've got Steak Diane or Lamb Korma. You choose.'

'You're kidding,' I say.

Mick's a little confused. His eyes shoot up at me then settle back on the dinners. 'What?'

'I just got out of juvie,' I say.

'And?'

'I'm not eating that.'

'They're gourmet.'

'They are not. They're garbage.'

'Well, don't eat it then. Go hungry for all I care.'

'Why can't I have the chicken and rice?'

'Because it's not for you.'

I glance down at Barry. He's sitting by the fridge, eyeballing me.

'If you must know, Barry's got allergies,' says Mick.

'Are you serious?' I say.

'Yeah, I am. Don't worry, though. You won't go hungry. Check this out.'

Mick cracks a victorious smile, reaches a hand out and opens the freezer door. Inside, the entire space is packed tight with frozen dinners.

'Five bucks each at Chester's,' he says. 'I bought the lot.'

I stare at the frozen dinners and their neatly labelled

edges. I'm starting to realise what the girl at the store meant about expectations.

'So what'll it be?' says Mick.

I look down at the choices and sigh. 'I think I'll go the steak.'

A rectangular, open-framed servery separates the kitchen and the living room. Mick leads the way to a small dining table and I notice there's a place already set in front of one of the three chairs.

'Are you expecting someone else?' I ask.

Mick shakes his head.

I look around the room. On the mantelpiece above the fireplace are three large pieces of black metal. They're letters – two 'Ms' with an '&' symbol between them.

'What's with the letters?' I ask.

Mick looks at the mantelpiece, stares at the two black letters, and I see something different in his eyes.

'Mick and Malaya,' he says.

'Who's Malaya?' I ask.

'No one,' says Mick.

I've opened something I shouldn't have, found a soft spot in Mick's armour, but I decide that now's not the time to get into it. I sit down at the table instead and shift the focus to something else.

'So what's with the boat in the shed?' I ask.

Mick's miles away. 'What?' he asks.

'The boat,' I repeat. 'In the shed?'

'It's nothing,' he says. 'I've always wanted to build one, so I started a few years ago when we found out . . .'

I wait for him to finish what he's going to say, but it doesn't come.

'When you found out what?' I say.

'Nothin'. The boat's off limits, anyway. I don't want you in there, all right?'

'Okay.'

I stab my fork through the congealed gravy and hear Barry guzzling his specially prepared dinner on the verandah. I start on a piece of steak and it's like chewing rubber. Mick's watching so I roll my eyes and manage to get a few words out. 'Gourmet, you reckon?'

We eat in silence for a bit, and I think about our scrappy conversation over the last few minutes. It's not what Mick's said that's got me thinking, it's what he didn't say, it's the secrets and the questions he's left unanswered. I spike a few soggy carrots and he starts up again.

'You'll be needing some clothes,' he says. 'I've left a few bits and pieces on the bed in there. Stuff I got from the op shop at the church. Took a punt on your size.'

I hadn't really given much thought to what I'd need when I got out. All the basics were taken care of in Croxley. You got what you were given, and that went for the company as well. Boys would come and boys would go, and each new day would be slightly different from the one before.

'So, how does this work, then?' I say.

Mick swallows a mouthful of Korma.

'How does what work?'

'This,' I say. 'You and me. Us. Everything.'

'Well, we take it a day at a time, I s'pose. Work it out as we go along. That's if you hang around, of course.'

I'm not sure why I didn't notice it when I first arrived or if it was even there, but when I turn my head slightly

I see a photo of two teenagers on the side table. The girl's hair is wet. She's wearing a bikini and she's sitting on the jetty, smiling, with her arm around the boy. Their blue eyes are happy. It takes a moment to sink in but, when it does, I'm shocked. It's my mum and Mick.

I'm not ready to see her like that, here, in this place, so I look away. I look down at my food but I can feel her pulling me back, like she's wanting me to look. I raise my head up and my eyes find her freckled face and lock onto it. I try to smile back. I try to miss her and remember what was good, but that familiar ache is there, the one that comes with knowing she's gone, the one that comes with knowing I'll never see her again. It's anger and guilt, a whole lot of stuff rolled into one, and I feel the ache rise up in my throat. I place my knife and fork down and push my plastic tray forward.

'I'm not feeling good,' I say.

Mick leans forward a little and eyes my food suspiciously.

'Is it okay if I sleep in the boathouse?' I ask.

Mick looks up. He seems surprised.

'What?' I say.

'Nothing,' he says. 'It's just . . . you reminded me of your mum, just then.'

'My mum?'

'When she was little, I mean. She was always asking if she could sleep in the boathouse. Can I, can I, can I? God, she used to drive everyone mad. Even when Dad said no, she'd sneak out her bedroom window and we'd –'

'Don't,' I say.

Mick looks up. 'Don't what?' he says.

'Don't talk about her like you knew her.'

'I did know her.'

I'm surprised at how quickly the anger comes back. I force myself to look at him, at the stranger in front of me, and I think about my mum, about everything she endured.

'Really?' I say. 'What night did she have book club, then?'

Mick looks at me blankly.

'No? Okay, what was her best friend's name?'

'Nate, come on.'

'No, no . . . How many shifts a week did she do at the hospital, Mick? What was her favourite drink? Where did she hide our leftover money? Where did she take me when he got pissed and started lashing out? You didn't fucking know her. You didn't know anything about her. And you didn't know me either. It's easy to call yourself an uncle, but calling yourself an uncle doesn't make you one.'

Mick's not smiling anymore. His eyes shift away to something behind me.

'You'll need some blankets,' he says. 'There's some in the cupboard, just there. I think there's a torch as well. And mozzie spray.'

I'm not sure I can do this with Mick. I grew up not knowing anything about him. Had I bumped into him on the street, I wouldn't have even known who he was. Seeing him in the photo with Mum, seeing them together, has changed things, made things real. And I'm not sure what to make of that.

I get slowly to my feet and push the chair back in under the table. I stand there for a moment and try to think of something to say. But there's nothing to say. Not tonight, anyway.

I grab my backpack and the bag of clothes and head down the gentle slope towards the river again. Barry comes with me and seems excited by the change in his evening routine. I don't need the torch on my walk down. The moon is full and its milky light is enough to guide me to the boathouse.

When I get there, I open up the double doors. I push them out as wide as they'll go, then step inside and set things up. It only takes a few minutes. I lie down on the bed and when I rest my head against the musty pillow, Barry comes over and wants to know what's going on.

'Goodnight, Barry,' I say. 'You can go now.'

But Barry doesn't go. He trots over to the double doors, then drops himself down and gazes out into the night. I look out too. I look up at the sky and all I can see are stars, millions of glittering stars. I've never seen so many. I lie there, quiet and still, and I start to hear noises in the night. I hear the rustle of leaves and the kissing sound the boat makes with its gentle bobbing in the water.

I reach for my backpack and pull out my mum's copy of *The Old Man and the Sea*. I don't know why I chose to keep the book and nothing else. I don't even know if Mum liked it, but it was in her handbag the day of the accident, the day she died. Knowing she was reading it made it special.

I open the book and see her name written on the first page. I sink my head into the pillow, rest the book on my chest and look out at the stars again.

I pick one out, a bright and twinkling star on its own, away from the others. I take a deep breath and taste the cool of the river in my mouth. I fill my lungs with it again and

I wonder if my mum lay on this very bed and did the same thing. I let myself think of her and for a moment it's the two of us, together, like it was before.

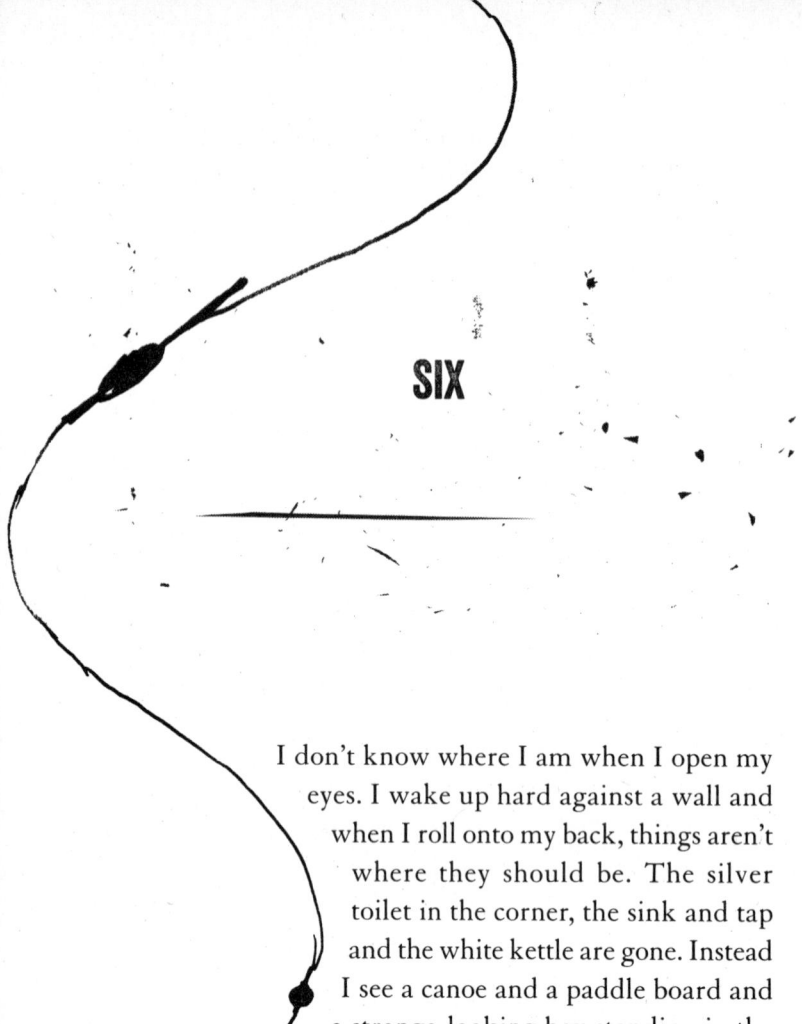

# SIX

I don't know where I am when I open my
eyes. I wake up hard against a wall and
when I roll onto my back, things aren't
where they should be. The silver
toilet in the corner, the sink and tap
and the white kettle are gone. Instead
I see a canoe and a paddle board and
a strange-looking boy standing in the
doorway with a dog by his side.
'What the fuck?'
When I sit up, the boy takes a step back.
'You sweared,' he says.
He's a scruffy-looking kid, about eight years
old, with fair skin, crazy hair and darting eyes. My
senses are dull, still foggy with sleep, so I wipe my eyes

and see he's holding something in his right hand.

'Have you been going through my shit?' I say.

'You sweared again,' says the boy.

'Yeah, and I'll keep swearing too. That's my book.'

'It was on the ground,' says the boy. 'I was only looking.'

'Yeah, well don't. It's my stuff. It's private.'

At least I'm wearing boxer shorts. After slinging the blankets off, I haul myself up, walk over to the boy and snatch my mum's book from his hand. I toss it back onto the bed and start rifling through the bag of clothes. There's not a lot to choose from so I decide on a pair of faded denim jeans and a black Billabong t-shirt. I'm not sure surfing gear is my thing but, for an older bloke, Mick's done surprisingly well at the church store and it feels good to be out of my old clothes. There's even a twenty-dollar note in an envelope that has my name on it.

'What's it about?' says the boy.

I turn around. He's standing with Barry on the wooden deck outside. The two of them look like old friends.

'What's what about?' I ask.

'The book,' he says.

'It's not about anything,' I say.

'It must be about something.'

'Well, it's not.'

It feels strange not to be doing what I normally do. Normally I'd be off to the shower block first thing. I'd be off with my toiletries bag and a towel, with all the other boys from the even-numbered cells. I look up at the kid standing in the doorway.

'Listen, I've just woken up,' I say. 'Who are you, anyway?'

'Is it about fishing?' asks the boy.

'What?'

'The book,' he says. 'There's a man on the front in a boat. And there's a fish.'

I glance down at the book on the bed beside me.

'Okay, yes,' I say. 'It's about fishing. Well, kind of.'

And just like that the boy's interest in the book seems to vanish. There's a moment of nothing in his eyes, a kind of blankness, but when I get up and walk past him, the movement seems to spur him to life.

He follows me towards the jetty with Barry at his heels. When we reach the landing, he pipes up again.

'You're Nate,' he says.

I stop and turn around.

'How do you know that?' I ask.

'Mick said.'

'Oh, he did, did he?'

'Yeah. He said your mum died. He said your mum died and you got sad.'

'What else did he say?'

'He said you did some bad things and they sent you away.'

'Oh yeah?'

'And he said your dad's a mean, angry, drunk piece of shit.'

I glance at the house, then look back at the kid.

'You sweared,' I say.

The boy looks into the sun, screws up his face and smiles.

'Yeah.'

'What's your name?' I say.

'I'm Henry.'

'Well, Henry. It was nice to meet you. Now bugger off. I've got things to do.'

But Henry just shrugs. He turns around and lies on his stomach on the landing, with his head over the edge. Barry snorts then shoves past me. He lies down beside Henry and the two of them gaze into the sun-kissed water, like it's something they've done a hundred times before.

I met a lot of boys in Croxley, but this one is odd. Really odd.

After splashing some water onto my face, I leave them to it. I head back to the boathouse and find a pair of white Converse in the bag, along with a pair of grubby, pre-loved sport socks.

As I walk up past the house, Mick's sitting on the verandah, nursing a cuppa.

He calls out as I go by. 'Morning!'

I wave and walk on quickly, hoping no one decides to join me. The only sounds I can hear are the birds in the trees, but all that changes when I get to the turn-off where the gravel road widens. Soon I hear another sound, a motor chugging away somewhere in the distance. Surrounded by trees and scrub, I'm not sure where the noise is coming from at first, but as I walk further along the gravel road it gets louder and louder. I glance over my shoulder again and see Henry on one of those four-wheeler motorbikes, the ones with knobbly tyres that you see people hooning around on in the bush. I turn back and keep walking for a bit until he rumbles up beside me.

'Where are you going?' he says.

'To the shops,' I say. 'Not that it's any of your business.'

'Can I come?'

'No, you can't. Haven't you got somewhere else to go?'

Henry shakes his head. 'Do you want a lift, Nate?'

'No, thanks,' I say.

'You sure?'

'Yes, I'm sure. What are you doing riding a motorbike anyway? Aren't you like eight years old?'

'Mick taught me,' he says. 'I'm not allowed to go all the way, but. Only to the end of the dirt bit.'

I start walking again. After eighteen months without privacy or space, without any real thing I could call my own, I'm desperate for some peace and quiet. Unfortunately, Henry has other ideas. He motors along beside me, smiling every now and then for no good reason at all. Fifty metres down the road and his presence starts to grate. I stop walking and pull up beside a tree.

'Look, Henry . . . I'm serious. Haven't you got something else to do?'

Henry looks to his right as if the answer might be hiding somewhere in the trees.

'Nuh.'

'Well, there must be something,' I say.

'There's not. I like it at Mick's place.'

'What about your friends?'

'I haven't got any friends.'

'No friends? A bloke who rides a quad bike? You must have some friends.'

Henry shakes his head.

There was always someone trying to prove something in Croxley. In fact, most of the time, it was impossible to work out who was telling the truth. After all the game playing and lies it's hard not to like Henry's honesty.

'All right, then,' I say. 'I'll get on. But no talking. It's driving me mental. I don't want to talk, okay?'

'Okay, Nate.'

After hopping up into the passenger seat, I get comfortable, and the two of us rumble along at a slow and steady speed. I sink into the seat and close my eyes and listen to the sounds of the bush. In a tree nearby, a bird makes a high-pitched squawking noise.

'That's a lorikeet.'

I open my eyes and look at Henry. 'What?'

'That bird,' he says. 'It's a rainbow lorikeet.'

'I thought I said no talking.'

Another bird makes a strange whipping noise.

'That one's a whipbird,' says Henry. 'I can do 'em, you know?'

'Do what?'

'The birds,' says Henry. 'I can do the sounds. Go on, say one. Say one, and I'll do it.'

I look around, hoping for inspiration. I can't see any birds so I go with the one I saw by the river yesterday evening.

'What are those black-and-white birds?' I say. 'The ones that dive into the river after the fish?'

'That's a cormorant,' says Henry.

'Okay,' I say. 'Do one of them.'

Henry makes a tuneful gargling sort of noise in his throat. It sounds remarkably authentic.

'How did you learn that?' I ask.

'I just listen,' says Henry. 'I listen to the sounds and do 'em. Sometimes they do 'em back. The birds, I mean. I've got a pet snake at home. He doesn't make any noise, but.'

We motor along for a few more minutes until we get to the end of the dirt road. Once we're there, Henry parks the quad bike in a clearing off to the right. He kills the engine then walks over to a row of four letterboxes. He lifts the lid on the third in line, number eight, then places the keys inside.

The shops aren't far from the start of the bitumen road so I begin walking, and Henry follows me.

'Where did you go?' he says.

I glance sideways at Henry, strolling along beside me, his oversized thongs slapping at his heels.

'What do you mean?' I say.

'When they sent you away,' says Henry. 'Where did you go?'

I think about making something up, but Henry's honesty seems to have rubbed off.

'I went to prison,' I say. 'A prison for kids. For teenagers.'

''Cause you were bad?'

'Yeah.'

'Mick said you got it from your dad. Being bad, I mean. He said it's in your blood.'

It doesn't feel right to hear Henry say that. But it's not like I haven't thought it myself.

Genetics and blood – that whole family thing was something I thought a lot about in Croxley. I thought about my mother's good and my father's bad and what it might mean for me. I'd never really considered it before – the possibility that I was like my father. I never really thought I had much of him in me, but when my mum died and the guilt set in, everything changed. I began to feel the bad pulsing inside me, running through my veins, the kind of bad that made me angry with the world, made me do things I never thought I'd do.

After Mum died, I couldn't handle being in the same room with my old man, couldn't stand the sight of him. I didn't have to pretend anymore so I began to spend less time at the flat. I stopped going to school. I stopped seeing my friends and hooked up with some people I met in the city one night. I started drinking and popping pills. I did whatever was going, and for a while those things made a difference and numbed everything I was feeling. But down the track they only made things worse. Whatever good was inside me seemed to vanish too. And the worst part was I didn't care. I didn't care about anything. Or anyone.

Henry's voice jolts me back.

'You don't seem bad, Nate,' he says.

'Well, I was,' I tell him. 'I was really bad.'

---

Soon enough a strip of six shops appears in front of us. The first shop on the corner is a takeaway place called Maria's, offering pizza, pasta, and fish and chips. There's a woman out the front with a white t-shirt and greasy hair. She's sitting in a chair studying the form guide with a cigarette trapped between her lips. She circles something with a red pen as we walk past.

When we get to the newsagent, I see a small group of people further up the footpath outside Chester's General Store. It's a loose circle of three boys and two girls, and they're laughing and backslapping and messing around. From a distance, I'd say they're all about my age.

Henry's gazing nervously at them. 'I'll wait here.'

'What's wrong?' I ask.

'Nothin'.'

'You sure?'

'It's too loud,' says Henry. 'I'll wait over here, near the seat.'

'Suit yourself. How about I get you something, then? What would you like? A chocolate bar? Chips?'

'A surprise, please,' says Henry.

I'm not really in the mood for games, but I play along all the same.

'I don't know you well enough to get you a surprise, Henry. You need to give me a hint. What kind of surprise?'

Henry looks confused. 'A Kinder Surprise.'

'Oh, you mean those chocolate eggs? You like them, do you?'

'I like the things inside them. I collect them.'

Henry turns away and heads over to the wooden bench while I walk up the footpath towards Chester's. They pretend not to notice me, but as I approach the group milling about on the footpath, I can feel their gaze poring over me. I can feel the boys weighing me up, marking their boxes with a tick or a cross. The same thing happened when I walked into Croxley. I was someone less, someone not to be trusted, just because I was new. It's weird how people do that. They do it everywhere. Instead of looking for the good, they look for the worst in a person straight off — a reason to keep them out.

I walk slowly past the circle and make a point of

nodding at the biggest bloke, before continuing on and into the store. People don't know what to do with a blank face and steely eyes, even if it's a bluff. I learnt that in Croxley.

There's no one behind the counter when I go in. The store seems unattended, and a little sadder than it was yesterday. I look around at the tacky Christmas decorations that should have come down weeks ago, the sun-faded tinsel in the window and the wonky plastic tree behind the door.

I'm about to call out, when I hear voices somewhere near the dairy section at the back of the shop. I head down an aisle towards the fridge and see the girl with the wisp of purple hair. She's wearing purple tartan today and she looks tense. There's a blond guy standing beside her, just a little too close.

I size him up and decide we're not that much different in height and weight. He's wearing board shorts and a loose-fitting singlet. He glances over his shoulder when he hears me and dismisses me with a look. I'm not sure the girl's all that happy to see me either. I try to remember her name – I think Mick called her Gem.

'So, what do you reckon?' the boy says to her.

'No, thanks,' says Gem.

'Why not? It'd be fun.' The boy cocks his head and blows air from his mouth. 'You like fun, don't you? I know you like fun.'

'Go home, Marty.'

Gem checks some items on the shelves in front of her then ticks a checklist in her hand.

Marty laughs. 'What? Do you like girls now?'

Something about the way Gem glances back at me

doesn't feel fair. It's one of those 'you're all the same' kind of looks.

'That's it,' says Marty. 'It all makes sense now – the clothes and the hair . . . why you don't want to –'

Gem puts a hand up to stop him.

'Don't flatter yourself, Marty. I'm not into girls. The reason I don't want to go out with you again is because there's nothing about you I find remotely interesting.'

I laugh. It's more of a snort, really.

Marty swings his head my way. 'Who the fuck are you?'

'I'm Nate,' I say. 'And it sounds to me like you've just been told.'

Marty's done with Gem. He's embarrassed now so he shifts his focus to me.

'You're that prick from the city,' he says. 'The tough guy, yeah?'

Marty runs his eyes over me, then takes a half step forward. A full step would have been different. A full step would have told me he was serious.

'This has got nothing to do with you,' he says.

I raise my hands innocently in front of me. 'I'm just getting some milk.'

I step past Marty and grab two litres of full cream from the fridge, then I close the door and turn to Gem.

'You got any of those sour strap things?' I say.

'I think we're out,' says Gem. 'I'll have a look in a minute.'

Marty's had enough of being ignored. As Gem walks off, he takes another half step forward.

I smile to make it clear I'm not impressed by the lack of

commitment in his footwork.

He musters some courage and leans in a little. 'Keep out of my way,' he says.

'Don't worry,' I reply. 'I'm not planning on staying long.'

When I pass Gem, she looks at me like she wants me gone. I totally get that. I mean, we barely know each other and the first time I met her I was hardly what you'd call impressive. Now that we're face-to-face, I've gone all stupid again. I nod my head, smile a stupid smile, and walk to the chocolate section to grab a Kinder Surprise.

On my way back I take two choc muffins from a cake rack. By the time I get to the counter, Marty's gone and it's as if nothing's happened. Gem's busy with some paperwork, chewing on the end of a pen. She doesn't even look at me. She raises her head a little, just enough to see my things on the counter.

'Do you want a bag?' she asks.

'Yeah,' I say. 'A bag would be good.'

After ringing everything up, she places my stuff into a plastic bag and pushes it forward across the counter.

'Are you okay?' I ask.

But Gem doesn't answer. She underlines something on the invoice in front of her, walks around the counter and heads for the back of the store.

# SEVEN

As we walk up the driveway, I hear banging noises and music coming from the workshop near the jetty. Henry quickens his pace and when he reaches the house, Barry launches himself off the verandah as if he's been waiting for Henry's return. The two of them race off towards the workshop.

I walk slowly, take off my shoes and socks at the boathouse and then continue on. When I get to the workshop I see Mick inside wearing a t-shirt, board shorts and thongs. He's bent over the boat, a face mask pushed up onto his forehead and safety goggles hanging around his neck. Henry's beside him wearing what looks like a

Viking helmet – a brown plastic headpiece with two ivory horns sticking out from the sides. For some reason, I'm not surprised.

'Morning,' I say.

Mick straightens up and half smiles, but it's not enough to hide the disappointment in his face. It's as if he's just woken from a deep and contented sleep and seeing me is a sudden reminder that his life has taken a wrong turn. I feel like that chore again, the unwanted nephew forced upon him by a sister he hardly knew.

'Sleep all right?' he asks.

I move into the workshop so I'm not straining to hear. Mick's covered in wood dust.

'Like a baby,' I say.

I stand there for a bit, feeling useless, then I hear some familiar words in the music that grab my attention.

I look over to the speaker sitting on a table. 'Is that the Bee Gees again?'

Mick looks up for a moment then returns to the boat. 'It's Malaya's favourite song,' he says.

'So that's why you play the Bee Gees all the time,' I say. 'It's because of Malaya. You said she was no one. Who is she?'

Mick takes a deep breath and closes his eyes.

'Come on,' I say. 'You'll have to tell me sooner or later.'

'She's my wife,' he says.

For some reason I look around the workshop as if she might be hiding somewhere. 'You've got a wife?'

'Yeah.'

'Well, where is she?' I say.

'Broome,' says Henry, straightening his Viking helmet.

'Malaya went to Broome.'

'Broome? Isn't that in Western Australia?'

Mick puts the goggles back on. 'Last time I checked, yeah.'

'Has she gone on a holiday, or something?'

Mick doesn't answer. He stretches his arm out and feels for something on the underside of the boat.

'Okay, so when is she coming back?' I ask.

'Soon,' says Mick.

'Soon? What does that mean?'

'It means I'm not sure.'

'Not sure?'

'Yeah, as in uncertain. Don't know.'

'But you must know when she's coming back. How long's she been away?'

'Eleven months,' says Mick. 'Eleven months and fifteen days to be exact. It's just a break. Some time away. She'll be back.'

All of a sudden, things start to fall into place – the Bee Gees, the table setting, the two metal Ms on the mantelpiece and the name on the fishing boat, *Forever One*.

I stand there and look at Mick fussing over something. I watch him go to the table, grab a wooden mallet and hand it to Henry who kneels midway along the boat. He only takes a few steps but the movement is enough to stir things up. It whips up particles of wood dust and they dance about in the shaft of morning light spilling in through the window.

I go back to Croxley, to the day I first met Mick, and I realise now what's responsible for the hurt I saw in his eyes. It's a broken heart.

Before Henry can get to work on the boat, a bell starts

to ring somewhere in the distance. It's a clanging sound like one of those hand-held bells they used to ring at school to signal the start of classes. Henry turns his head to the sound, lifts the Viking hat from his head and places it on a shelf at the back of the workshop.

He heads for the door and, just before he disappears outside, Mick calls out after him. 'Bye, Gunter,' he says.

I stare at the open doors, but I give it away after a few seconds when I realise there's no point trying to make sense of what just happened. When it comes to Henry, things are what they are, and I'm starting to think that it's best to roll with it.

But it's awkward when he goes. It makes me wonder what Mick and I would have without him – if we'd have anything in common at all. I stand there for a bit, not sure what to do.

'Righto, then,' says Mick.

He picks up the mallet and starts banging, so I turn and walk away.

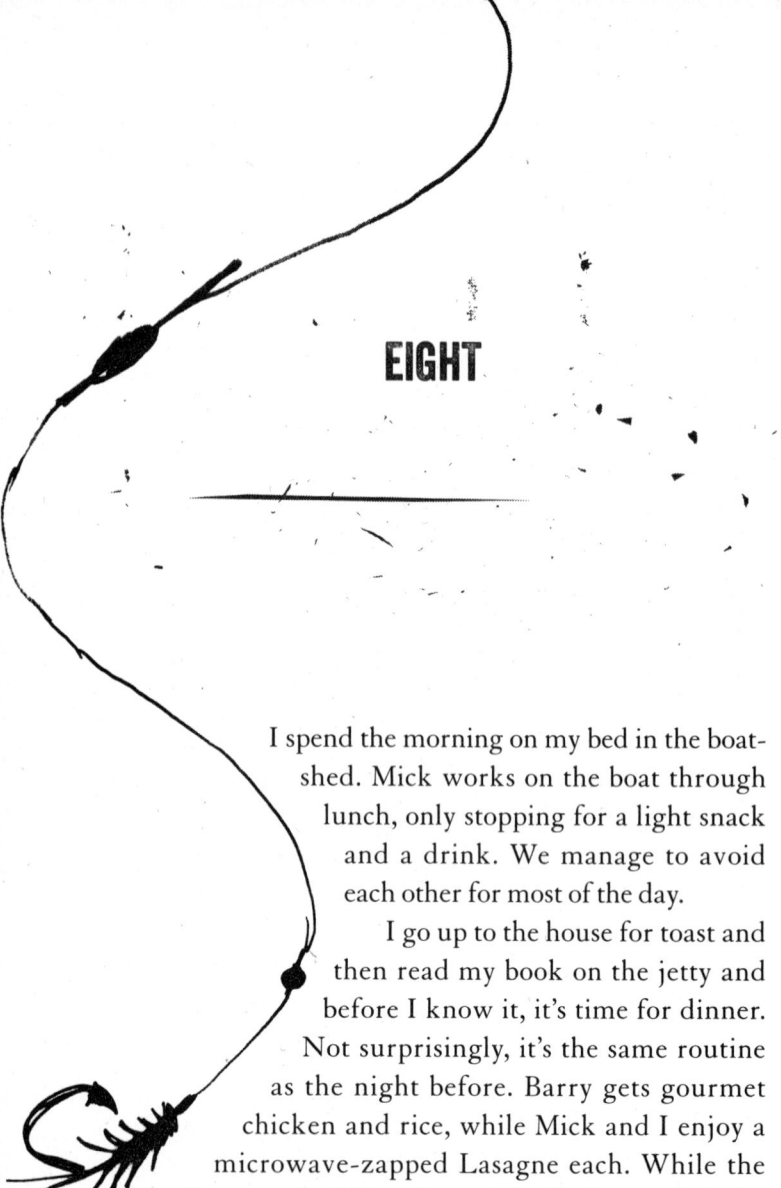

# EIGHT

I spend the morning on my bed in the boat-shed. Mick works on the boat through lunch, only stopping for a light snack and a drink. We manage to avoid each other for most of the day.

I go up to the house for toast and then read my book on the jetty and before I know it, it's time for dinner. Not surprisingly, it's the same routine as the night before. Barry gets gourmet chicken and rice, while Mick and I enjoy a microwave-zapped Lasagne each. While the Lasagne itself is only marginally better than the Steak Diane, I'm surprised Mick's allowed us to have the same thing on the same night. I wonder if it might upset the balance of numbers and the meticulously labelled, neatly stacked frozen dinners in the freezer. After a few mouthfuls of cheesy slop, I decide to voice my concern.

'Is this allowed?' I say. 'Both of us having the Lasagne, I mean?'

'Not really,' he says. 'But it's Friday. Let's go crazy, hey?'

We eat in silence for a bit until Mick clears his throat.

'There's something I want to run by you,' he says. 'I was going to wait a few days, but we may as well get into it now.'

I stop chewing and sit up.

'Thing is, we used to farm oysters here,' continues Mick. 'Your grandpa Walt started it all. Anyway, about two years ago, this virus appeared from nowhere. Wiped everyone out, everyone who was farming along the Glamorgan. The local industry went balls up.'

It's hard to imagine a virus in the Glamorgan River. It looks so perfect and clean.

'So the water,' I say, 'is it . . .?'

'The water's fine,' says Mick. 'Clear and pristine like you wouldn't believe, and the fishing's never been better. This virus only affected the oysters. Killed them off overnight. Bloody devastating, it was. Anyway, the months ticked by, a year, and then families, friends, people who'd been in the business for a hundred years, they started selling their farms, packed up their things and left.'

I rest my fork on the plastic dinner tray. 'But not you?'

Mick sits back in his chair and half smiles. 'Where would I go?' he says.

'What about Broome?'

'Nah, it's home here. And, anyway, they're doing what

**59**

they can – the scientists, the marine biologists. Actually, there's been some good tests of late so the green light might not be far away.'

'So, what do we do?' I say.

I check myself without letting on and wonder where the 'we' came from.

'I mean what do you do?' I say. 'For work. For money.'

'Well, that's what I wanted to talk to you about. Your mum left some money for you. It's not much, but it was all she had. Anyway, I've set up a bank account with a card attached so you can dip into it if you need to.'

Mick looks up with a serious kind of face. 'I'm trusting you with this, Nate. Do you understand?'

'Yeah, course.'

'I mean it, Nate. Taking off, leaving now . . . it'd be a really bad idea.'

While Mick might not rate much as an uncle so far, he's smarter than I thought he was. With a bit of money behind me I could go back – back to my old life in the city. It wasn't much, but it was familiar, and I knew people there. It'd breach my parole, but maybe it'd be worth it. Maybe I could get a cash job, get a room with some friends. Live someplace where things actually happen.

'Nate?'

'Relax, Mick. I'm still here, aren't I?'

'You are,' he says. 'Do I need to tell you about responsible spending.'

It doesn't really sound like a question so I don't answer. He turns himself around on the chair and reaches a hand into a ceramic bowl on the servery bench. He grabs a red card and pushes it across the table towards me.

I've never had a bank card before. I don't pick it up. I just sit there and stare at it, stare at my name, Nathaniel Cole, branded into the bottom of the card in silver typewriter font.

'I think you should get your boat licence,' says Mick.

I can tell Mick's put some thought into what he's just said. It sounds important, like the start of a story.

I look up. 'Really?'

'Yeah. I've been thinking it through all day and I've decided – I want you to take over the deliveries.'

'What deliveries?'

'People come from all over the place to holiday on the Glamorgan and its islands,' says Mick. 'You'll see them in town. It's mostly city folk, really. In the summer. For some reason they seem to like the isolation. They think there's something romantic about a holiday house on an island that's only accessible by boat. Truth is, it's a pain in the arse.'

'Sorry,' I say. 'I'm not following.'

Mick takes a deep breath, then downs his fork as if the utensil is somehow interfering with what he's trying to tell me.

'When the virus hit, I had to think of something else besides oysters,' he says. 'I racked my brain for weeks but couldn't for the life of me think of anything that might turn a few dollars. I thought about fishing, but competing with the established fishing families wasn't going to work. Anyway, one day I was in Chester's buying a few things and this couple from the city were stocking up on supplies, whingeing about how much of a hassle it was having a holiday house on an island, having to do the back-and-forth trips to the store and lug all their food in a tinnie. And that's how we came up with the delivery idea.'

'We?' I say.

'Singlets and me. Tom Chester. You met him.'

'Hang on,' I say. 'Are you telling me that Tom Chester and Singlets are the same person? That the old bloke in the footy shorts who sits out the front of the store actually owns it?'

'Yeah, I am. We started a business together. It's all online now. People order what they want beforehand. They buy the stuff at Chester's, and I boat it out to their house so it's all there when they arrive. People pay good dollars for convenience.'

'So you want me to be the delivery boy?'

'That's the plan. Gem does most of the computer stuff and invoicing now, and I could do with a break, to be honest. I'll deduct some money for board, naturally, and pay you a wage into your account. It won't be much, but at least it's something. Sound all right?'

No one's ever offered me anything like this before. It feels serious and heavy in a grown-up kind of way.

'You do understand what this means, Nate?' asks Mick.

'I think so.'

'Part of delivering hampers requires you to enter peoples' homes.'

I think about what Henry told me that Mick said – about the bad blood.

'You don't trust me,' I say.

'Actually, I do trust you, Nate. Or I wouldn't have asked. But the people who own those houses might not be so understanding. I'm sticking my neck out, Nate.'

'I know,' I say.

'Good.'

The two of us look at each other and when our eyes meet it feels like a handshake.

'Is it hard to get?' I say. 'The boat licence?'

'Nah. There are two parts to it. I'll teach you all the practical stuff, and then there's some general boating knowledge you'll have to learn. I've left the booklet in the boatshed on your bed. It's all multi-choice. Easy.'

'Really?'

'Put it this way. Doug Tomkins got his. Took him three goes, mind, but he got it.'

The two of us pick up our forks, Mick first and then me. We go back to eating but after swallowing a mouthful of Lasagne, Mick puts his hand on his stomach and grimaces in pain.

'Are you okay?' I ask.

'Yeah,' he says. 'I'm fine. Bloody indigestion, that's all.'

Mick expects me to tidy up so I make quick work of the dishes and wipe the benches down. After cleaning my teeth in the bathroom, I say goodnight to Mick and head for the boatshed. Barry comes with me. He trots along beside me and looks up at me as we go.

'Don't start, Barry.'

Barry responds with his eyes.

'Because I don't need you on my back, as well,' I say. 'You're a dog, okay? I know you might not think you are, the way Mick spoils you, but you are. You've got four legs, a tail and you lick your balls.'

Barry snorts.

'You do, Barry. I saw you, yesterday. You were lying

on the verandah in the sun.'

He rolls his eyes.

'There's plenty wrong with it, actually. It's gross. And the fact that you don't see that proves my point about you being a dog. People don't do that.'

When I step inside the boatshed and flick on the light, a small brown gecko scurries up the white wall and ducks behind a paddle board. The booklet is on my bed. On its front cover, there's a smiling family – a mum and a dad and two kids in a speedboat, wearing matching life jackets. I open it up and begin to read.

'Hey.'

The voice behind me is kind of familiar, but I startle all the same.

Barry jumps up and charges. For a second I think there's going to be trouble, but it's a friendly charge – he pins his ears back and his tail starts flapping wildly.

I turn around and see Gem standing on the deck. To say that I'm surprised is an understatement. I'm not sure how I feel about her standing there, how I feel about her rocking up unannounced. Technically, the boatshed is my bedroom.

Gem bends down and lets Barry lick her face, starts talking to him like he's a baby.

'Hello, there, my gorgeous boy,' she says. 'You're very handsome, aren't you?'

I look at Barry just in case I've missed something. 'Handsome?'

'Oh, yes, you are. You're a very handsome boy.'

Barry won't stop. He keeps licking, slobbering all over her face.

'Really?' I say.

It goes on for a bit until Gem finally straightens up. She reaches a hand into her pocket then pulls out a bag of lollies and tosses them to me.

'Sour straps,' she says.

'Thanks,' I say. 'You shouldn't have.'

And then it's awkward. I have no idea why Gem's here or where she came from. She reaches a hand up and pushes the wisp of purple hair back behind her ear.

'Can we . . . start again?' she says.

I turn around so that I'm facing her properly and can't help thinking how much worse it could have been had I got undressed for bed.

'What do you mean, start again?' I ask.

'I like good starts,' she says. 'Good beginnings. They're important.'

'Right.' I already know the answer, but I ask the question anyway. 'What was wrong with our start?'

'It was average,' says Gem. 'Mediocre.'

'Was it?'

'Yeah, pretty much. We should rewind, I reckon. Go back to the start and pretend we haven't met. Do it again.'

Gem wipes her palms down the sides of her tartan skirt, then takes a few steps forward and extends her right hand.

'Hi,' she says. 'I'm Gem.'

'Hi, Gem. I'm Nate. I'm sure you've heard already. I'm the nephew from the city. That bloke who messed up.'

We shake hands, and Gem smiles a little.

'I'm . . .' She starts to speak, but it's clear she's not sure what to say or where to look. Her eyes do a lap of the boatshed and finally settle on mine. 'I'm the girl who works in the store,' she says.

I nod my head and it all feels weird. Not in a bad way, though. It's a good kind of weird – interesting.

I don't know what else to do so I lift two deck chairs off the metal hook.

'Do you want to sit down for a bit?' I ask.

Gem nods. I unfold the chairs and set them up on the deck about a metre apart. I turn off the light so we can see the stars, then the two of us sit down. I open the lollies for something to do and reach out to offer the bag to Gem.

'Sour straps,' she says. 'Your favourite?'

'Not really,' I say. 'I used to buy them when I was little.'

She nods her head.

'So that creep in the shop,' I say, after a pause. 'Is he always like that?'

It's too dark to see her face properly, but she seems to hesitate before answering.

'I can look after myself, Nate.'

'Yeah, I reckon you can. But I'm new here. Who is he?'

'His name's Marty,' she says. 'Marty Holland. Everyone calls him Dutchy. He's a complete arsehole really, but for some reason everyone thinks he's a legend, especially Marty.'

He sounds familiar. No matter where you go, there's always one guy like that. I think back to Croxley and Jackson Sinclair comes to mind.

'You should be careful about pissing him off,' says Gem. 'Marty, I mean. He's got mates. They're arseholes as well.'

'I'll be okay,' I say.

'That's right, I forgot – you're a tough guy.'

'Not that tough,' I say. 'You shouldn't believe everything you hear.'

Not knowing what to say to a girl doesn't matter when you've got stars. The two of us sit there for a bit gazing up at the night sky, and I feel the air brushing soft and warm against my skin. Barry's resting his muzzle on Gem's feet.

'So, how's it going?' says Gem. 'With Mick?'

'Okay,' I say.

'Really?'

'Yeah. It's early days. He's a bit grumpy, kind of sad too, but it could be worse. Way worse. He wants me to get my boat licence and help with the deliveries.'

Gem looks surprised. 'You?'

'Yeah, me. Why not?'

'I just can't imagine you in a boat.' Gem looks over at the jetty. 'In that boat, especially.'

'Why not?' I ask.

'I don't know. You don't seem the type.'

'Here we go.'

'What?' asks Gem.

'Why does everyone keep telling me what type I am? And, anyway, you don't even know me. We just did a rewind, remember, so technically we only met a few minutes ago.'

'I'm not telling you what type you are,' says Gem. 'I'm just not sure a city kid like you can handle a powerful boat like *Forever One*. She's a Randell Thirty-Two – even took me a while to get the hang of it.'

'Hang on, you mean you've got your boat licence?'

She laughs. 'What?' she says. 'I'm not the type? You're not about to tell me what type I am, are you, Nate?'

She's clever, Gem. I sneak a look and let my eyes linger on her moonlit face, on the grains of sugar stuck to her lips.

She turns her head and catches me looking.

'I hear you've made a new friend,' she says.

'Huh?'

'Henry,' she says. 'You must have done something right. He doesn't like many people, but he seems to like you.'

'Tell me about it. I don't think I was even that nice to him. But he's a stubborn little kid. You know him, do you?'

'Yeah, you could say that. He's my brother. Well, not by blood. But that's how I think of him.'

Gem points to the thick wall of trees that runs along the west side of the workshop.

'Behind those trees there's a house,' she says, 'It's about five hundred metres in. Well, it's a cottage really. That's where we live.'

There's nothing to see in the dark, but I look anyway.

'So, that means we're . . .'

'Neighbours,' says Gem.

I like the idea of that, being close to a girl like Gem. It feels like a treat so I tuck it away for later. I look out into the darkness, and I go back to the morning, back to Henry staring at the water with Barry by his side.

'Henry said he didn't have any friends.'

'He hasn't,' says Gem. 'Except for Mick. He gets teased at school because he's a bit different. But he likes the water, always has, so he helps Mick with the boats.

Especially lately, since Malaya left.'

'I can't imagine Mick with a wife,' I say. 'Was she . . . nice?'

Gem turns her head my way. 'Yeah, she was. She was really nice. And beautiful. Kind of crazy, though. She loved to dance and wear sarongs and she loved the Bee Gees. God, she loved the Bee Gees.'

'So, what happened?' I ask.

'Well, I'm not sure exactly,' says Gem. 'I think it started around the time the virus hit and their business went bust. Or a bit after. But about a year ago, she just packed up her things and left. Just like that. And Mick hasn't been the same since. He was devastated.'

It feels strange that Gem knows more about my uncle than I do. While I'm thinking of what to say, something furry and medium-sized scurries through the bush nearby. I jump.

'Possum,' Gem says. 'You'll get used to them.'

'Mick seems to like the Bee Gees, too,' I say, as I watch the creature disappear up a tree. 'What do you like? Besides tartan, of course.'

'I like a lot of things,' says Gem.

'Like what?'

'I'm not telling.'

'Why not?'

'You'll have to find out. That's half the fun.'

Our eyes meet and I hope like hell the night sky is hiding the burning red in my cheeks. I raise my hand up and point a make-believe remote control at Gem's face. I press a button with my thumb.

'You're like a movie,' I say.

Gem screws up her face. 'Really?'

I don't know what I was thinking. The remote control was a bad idea, but it's too late now, I'm committed.

'Yeah,' I say. 'You made us rewind and go back to the start. And now you just hit pause.'

Gem laughs. 'Pause isn't so bad,' she says. 'It's better than stop.'

I turn my head and look for her words in the dark. Maybe I've got lucky.

Gem hauls herself up and gets slowly to her feet. I get up too and stand beside her in the moonlight, looking down at the scuff marks on her Doc Martens. I raise my eyes up slowly and see bruises on her wrist and hand. I wonder if they might be birth marks, but I know deep down they're not.

I know bruises. I've seen them plenty of times before. I've seen them on my mum's arms, around her eyes and on her lips. I've seen bruises that are old and ones that are new. I've seen rainbow-coloured bruises, bruises that are black and purple, yellow and red.

'I'd better go,' says Gem.

I feel shattered. There's lots of ways to get a bruise, but I can't shake the feelings they give me. Oyster Bay is supposed to be something new, something fresh. I look at Gem and try to smile.

'I'll walk you home,' I say.

Gem shakes her head.

'Walk me home?' she says. 'I'm a big girl, Nate. I don't need walking home.'

I shrug my shoulders, embarrassed. 'I know,' I say. 'But I want to. I feel like a walk.'

Gem steps off the deck, walks a few metres then turns.

'C'mon then,' she says.

I follow her past the workshop and towards the trees. As we go further in, the bush begins to thicken and she walks faster, starts to weave between the trunks as if she's playing a game. She pulls away, about ten metres ahead, and when we get to a clearing she spins around and her tartan skirt balloons like a tutu. She's breathless. When she stops spinning she stands there, lit by the moon, and all of a sudden Oyster Bay just got a whole lot better.

'So, what kind am I?' she says.

I'm about to ask what she means, but she beats me to it. 'If I'm a movie. What kind would I be?'

'Well, I'm not sure,' I say. 'You've only just started really, so it's hard to say. From what I've seen so far, though, I'd say you're unique, kind of kooky, and you're . . .'

'I'm what?' asks Gem.

'You're impossible not to watch,' I say.

I catch up to where she's standing, and she smiles. 'Good answer,' she says.

We walk on, side by side, and I can hear Gem breathing. We break through the trees, and in front of us is a house with a small white sedan out the front.

Gem stops again and turns my way. 'Goodnight, Nate. And thanks for walking me home.'

I nod my head and smile, and as she walks off towards her house, I call after her. 'Gem . . .'

She pulls up and turns slowly around.

'Yeah?' she says.

I'm not sure where the words go. I thought I had them all ready so I stare at the ground and buy myself some time.

'I think I should . . . I mean, I really need to . . .'

'Just say it, Nate.'

I look up. 'I'm not a good idea, Gem.'

'That's okay,' she says. 'Neither am I. Maybe we can be bad ideas together.'

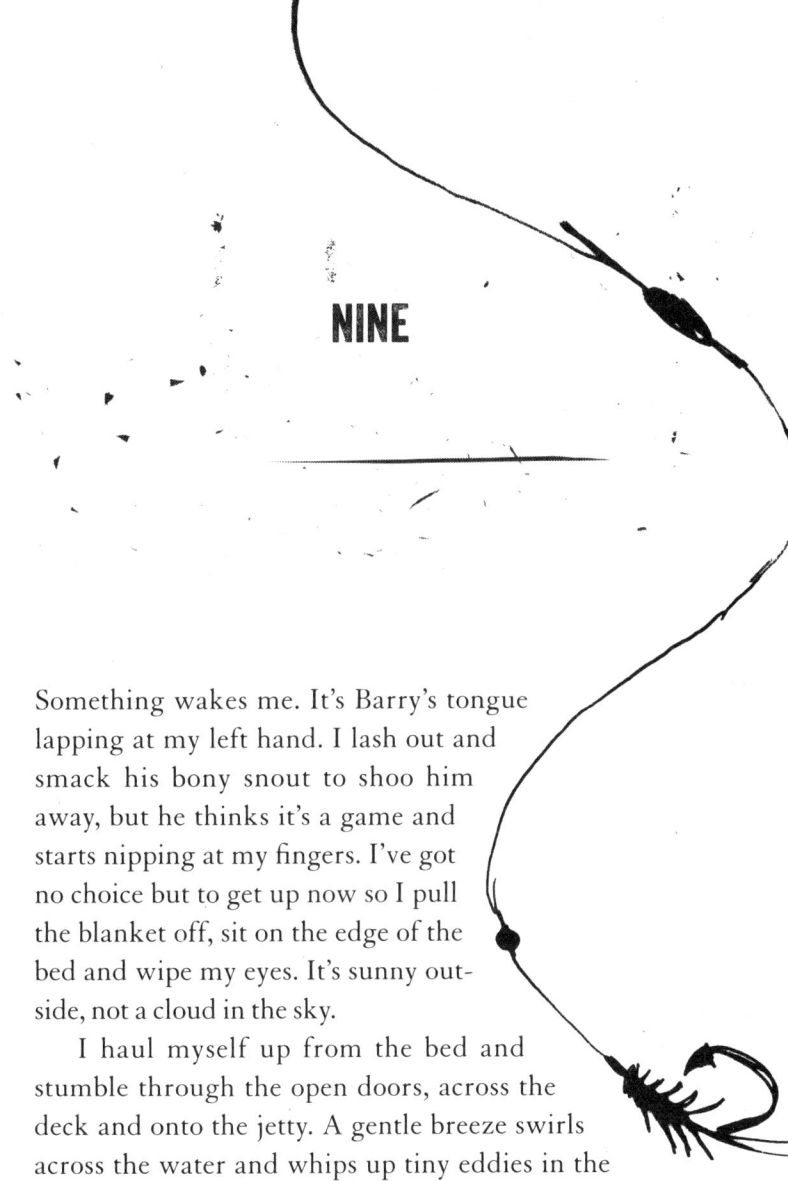

# NINE

Something wakes me. It's Barry's tongue lapping at my left hand. I lash out and smack his bony snout to shoo him away, but he thinks it's a game and starts nipping at my fingers. I've got no choice but to get up now so I pull the blanket off, sit on the edge of the bed and wipe my eyes. It's sunny outside, not a cloud in the sky.

I haul myself up from the bed and stumble through the open doors, across the deck and onto the jetty. A gentle breeze swirls across the water and whips up tiny eddies in the blue. I spot a dragonfly, its rainbow-coloured wings flittering in the sun.

It's peaceful and calm out by the river, but when I step down onto the landing I see a shape in the water, a body.

I hear myself yell out, and when I run to the edge for a closer look, I realise it's Henry. He's under the water and he's not moving. Without thinking I jump off the landing and feel my feet hit the sandy bottom. Frantically, I rush over to Henry near one of the pylons, then I duck under the water and swim.

I don't know what's happening when I try to haul him up. It's confusing. Rather than a dead weight, Henry seems to be resisting.

He's alive. When his head breaks the surface he starts shouting, starts lashing about with his arms. Despite the adrenaline pulsing through me, I'm overcome by a wave of relief.

'What the fuck, Henry?'

Henry seems annoyed. He pushes his goggles up onto the top of his head, and I let him go.

I hadn't noticed the metal ladder at the end of the landing. Henry dog-paddles over, and when he starts to climb up I see he's wearing a weight belt around his waist. Once he's on dry land, I climb up the ladder myself and sit on the landing beside him.

I take a moment and try to slow things down.

'Jesus, mate, I thought you'd drowned,' I say. 'What the hell were you doing anyway?'

Henry wipes water from his face.

'I like it,' he says. 'It's quiet.'

'Quiet?'

'Really quiet,' says Henry. 'I like the fish too.'

I look at Henry in his board shorts and rashie, his

goggles and his weight belt, and I feel myself smile.

Hearing him talk about the river and seeing the joy in his face, a strange mixture of happy and sad creeps under my guard.

'Sorry, Henry,' I say. 'I thought you were . . . I guess I panicked.'

A pelican flies into view above the tree line to our right, and the two of us watch it descend until it's only a few metres above the water. I've never seen a pelican before, in real life I mean, and I'm struck by its size, by its strange and unusual elegance. I wouldn't have thought a pelican would be known for its flying, not like a smaller bird anyway, but there's a gracefulness about its barrel-shaped body, the way it glides effortlessly above the water. When it draws level with where we're sitting, its wings make a whooping sound. Its large webbed feet lurch forward and it skitters across the surface of the water.

Henry starts to make pelican noises with his throat. As he gargles and groans, the pelican looks our way.

A voice rings out behind us. 'Morning, lads.'

It's Mick. He's standing on the jetty wearing jeans, a pale-blue cotton shirt and sandals. He's all dressed up.

'I have to go into the city for a bit,' he says. 'Run some errands. Do a few things.'

He coughs a few times, heaves a breath when he's done, and his chest makes a hideous rattling sound.

'Jesus, are you all right?' I say.

'Yeah, yeah. Fine. I might be gone for a bit. You two be right?'

I go to get up, but he raises a hand in the air and shows me a palm.

'Help yourself to whatever's inside,' he says. 'Take the quad bike to the end of the drive if you need to go into town. I should be back in the arvo sometime.'

I nod my head, but Mick still seems a little hesitant.

'Okay,' he says. 'I'll see you later . . .'

As he goes to move off, he seems to remember something and turns around.

'Oh, and we had a few delivery orders overnight. I'll organise someone to take you out on the river and show you the ropes. Shouldn't take long.'

I nod my head again. I shield my eyes from the morning sun and watch Mick walk back towards the pick-up. Barry seems okay with that. He drops himself down near the edge of the landing and eyes the pelican.

I turn to Henry beside me. 'You hungry?'

'Yep.'

'How about I get us some breakfast? We can eat on the landing, if you like.'

'Okay,' says Henry. 'I'll wait out here. I might go under again.'

---

It's strange to be in the house by myself – in the house where my mum grew up. Without Mick hovering about and watching me, I can take my time and have a look around, get a proper feel. I go straight for the photo on the sideboard, the one of my mum and Mick as teenagers, sitting on the jetty in their bathers. I pick it up and look at my mum's happy, smiling face. I never saw her smile like that so I touch the glass with my finger and gently swipe her face just to make sure the smile is real.

I put the photo down and look around the house. I walk past the mantelpiece, past the two black Ms, and then continue on towards the kitchen. The white plate on the table, the knife and fork, and the folded red napkin look even sadder now I know why they're there.

There's not much else to see on the fridge, just the card, a few magnets and the photos. The rest of the stuff is mostly bills. I'm getting hungry so I open the fridge door and look inside for something that might pass for breakfast. Not surprisingly, there's not a lot to choose from. I've eaten the bread so there's just the milk I bought the other day. I look in the fruit bowl, but it's bad news.

After a full sweep of the kitchen I've come up empty-handed so I lean against the bench and look back at the fridge, at the freezer section at the top. I can't believe I'm even considering it.

Even with the quad bike in the shed outside, I can't be bothered heading into town so I open the freezer door. A gust of cool brushes against my face and when the chill cloud clears I scan the handwritten labels on the ends of the frozen dinners. I read them aloud and try to find something that sounds like breakfast – Thai Green Chicken Curry, Shepherd's Pie, Linguini Carbonara, Roast Lamb and Vegetables, Beef Stroganoff . . .

It's not an easy decision, but in the end I go for the Shepherd's Pie. I pluck two from the freezer and get one going in the microwave. While I'm waiting for it to cook, I gather up the things I need and soon I'm ready to head back out.

Barry meets me at the end of the landing and looks

hopefully at the food. Henry's underwater so I balance the two food trays on the top of a pylon, warn Barry to behave, then walk back to the boatshed to pick up two chairs. I grab my boating booklet while I'm there and double back to the landing.

Everything's set up when Henry breaks the surface of the water, heaving in air. He pushes his goggles up and spits water.

'Visibility okay?' I ask.

'It's all right,' says Henry. 'Barry kept barking, though.'

As soon as Henry climbs the ladder and steps off onto the landing, Barry starts to lick the salt from his legs. I sit in my chair and watch the pelican cruising up and down in front of us, about ten metres out.

Henry grabs the black plastic tray from the pylon and sits down beside me. 'What is it?'

'It's called Shepherd's Pie.'

'I have cornflakes for breakfast,' he says.

'Yeah, well, it's the best I can do, I'm afraid.'

'Have you got any sauce?'

'No, Henry. I don't have sauce.'

He looks unimpressed. 'You can't have a pie without sauce.'

'It's not actually a pie, Henry. It's minced meat with mashed potato on top.'

'Why do they call it Shepherd's Pie, then?'

'I don't know. Just eat it, mate.'

Henry doesn't eat it, not straight away. He digs his fork into the tray and scrapes the top layer of potato off to one side. I watch him arrange his food for a bit, then I open the booklet and flick through the 'nice to know' bits until I get to the important stuff, the sample questions for the test.

'Here we go,' I say. 'Where should you drive a vessel when in a channel? Possible answers are: on the port side, on the starboard side, in the middle, or on any side, it does not matter as long as a collision does not occur.'

I look out across the water, at the solitary sailing boat cruising up the middle of the river.

'It's starboard,' says Henry.

'Yeah, yeah, I knew that,' I say. 'Okay, what about this one, then? When driving a vessel at six knots or more, or towing a person, what is the minimum distance both the vessel and any towed person must keep from power-driven vessels, land or structure?'

I scroll down to the answers underneath, but Henry beats me to it.

'Thirty metres,' he says.

I run through a few more questions, but Henry knows all the answers and gets bored. He puts his tray back on the pylon and stands on the landing to look south along the river towards the bridge. We watch a silver tinnie zip by.

'Can I get the book?' he says.

'What book?'

'Your book,' says Henry. 'The one about fishing.'

I'm not sure how I feel about that. I would never have shared my mum's book with anyone in Croxley. Not even with the blokes I knew before that. Or Amy. Some things aren't meant to be shared. But this is different. Henry's different.

'Okay, then,' I say. 'Go on.'

He tears off for the boathouse and returns a minute later with the book in his hand.

'I'm not very good at reading,' he says. 'Can you read me some, Nate? The bits about fishing?'

'Sure, Henry. Give it here.'

Henry hands me the book and sits back down in the chair beside me. As I flick through to the start of the text I see my mum's name again, but I don't feel the ache quite like I did before. It still hurts seeing her name. It's still hot and raw and real, but the ache itself, the thing in the centre of it all, feels a little different. I look up and gaze out over the blue water. I feel the sun on my face and the breeze against my skin. I look at Henry and he smiles. He just smiles.

'You ready?' I say.

Henry nods and I read.

I tell him about Santiago, the man who fished alone in his skiff. How he fished all along the gulf stream. I tell him how Santiago had gone eighty-four days without catching a fish.

'Eighty-four days?' says Henry.

I look up from the book and imagine the two of us sitting in our chairs six months from now, still working our way through chapter one. Henry interrupting, peppering me with questions.

'Yep,' I say. 'Eighty-four days.'

Henry gazes out across the water. 'What bait was he using?'

'Tuna,' I say.

'No wonder. Live bait's the best. Worms. We should go in the fishing comp.'

'Fishing comp?'

'Yeah,' says Henry. 'You and me.'

'I don't know the first thing about fishing, Henry. Although, I think I remember catching a toadfish once.'

'This comp's mulloway only,' says Henry.

'What's so good about mulloway?' I say.

'They're smart,' says Henry. 'And sneaky. They're good at hiding too, which makes them very hard to catch.'

'And why is that a good thing?'

'Because I know where they are. Can you read some more, Nate?'

I look down at the book again and start reading where I left off. I read about the young boy called Manolin who went fishing with the old man until, after eighty-four days without a fish, the boy's parents banned him from going out in his boat. They told him that the old man was *salao*.

'What's *salao*, Nate?'

'It means unlucky.'

'And what's the man's name again?' asks Henry.

'It's Santiago.'

'And the boy?'

'He's Manolin.'

'And where do they live?'

'In Cuba.'

'Is it nice in Cuba?'

'I don't know. It sounds nice.'

'We should go there, you and me. After the fishing comp, I mean.'

Henry points to the book, and I continue reading about the old man and the sea.

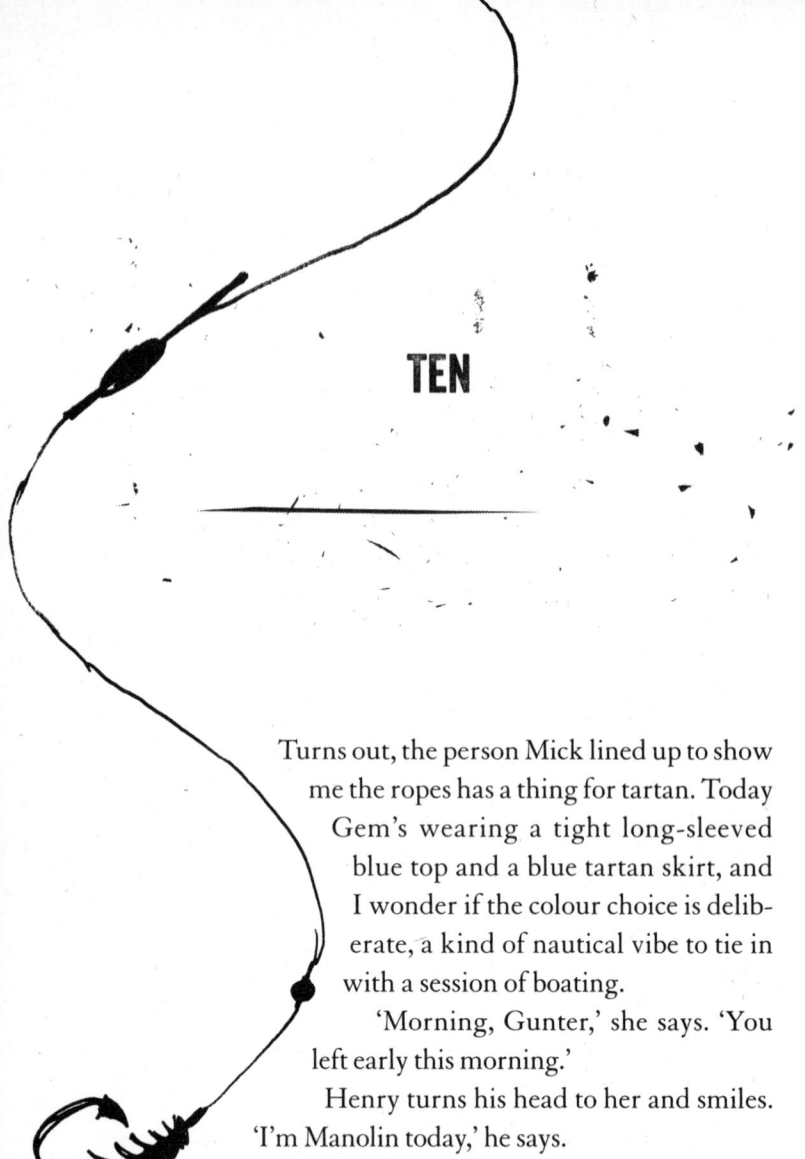

# TEN

Turns out, the person Mick lined up to show me the ropes has a thing for tartan. Today Gem's wearing a tight long-sleeved blue top and a blue tartan skirt, and I wonder if the colour choice is deliberate, a kind of nautical vibe to tie in with a session of boating.

'Morning, Gunter,' she says. 'You left early this morning.'

Henry turns his head to her and smiles. 'I'm Manolin today,' he says.

'Manolin?' says Gem. 'Why are you Manolin?'

'We're reading a book,' says Henry.

Gem looks over, and I angle the cover so she can see it better.

'Hemingway?' she says. 'Really?'

'It's about fishing,' says Henry.

'Well, it kind of is,' says Gem. 'Definitely wouldn't have picked you for a Hemingway kind of guy, Nate.'

'I'm not, really. It was my mum's. I've lost count of the number of times I read it.'

Gem nods. 'Did Mick happen to mention the deliveries?' she says.

'Yeah, he did. He didn't say it was you, though.'

'I'm coming too,' says Henry.

'No, mate,' says Gem. 'Mum wants you home.'

Henry seems to know not to argue. He gets out of his chair and pushes his goggles down so that they're hanging around his neck.

'Bye, Nate,' he says.

'Bye, Manolin.'

As we're walking back to the house with the breakfast things, a battered four wheel drive comes bumping up the drive. It's decked out with an assortment of outdoorsy off-road extras – an awning, a winch, a metal shovel, water tanks and a heavy-duty aerial. Three serious-looking fishing rods arch over the white bonnet, their handles housed in the hollow metal pipes attached to the front bull bar, their tips tethered somewhere above the cabin roof.

Two P plates adorn the front and back windscreens so I'm guessing the driver's just turned eighteen. I look at Gem for a heads-up, but the new arrival seems to have made her uncomfortable. She shifts about and mutters something into the dust.

The driver doesn't go all the way to the end of the driveway. He stops about five metres short, then pulls hard on the steering wheel and swings the beast around in a grinding half circle. After straightening up, he reverses back to the edge of the grass.

The guy who gets out is stocky, medium height, wearing jeans and a hoodie.

He puts a foot on the running board and steps down. He looks me over and smirks.

'Morning,' he says. It's like Gem isn't even there. 'I'm Stevie Chester,' he says. 'You must be the tough guy.'

I glance at Gem who shakes her head as a warning.

'Nate,' I say.

'Just out of juvie, yeah?' says Stevie. 'Break and enter, I heard. Bashed some old guy. Doesn't sound all that tough to me.'

He opens the back of the four wheel drive and starts to unload the hampers. There are three in total – three silver-coloured coolers stocked with provisions. Each cooler has a plastic pocket on its side, and inside each pocket is a cardboard card with a handwritten address.

Stevie finally looks at Gem, then back at me as if we're an item. He makes it obvious.

'You don't muck around, Gem,' he says. 'Moving quick, hey? Give him a welcome present, did ya?'

'Shut up, Stevie,' says Gem.

Stevie's got one of those faces you want to punch. He off-loads the last of the hampers, and I walk forward to get one. The quicker this is over, the less likely there'll be trouble.

He eyes me off, making sure he's got my attention.

'You're not the first, you know,' he says.

'Sorry?'

He nods his head at Gem. 'Dutchy reckons she's a dud. Reckons the slut's not worth the effort.'

Gem flinches. 'Drop dead,' she says.

I feel my fists clench tight beside me. 'You should go,' I say.

'Or what?' Stevie says. 'You're on parole, tough guy. What are you going to do?'

All of a sudden I'm back in Croxley, trapped inside its grey walls, standing on its shiny, polished floors. I feel the rush of adrenaline as I size him up and imagine how things will go. It'll be fast, of course. I'll close the gap with a lightning step, dip my left shoulder and launch a swinging right hand into his jaw. I wouldn't have given it a second thought in Croxley. I wouldn't have cared about the consequences.

But it's different now. I'm not sure when I realised it exactly, maybe it snuck up on me this very second, but I've got *things* now. I don't know exactly what those things are yet or what they even mean – but they're new, and they feel kind of good so I don't want to throw them away.

Stevie turns slowly and steps up onto the running board. He laughs down at us, blows Gem a kiss and looks at me.

'Maybe you and Dutchy can compare notes,' he says.

Stevie closes the door. Gem doesn't say a word as the four wheel drive disappears around a bend. She grabs a hamper. It's heavy and she struggles with it as she heads for the jetty, but I know better than to ask if she needs help.

I pick up the second and follow her, then go back for the third. When I step onto the deck, I pack the hampers next to the first one in a wooden crate in the back, then head to the front of the boat. Gem's behind the wheel when I get there. When I slip in front of the passenger seat next to her, she turns away like I'm not even there.

'Gem.'

It's like we don't even know each other. Gem turns her head back and indicates the area in front of us with her hand.

'So, the front's called the bow,' she says. 'The back is the stern. Right is starboard and left is port.'

'Gem. Stop.'

'Fuck stop. Do you want to get your boat licence or not?'

'Not when you're like this, I don't.'

There's no hiding this time. Gem turns my way and stands in front of me. She extends her arms out to the side as if she's asking me to look.

'Like what, Nate?'

'Well . . . upset.'

'Upset? Upset?'

'Yeah. Upset.'

'Too right, I'm upset.' Gem's going at a hundred miles an hour. 'Do you have any idea what it's like to have people say things about you like that? Apparently I'm a slut, Nate.'

'I don't care about you and Marty Holland,' I say. 'And I don't care about Stevie or what anyone says. I know what you are, Gem.'

'Yeah? And what am I then, Nate? What do you think I am?'

'I think you're amazing. And you're wrong, by the way.'

'Wrong about what?' she says.

'I do know what it's like to have people say things that hurt.'

All of a sudden Gem's eyes seem a little softer somehow. The two of us stand in front of our seats a metre apart and we look at each other as if nothing else matters. We look deep into each other's eyes, and we say things without words, kind things, gentle things, things that maybe only eyes can say.

It's weird. After all the rubbish I put into my body, I thought I'd be fried. I thought the numbness I felt might stay with me forever, and maybe in a way that's what I wanted. But Gem's like some magic potion that's sparked me to life and rewired all the parts of me that were dead.

I know we've only just met, but I can see things clearer with Gem, and I can feel things that I never felt before.

# ELEVEN

A yellow speedboat fangs by not far from the jetty and brings us back. It takes a few seconds to re-focus and when we do it's all hands on deck. After untying us from the pylon, I scramble back to the cabin next to Gem, and she starts the boat. She pushes gently on the throttle and the boat lurches away from the jetty and into deeper water.

As we chug slowly south, towards the first of the metal bridges, Gem takes me through some of the things I need to know about *Forever One*. Basically, it's an all-rounder, a fishing boat that can double as a go-anywhere cruiser or charter boat. It's nine metres in length with a fibreglass hull, and the original engine has been replaced with a Yanmar 315 diesel. The instrumentation and controls are simple enough, as is the radio, and its emergency frequency number is written on the dash just in case.

Before Gem can really let loose and give the engine a nudge, she runs through the gear and safety checks that need to be done and shows me the emergency flares. Then we're pretty much ready to go.

I clap my hands together as Gem pushes the throttle forward again and the engine responds.

'God, you're such a boy,' she says.

'Who me?'

'Yeah, you. Look at you – you're practically salivating. Can't wait to get your hands on the wheel.'

'Well?'

'Well, you can't,' says Gem. 'Not until you do the theory and prac. They're the rules.'

There's a map of the Glamorgan River and its islands stuck to the cupboard doors to my left.

'It's a tidal river,' says Gem. 'Where we live, our houses, I mean, that's pretty much the start of the Glamorgan.'

I like the sound of 'where we live', especially when the words come from Gem. I look at her mouth and imagine kissing her.

'The river comes in from the sea,' she continues, 'and runs all the way through to the reservoir at Finton. But we're only interested in the section before Hartnell, which is here.'

Gem points to the map.

'So, our section is basically a set-up of threes,' she continues. 'There are three bridges that span the straight section of water – Coppins, Darling and Franklin. Franklin is the last bridge, a railway bridge, and after that the river pans out into a big body of open water. That's where our three islands are.'

Gem points to the map again.

'That's them there,' she says. 'The green blobs that aren't attached to the mainland. There's Pine Tree Island, which is the first and the biggest, then there's Horseshoe Island and Blue Island is the last. Make sense?'

'Yeah.'

'The best way to learn is to get out on the water, really. Look at the map if you get stuck. Mick drew a few things on it for me when I was learning. Made it so much easier. Tricky thing is the river itself. There are a few no-go areas. Snags, shallow bits. They're on the map as well. I'll show you them later.'

It's strange to see Gem behind the wheel of *Forever One*. She looks out of place in her tartan skirt and Doc Martens, with her wisp of purple hair. But hearing her talk, watching the way she handles the boat . . . it's clear she's been doing this most of her life.

We pass under the Franklin Bridge, the last of the three bridges, and Gem steers us left, away from the moron in the yellow speedboat doing circle work on the other side of the river.

'Dickheads,' she says.

It feels like the boating lessons are on hold so I sit back in my seat and gaze out towards the mainland on the port side. There are houses on its slope, dotted amongst the trees. I see one that looks similar to Gem's, an old fibro shack with a leaning verandah.

'So, tell me about your family,' I say.

'It's messy,' says Gem.

'Whose isn't?'

Gem takes a deep breath before she starts.

'My mum's Chinese and my dad's Scottish.'

I laugh. 'That explains the tartan.'

Gem smiles. 'It's nothing to do with him really,' she says. 'I just like tartan. My mum's name is Karen. I live with her and Henry. Henry's dad's never home, though. He's out of the picture basically. He drives trucks. Long haul.'

I'm not sure if Gem minds talking about her dad so I hesitate for a few seconds before asking. 'And where's your dad?'

She doesn't seem bothered. 'Up north,' she says. 'Last I heard, anyway. He's got a different wife now. Another kid, too. He coaches soccer and works behind the bar at a Leagues Club up there.'

'Do you see him much?' I ask.

'Not for ages. He freaked out when I went up last time. I think it was the tattoo.'

'You've got a tattoo?' I ask.

Gem's got her foot up on the dash. I glance at her leg, but all I can see is a purple bruise on her calf. It brings back memories again.

It makes me think about Mum, and how she had to wear the bruises my father gave her. She took them with her everywhere she went. Despite her attempts to hide them with make-up, she always knew they were there. She caught glimpses of them when she passed by a window or a mirror. In the street and on the bus, people sometimes baulked when they saw her up close. Well-meaning work friends asked what had happened so she made things up. She told them she bruised easy. She told them she was clumsy. She said she'd fallen over, bumped into something.

With my father, it was never just the physical act, the assault. My mum had to endure the aftermath as well. But that's not now. That's not Gem. So I shake those thoughts away and talk about something else.

'What kind of tattoo did you get?' I ask.

'It's a seahorse,' she says. 'It was pure rebellion. I got it to piss everyone off.'

'Where'd you get it?' I ask.

'The city.'

'No, I mean where . . . as in on your body.'

'None of your business.'

Gem pushes forward on the throttle with her left hand and the engine roars.

The first stop is Pine Tree Island. Gem tells me it was called that because of the line of pine trees that run along the ridge at the eastern end of the island. She cuts the revs on the throttle and expertly glides *Forever One* into one of the five jetties. As soon as its port side kisses the wood, I leap onto the jetty with the rope line and secure the boat to the white-tipped pylon.

Gem kills the engine and then joins me with one of the hampers. I take a handle and the two of us walk slowly up a series of steps towards a two-storey wooden house with big glass windows and a huge deck.

According to Gem, most people leave their houses open, but there are a few families who like to lock up, so it's important to know where the different keys are hidden. When we get to the house, she veers left and stops on a smaller wooden deck underneath an outdoor shower. She reaches a hand up to the wooden upright and lifts a silver key from a metal hook.

'I love this place,' she says. 'It's my favourite.'

I follow her up some more steps to a door on the ground floor. She unlocks it and heads up to the main part of the house. She looks tired and hot after the walk up, and when we off-load the hamper onto the kitchen bench she stops for a moment to enjoy the cool of the house.

We unpack the provisions and Gem puts them away. To finish things off, she pulls a card out of her pocket with a picture of a smiling hamper on its front. Below the hamper are the words *HAPPY HAMPERS* and an email address.

'And that's it,' says Gem. 'Easy-peasy.'

After a final check, Gem looks up and runs her eyes lovingly around the open-plan living room. She glances at me as if she's not quite sure about something, then she walks over and takes my hand and leads me to the puffy white sofa. She falls onto the cushions and pulls me down next to her.

'Is this allowed?' I say. 'I mean, shouldn't we . . .'

She raises her hand up and places her finger over my lips.

'Last night,' she says, 'you wanted to know what I like, remember?'

'Yeah,' I say. 'I remember.'

'Well, this is what I like,' she says.

I look around, thinking I might be missing something. 'You like doing deliveries?'

'No. I like sitting in other people's houses. When they're not home. I know it's completely mental.'

I'm not sure why I shake my head. It is mental.

'I like to pretend,' says Gem.

'Pretend what?'

Gem points to the sideboard, to a framed photo of a deliriously happy family. There's Mum and Dad, a boy and a teenage girl.

'I pretend I'm her,' she says. 'That girl, I mean.'

'Okay . . .'

'I pretend that's my family,' says Gem. 'Mum and Dad love each other to bits. They hold hands in public like teenagers. And we do things together, the four of us. We go for walks and we swim and we talk. No one shouts or fights, no one lashes out, no one tries to control anything or turn someone into something they're not, and no one rings a goddamn bell when they want someone to come home.'

'And the girl?' I say.

'She's popular,' says Gem. 'Everyone loves her. No one whispers when she walks past, no one laughs or makes stupid jokes. She's smart. And she's going to be something. She's going to be anything she wants.'

I'm surprised to hear Gem talk like that. Despite what happened with Marty and Stevie, she seems to have everything under control.

'Wait, let me get this straight,' I say. 'You actually want to be that girl?'

'No, Nate. I don't want to be her. God, that'd be really weird.'

'What do you want then?'

'I want what she's got.'

'And what has she got, exactly?'

'She's got easy.'

I screw up my face and look at Gem. 'Easy? What does that mean?'

'It means nothing bad happens to her. Everything is cruisy and sweet.'

I crane my head forward and stare at the girl as if a few centimetres closer might make me see things clearer. 'And you can tell that from a photo, can you?'

'Look at her, Nate. Why does she get easy? Why does she get whatever she wants, whatever she asks for? I want that too. I want it just for a bit.'

'It's a photo, Gem,' I say. 'And if you haven't noticed, people smile in photos. That's what they do. It doesn't mean they're happy.'

'Well, they look happy. They look really, really, happy.'

I look hard at the photo and twist things around in my head.

'The dad's an arsehole,' I say. 'He's a drinker.'

Gem swings her head my way. 'He is not.'

'He is,' I say. 'And the mum's exhausted and scared all the time. She barely has the energy to talk to her kids. And the boy's a complete twat. Don't get me started on the boy.'

Gem punches me on the arm. 'You're ruining my family.'

She leans sideways and rests her head on my shoulder. 'Do you miss her?' she asks.

I knew this moment would come, and I knew I wouldn't be ready.

'Yeah,' I say. 'I miss her.'

I snatch a look at the photo on the sideboard again, but the family inside has disappeared. I see an image of my mum instead, lying lifeless and grey on a hospital bed.

Gem lifts her head from my shoulder, and I feel her eyes on the side of my face. I notice Gem's hand on mine and I wonder how long it's been there.

'I didn't get to say goodbye, Gem. And I should have looked after her better. I should have done something to help.'

'What would you have done, Nate?'

'Something. Anything.'

I feel Gem's finger on the side of my chin. She turns my head.

'I don't know what happened,' she says. 'But I know it wasn't your job to protect her.'

There's something in Gem's eyes now, a kind of knowing that pulls me in.

'Things aren't always fair, Nate,' she says. 'Believe me, I know. It's called life. It doesn't always make sense.'

I sink further into the couch beside her and place my hand on the side of her face. I smooth my thumb across her cheek. When I run my fingers through her hair, it sounds like the wind.

She smiles at me and kisses me softly on the lips.

Mr and Mrs Happy and their happy, smiling kids are back in the frame. I catch Gem's eye and nod my head their way.

'I'm glad you're not that girl,' I say.

———

The first time I saw Gem, stacking the bait fridge in the store, I knew she was a breaker of rules. It was her appearance that stood out first, but that was only a layer, a wrapping of 'up yours' and 'go to hell'. The real rebellion is in Gem's head.

As we cruise towards the next delivery, I try to tap into that with some begging and pleading.

'Come on, Gem,' I say. 'I've been studying. I'm all over the theory.'

'You are not. I bet you haven't even read it.'

'I have read it. I've been going through it with Henry. I could take the test now. Ask me something. Go on.'

Gem gazes through the front windscreen and tries to recall a question from the quiz.

'Okay, then,' she says. 'If you're approaching another vessel head on, what should you do?'

'Both vessels should turn to starboard,' I say.

Gem smiles.

'And at what age is the wearing of a life vest compulsory?'

'Twelve and under, of course.'

I'm in luck. There's not much traffic on the river so Gem finally relents. I slide in front of the driver's seat and place my hands on the wheel of *Forever One*. According to Gem, getting the throttle right is the key. We get moving, and after a quick demonstration she lets me work it back and forward, making up different scenarios and problems as we go.

Our last two deliveries are to Horseshoe Island. Of the three islands that matter to us, it's Gem's favourite because of the stretch of white sandy beach on its northern side. Unlike Pine Tree, however, Horseshoe has no private jetties. The only access to the island is by way of a shared jetty on the eastern side, a long wooden structure that runs out thirty metres from the shore. There's only a small tinnie and two kayaks tied up when we get there so Gem lets me stay behind the wheel. She points to a pylon about halfway along the jetty, and I steer *Forever One* in, slow and steady.

'Ease off the throttle,' she says. 'And come in side on, like I did at Pine Tree . . . That's it . . . ease off . . . ease off . . . and . . . nice.'

It's not bad for my first go. The starboard side kisses the black rubber tyre around the pylon just a little too hard and Gem makes a face.

When she jumps onto the jetty and ties us up, I kill the engine and retrieve the two hampers from the back. We take a hamper each and the two of us lug them along the jetty towards the shore. There are no cars on the islands so instead of the usual system of roads there's a network of tracks and paths instead.

Gem knows her way around. She leads me up a path that meanders along through a thick wall of tea tree. After a few minutes of walking, the tea tree begins to thin and the sand underfoot becomes a dark-coloured soil. At the end of the path, a dirt track runs sideways in front of a row of houses. They're much more basic than the ones on Pine Tree Island. Some are fibro and some are wooden, but all of them are classic beach shacks.

We stop in a grassy clearing with makeshift tree-trunk seats, and Gem tucks a hand into her pocket. She hands me a business card and points to the green house off to our left.

'It's open,' she says. 'You do number nine and I'll do three.'

The green house is called 'Tarcoola', and when I walk inside it's pretty much as I thought it would be. Old furniture and second-hand knick-knacks fill up the living-room space. Pictures adorn the walls, bush land-scapes mostly, except for the one above the small pot belly stove. It's a painting I've seen before, a cricket scene in a dusty, deserted street at sunset. A long imposing figure with an arched back is charging in to bowl to a small boy. The boy is dwarfed by an enormous brick building behind him. I can't recall where I saw the painting before or even how old I was when I saw it, but I remember feeling sad for that boy facing up with the bat, just standing there with nowhere to go.

Pots and pans and various kitchen tools hang from the line of hooks screwed into the beam above the bench in the kitchen. I start to unpack the hamper and divide it into sections the way Gem did. I put the perishables into the fridge then rummage through the cupboards and find a large glass bowl. I arrange the fruit as best I can and leave the Happy Hampers business card leaning against a Granny Smith. I check the delivery one last time then grab the silver cooler and head outside.

Gem's waiting on the tree-trunk seat in the clearing so I walk over and sit down next to her. We look at each other and smile, and all of a sudden everything feels different. There's an urgency between us, a kind of craving – it's like wanting something really badly, needing it. But I'm afraid now. I'm afraid I don't deserve her.

'You know what I did, right?' I say.

Gem nods her head. 'I know.'

'And you still want to?'

'Yep.'

'But what if I'm like him?' I say. 'What if I'm like my father?'

'You're not like him, Nate.'

'How do you know?'

'I just do.'

I reach for Gem's hand and the two of us sit in silence for a bit.

There are things I want to say. I try to say them, but I'm not sure how.

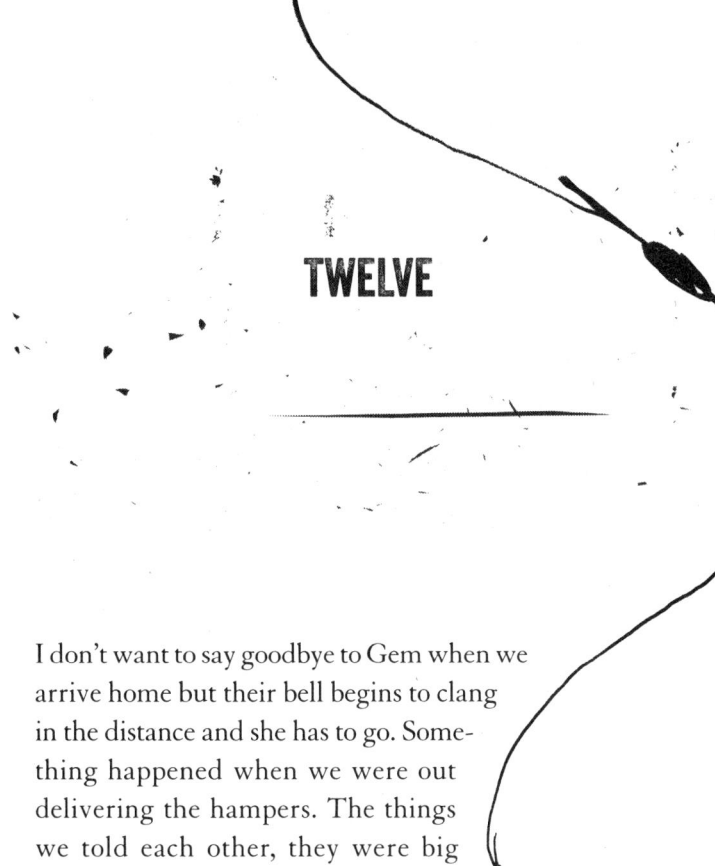

# TWELVE

I don't want to say goodbye to Gem when we
arrive home but their bell begins to clang
in the distance and she has to go. Something happened when we were out
delivering the hampers. The things
we told each other, they were big
things and you don't tell a person big
things unless you want to, unless it feels
like they're the right person to tell. I've
never had a person to do that with before,
but something about Gem made it easy. It was
like opening a door and asking her in.

I miss her as soon as she walks away. I stand
there and watch her go, watch her thread her way
through the columns of peeling tree trunks. She looks

small in the shadows and just for a moment she reminds me of the little cricket boy in the painting, standing alone, dwarfed by the giant building behind him.

More and more of Gem gets lost behind the trees and when she's finally gone I turn around and head towards the house. It's warming up, and Barry is overacting like you wouldn't believe. He's done nothing for the best part of three hours, but as we climb the verandah steps he glances up and throws me a pathetic look like he's been out in some dusty paddock all morning rounding up sheep.

As he wobbles over to his bed, I walk into the darkened house, grateful that Mick's thought ahead and drawn the curtains to keep out the heat. The Shepherd's Pie hasn't done much for my stomach, and I'm craving some proper food. I can't bear the idea of another frozen dinner, and with nothing in the fridge I decide to put off eating for a bit.

I wander aimlessly around the living room, checking things out, and I realise that Mick has no TV. He has a bookshelf instead, stacked with a collection of books with brightly coloured spines. Most of the books on the shelf seem to be non-fiction, arty-type hardbacks about music, travel, photography and art. Sticking out from under one of them is a council brochure. I pick it up and read it.

*The Book Bus*, it says. *Karinga Mobile Library. Monday and Friday, 11.30am–2.00pm. Oyster Bay shops carpark.* Inside the brochure there's a library card with Mick's name on it. I tuck the card into my pocket and put the brochure back where I found it. I turn around and as I start for the door, I knock a pile of pamphlets to the floor.

The top pamphlet is headed *Leukaemia – When*

*Treatment Stops Working.* I crouch down and gather up the bundle of pamphlets, try to straighten them up like a deck of dropped cards. I go through them one by one and read the headings on each – *Coping with Cancer, Palliative Care, Practical and Emotional Support.* I'm stunned and confused.

I sit back in my chair and stare at the pamphlet on top. *Leukaemia.* I stare at the word, at the strange and sinister way it's put together. I don't know much about it to be honest, but I know it's a nasty type of cancer that has something to do with the bone marrow and blood.

I shift forward, flick through the brochures again and this time I become aware of three words instead of just one. Before, I was focused on the leukaemia itself. It was as if that word was all I saw, but now I realise there's more. A number of the brochures are more specific, and I don't like the sound of them, not one bit.

*Acute Myeloid Leukaemia.*

I pick one of the brochures and start to read.

I read about red cells and white cells, about platelets, bone marrow, infection, bleeding, chemo, radiation and stem cells. I read about symptoms and treatments and prognoses. I read about blood transfusions and palliative care. I hurtle through it and my head starts to spin.

And then I open the first one – *When Treatment Stops Working.*

I begin to panic. I backtrack over the past few days with Mick and replay our short time together. I pluck random moments from the slide show in my head – Mick at Croxley, Mick driving the pick-up, Mick making dinner and working on the boat in the shed. Nothing about his behaviour seems odd at first, but then I start to see things smaller and closer than I did before. It's as if I'm looking through a lens and I've zoomed in. I see things I didn't clock before. I see Mick at the end of our long drive when we pulled up at the house for the first time. I see him get out of the pick-up all dizzy and reach for the back tray to steady himself. I add that to the first night at dinner, when he touched his stomach and grimaced in pain. And I hear his rattling chest when he coughed on the jetty this morning, the sweat stains on his shirt and the strange moment of hesitation before he left to run so-called errands in the city. It seems so obvious now when I throw all those moments together and tie them up with that strange sounding word, leukaemia.

I'm not sure what to do. If Mick had wanted me to know he was sick, he would have told me.

I sit back in the chair again and my stomach begins to grumble. I glance over my shoulder and stare at the freezer in the kitchen. Food. The brochures said that eating well was important for cancer patients. It's not much, I know, but maybe there is something I can do without making it look too obvious, something small that might make a difference.

I've got half an hour before The Book Bus leaves town so I get up and run outside to the shed. It smells of petrol and turps, the way a shed should. The quad bike is parked on a slight angle beside a trailer so I head over and sit on the cool vinyl seat. I fire it up and after clicking it into gear, like Mick said, I motor up the driveway and out onto the gravel road.

The bush smells different in the midday heat. The

eucalyptus leaves seem to have a sharper scent and the bush floor, the shaded undergrowth below, smells earthy and rich. Birds perch on tree branches like divas and warble their tunes before the afternoon heat kicks in and it's too hot to sing. I don't stop at the end of the dirt track. I haven't got time.

I know it's illegal. I don't have a licence, or a helmet, I don't even know if the bike is registered for the road, but I decide to keep going all the way to the shops. I don't meet anyone on the way. When I turn left around the last bend, I see a large blue bus parked in the gravel carpark opposite Chester's. I head for the grass area and drive slowly beside the wooden safety rails until I find a spot to park.

After crunching across the gravel towards the bus, I walk up a set of metal steps and through the open door. Behind a desk to the right is a colourfully dressed woman, wearing pink-rimmed glasses and matching lipstick. Her long grey hair is gathered at the top of her head, held together by a single chopstick. A badge on her cardigan says, *I'd Rather be Fishing*. She narrows her eyes and tilts her head as if she's sizing me up for new clothes.

'Angsty,' she says. 'Kinda cynical, defensive, bit of a loner . . . a Holden Caulfield kinda guy.'

I stand there totally confused.

'Am I right?' she says.

'About what?' I ask.

'About you? Holden Caulfield? *Catcher in the Rye* and all that.'

'Ah, I don't know.'

'What do you mean, you don't know?'

'I'm only seventeen. I haven't worked out what I am. People seem keen to tell me, though.'

The lady shifts about in her seat, extends her right hand over the desk and smiles. 'I'm Jan,' she says.

'Nate,' I say, shaking her hand. 'I'm actually after some cooking books.'

Jan looks back, blankly.

'You are the librarian?' I ask.

'Librarian?' she says. 'God, no. I'm a psychic . . . actually, I'm not one yet. I'm doing a course. I'm supposed to be practising on people I don't know.'

I look around the bus and try to work out where Jan fits. 'So, you're . . .'

'I drive the bus,' says Jan. 'Bob's the library guy.'

Jan turns her head right, to the far end of the bus and calls out. 'Hey, Bob.'

Bob looks like a meerkat. He sticks his head up from behind a shelf and peers back along the narrow bus as if there might be danger lurking somewhere near the Children's section to my left. When he sees me standing there, he steps into the small space and starts walking towards me. He's late-thirties, early forties maybe, with a long, thin neck, brown shaggy hair and patchy ginger stubble. He's wearing jeans and sandals, and there's a badge that says *BOB* pinned to his black Ramones t-shirt.

As he comes our way, Jan leans forward across the desk. She cups a hand around her mouth.

'Nervy,' she whispers. 'Low self-esteem, kinda goofy. He's a cat lover and a green-tea drinker, single of course . . .'

Bob looks shiny under the lights. Just before he gets to us, I turn to Jan for an explanation, and she mouths the word 'moisturiser' to me.

'Welcome to The Book Bus,' says Bob. 'What can I help you with?'

'I need some cookbooks,' I say. 'Healthy ones.'

'Okay,' says Bob. 'Healthy, as in?'

'As in super healthy,' I say. 'Wholegrains, fruit and veg, fish, all that stuff.'

Bob does a thinking face.

'Let's see,' he says. 'Healthy . . . healthy . . . healthy . . .'

I follow him to a shelf about five paces away.

'This is it,' he says. 'We're a bit light on for super healthy, as you can see. Still, it might get you started.'

I thank Bob for his help and, when he leaves me to it, I work my way along the spines, plucking out things that interest me as I go. After looking through some pages, I decide on three books. There's *Healthy and Hearty*, *Simple Summer Salads* and an unexpected bonus called *Juicing for Life*. Bob's waiting at the desk when I take them up. I hand him the library card and he checks the details on its front.

'Mick Cole?' he says.

'I'm staying with him,' I explain. 'Can I use his card?'

'Sure,' says Bob. 'You might want to get one of your own, though. If you're hanging around, I mean.'

I hadn't given any serious thought to how long I might stay, but right now a library card feels like a serious commitment so I just nod my head and smile.

'And how is Mick, by the way?' says Bob. 'I went to school with him, you know. Actually, I was in his sister's year. Katie, her name is.'

It's not just any name. It sounds all wrong when Bob says it so I snatch it from him and make it mine.

'I'm Katie's son,' I say. 'I'm Nate.'

Bob takes a step back. 'Really?' he says. 'Wow, I didn't know Katie had a son. She moved away ages ago. Shacked up with that Shane Peterson bloke. How is she, anyway?'

I don't answer. I'm not sure how. I wait for Bob to scan the last of my books, then I grab all three off the desk and walk towards the door. I'm halfway there when I spot a small blue book, sitting face forward on the Classics shelf to my right. On its cover there's a man and a boat and a fish.

I turn around to Bob and Jan standing behind the desk.

'She's dead,' I say.

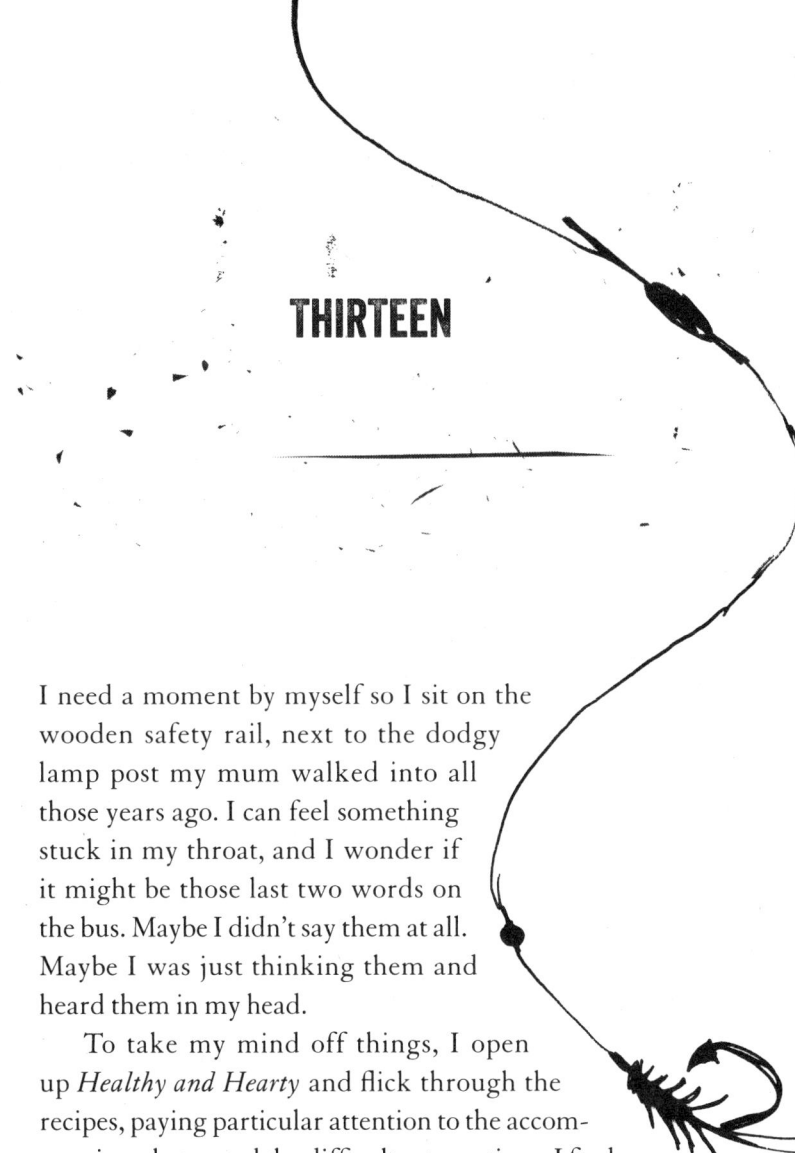

# THIRTEEN

I need a moment by myself so I sit on the wooden safety rail, next to the dodgy lamp post my mum walked into all those years ago. I can feel something stuck in my throat, and I wonder if it might be those last two words on the bus. Maybe I didn't say them at all. Maybe I was just thinking them and heard them in my head.

To take my mind off things, I open up *Healthy and Hearty* and flick through the recipes, paying particular attention to the accompanying photos and the difficulty star ratings. I find a simple fish recipe, dog-ear the page and go searching for a simple salad to go with it. I skim through

*Juicing for Life* and make a list in my head of all the things I need. Once I've got my menu sorted, I head towards the store.

Singlets is sitting in his usual spot and has swapped his navy footy shorts for a maroon-coloured pair with yellow panels down the sides. There's a newspaper open on the table and an untouched coffee next to it with a love heart shape decorating its foamy top.

I look at Singlets long enough to make him think an explanation is in order.

'What can I say? I'm the boss,' he says. 'Sweet, hey?'

Being mates and business partners, I wonder how much Singlets knows about Mick's leukaemia, and whether Mick's actually told him at all. I decide not to say anything, just in case.

I'm a little nervous about the whole cooking thing to be honest so I put the shopping on hold for a bit and pull out a plastic chair. I sit down next to Singlets and gaze out across the carpark like it's something you're supposed to do.

'Bad day?' asks Singlets.

He may not look like much, but Singlets is no fool.

'Yeah,' I say. 'It was great this morning, but it's turned to shit. Big time.'

'I see you've finally cracked,' he says, pointing at the books on the table. 'Lasted longer than I thought you would. What's on the menu?'

'Fish and salad, I think. That's the plan anyway.'

'You wanna buy your fish down at the Co-op,' he says.

'What's the Co-op?' I ask.

'The Cooperative,' says Singlets. 'Been around for years. It's on the main jetty, next one around from you.'

'Do you mean the green shed?' I ask.

'That's it. Stavros and Cass Kostas run the show. I think it's just Stavros on today. Tell him I sent you.'

'I will. Thanks.'

The Book Bus is preparing to leave. After its engine starts up, Bob walks down the metal stairs and folds the hand rails down. He walks back up, and Jan appears in the doorway in a flurry of pink and pushes a button somewhere inside. The stairs begin to lift automatically and when they're almost housed, she raises her hand and gives us a wave. Singlets and I wave back, and in a few minutes The Book Bus is gone.

When the dust in the carpark clears, the wooden lamp post is the only thing worth looking at. It seems to be leaning to the left a lot more than it was yesterday. I tilt my head for a better look.

'It does that,' says Singlets. 'Looked straight as an arrow, yesterday. I think it's the light. You met my grandson, Stevie, yet?'

I'm tempted to let rip and tell him exactly how I feel about Stevie, but I'm not sure it's my place.

'Actually, I have,' I say. 'I met him this morning.'

'He's a moron,' says Singlets. 'You probably worked that out yourself. Doesn't take long with Stevie. Unfortunately, you don't get a choice when it comes to family. Spoilt rotten, he is. I don't go in for all that New Age touchy-feely rubbish. What do they call it? Aeroplane parenting?'

'Helicopter,' I say.

'Yeah, helicopter. He's had things his way for too long. But I'm supposed to keep my nose out of it and watch on.

Breaks my bloody heart, it does.'

Singlets looks at me and nods.

'You've done all right, though, with your mum and Mick. You might want to count yourself lucky there.'

I'm not so sure about that. Ever since Mick came to pick me up at Croxley, and the more I've got to know him, I've been asking myself something, over and over again.

'Why didn't he ever come to find us?' I say. 'He must have known what was going on. How bad it was. Why didn't he help us?'

'It's complicated,' says Singlets. 'That's another thing with families. Maybe that's a question you should ask Mick.'

Singlets sips his coffee then sweeps his tongue over a small puff of foam on his top lip. I really want to ask him about Mick's leukaemia, but instead I push my chair out and gather up my books from the table.

'I'd better get into it,' I say.

'Good luck,' he says. 'You doing the fish on the barbecue or in the oven?'

'I don't know,' I say. 'I haven't got that far yet. What do you think?'

'I prefer the barbie, myself. Be careful, though, you don't want to dry it out. A couple of minutes on each side, that's all you need.'

I nod my head and leave Singlets to his lamp post, newspaper and coffee.

When I walk into the store, there's a girl behind the counter. She's vaguely familiar – then I remember her from the group mucking around on the footpath the other day. Her face is fake-tan orange and her strawberry-blonde hair is gathered in a loose bun at the back of her head. I grab a plastic basket near the door and she looks up and forces a smile.

With all the frozen food in Mick's freezer, I haven't paid any attention to the fruit and veg section in the store, but when I walk towards the back left corner, I'm surprised by the variety and quality of produce on display. No doubt it's got something to do with the cashed-up holiday-makers so I give thanks to the city crowd and grab a five-fingered hand of bananas. I grab carrots, tomatoes, avocados, strawberries, blueberries, peaches and pears and a strange-looking leafy arrangement called kale. I load up with all kinds of freshness and marvel at the pop of colours in the basket. When I'm done, I make my way back to the front of the store.

'Box?' asks the girl.

I don't know what she means.

'A cardboard box,' she explains. 'For the fruit and veg?'

'Oh, yeah,' I say. 'Thanks.'

She turns around and grabs a medium-sized box and lifts it up onto the counter.

'You're Mick Cole's nephew,' she says. 'Nate, yeah?'

'Yeah,' I say.

'Stayin' at his place, yeah?'

'Yeah.'

'Just got out of juvie, yeah?'

I'm getting a bit sick of 'yeah' so I nod my head instead.

'I heard you tried to kill someone,' she says.

'And where did you hear that?' I ask.

'Around. What was it like, anyway?'

'What was what like?' I ask.

'Juvie. Was it like it is in the movies?'

I shrug my shoulders and push the basket a little closer to her.

'Do you reckon you could ring them up?' I say. 'I'm kind of in a hurry, if you don't mind.'

'Suit yourself.'

Eating healthy isn't as cheap as I thought it would be so I have to use my new card. I don't know how much is in the account, but it seems to work fine when the girl taps it against the machine. She hands it back, and I thank her for nothing in particular.

Singlets is gone when I head outside with my cardboard box so I make my way across the carpark to the quad bike. I put the box onto the metal carrier frame on the back and tie it down with a blue-and-red bungee cord. I fire up the engine and after a quick look south along the road, I click the bike into gear and head off.

I don't want to get caught not wearing a helmet, but the Co-op is only a few minutes away. I turn right at the sign and the road continues on down to a carpark half-filled with cars and trailers.

It's busy on the foreshore. The smell of sausages and onions wafts up from the barbecues near the boat ramp. On the playground, kids hang upside down from the monkey bars and make faces at each other. Another group scoop handfuls of sand from the sandpit, pat them into balls and toss them into the air like grenades. There's a birthday going on. A gang of party-hatted children clamber up the drawbridge of a wooden castle and shoot down a slide on the other side.

It's quiet out at Mick's place, so seeing Oyster Bay in

holiday-mode feels kind of weird.

There's a mixture of people here too. There are rich people with fancy four wheel drives and shiny new boats, there are happy day-trippers and holiday-makers and there are grumpy locals, working.

I thread the quad bike through a backlog of cars, steer it left and reverse into a half-sized park beside a navy-blue Land Rover that seems to think it's entitled to take up two spaces.

I dismount and walk along the jetty towards the green shed. At the moorings along the jetty's length there are boats tethered to yellow-painted pylons. Couples walk hand in hand, stopping every now and then to get photos on their mobile phones. I pass a group of young boys in board shorts. One of them climbs up onto the metal railing, leaps into the air and back flips before bombing into the water.

A father and daughter sit happily in their fold-up chairs at the edge of the jetty. I slow down as I get closer and sneak a look into the white plastic bucket between them. It's empty. I follow the girl's blue rod all the way up to its tip, then I run my eyes down along its silvery spiderweb line. I try to follow it as far as I can, but the wind whips up and I lose sight of it completely.

The Co-op is bigger than I thought it would be. When I walk inside there's a middle-aged couple standing in front of a panel of frosted glass. They're obviously not locals. They're wearing boating gear, polo shirts and shorts, with matching pastel jumpers tied around their shoulders. The two of them are agonising over what to buy – crayfish or prawns.

I head over to the other end of the display, and the man behind the counter looks at me absently. His white apron is splattered with fish guts and blood.

'Are you Stavros?' I ask.

'That's me,' he says.

'I'm Nate,' I say. 'Singlets sent me.'

Stavros's face changes instantly. 'And what can I get you, Nate?' he asks.

I look down at the impressive catch of seafood laid out on the bed of ice in front of me.

'I don't really know,' I say. 'I haven't cooked fish before. Actually, I haven't cooked anything before, really. I'm thinking of barbecuing something. What would you recommend?'

'It's all good,' says Stavros. 'It's hard to stuff fish up if you keep it simple. Just don't cook it too long. If it was me, I'd go the blue-eyed bream. It's all filleted so you don't have to worry about the bones. Throw on some lemon juice, butter, then a couple of minutes on each side and you're done.'

'Okay,' I say. 'Blue-eyed bream it is.'

'And how many are you feeding, Nate?'

I'm starting to get nervous now. It's the first time I've cooked a proper meal with proper ingredients and I'm not sure I'm up to it. Surely Mick won't expect me to feed Barry as well.

'Just two, thanks, Stavros.'

Stavros weighs the bream and wraps it. I tap my card, and while we wait for it to process he glances at the couple next to me and rolls his eyes. I thank him for the fish and walk back to the quad bike. I toss the fish into the cardboard box with the other stuff and climb on.

I reach a hand down and go to start it up, but the keys I left in the ignition aren't there. I check the pockets in my jeans, just in case, then I jump off the bike and search the ground around me. There's no sign of them.

I'm wondering what to do next when I hear someone whistle loudly. I look across the foreshore and see a yellow speedboat in the shallows. It's the same one Gem and I saw hooning around when we were out delivering the hampers.

There are three teenage boys in the back. It's Marty and Stevie and someone else. Marty steps up onto a seat on the back of the boat and waves at me. I can't really see from this distance, but I'm pretty sure he's holding the set of keys above his head.

The boat's engine gurgles and coughs and the speed-boat glides slowly away from shore. I keep watching for a bit. When they're about thirty metres out, Marty cocks his arm behind him. He prepares for a throw, then he launches the keys into the water.

––––––––––

It's annoying more than anything. I'm not sure how Mick will react when he hears I've lost the keys and I'm running out of time, so I grab the cardboard box and start walking quickly back along the road.

I'd rather not have to walk if I had the choice, but it gives me time to do some thinking. I shouldn't have taken the quad bike off the gravel road without a licence and a helmet. I'm stupid sometimes. I don't think. I don't think about the consequences of things, the collateral damage, and how other people might be affected by what I do. Still, I suppose it could have been worse.

Unfortunately Barry seems to think otherwise. When I walk down the driveway with the cardboard box, my forehead dripping with sweat, he looks at me and shakes his head.

'What?' I say. 'It's not like you've never done anything wrong, Barry. He that is without sin, let him cast the first stone.'

I'm hot and bothered when I get to the house. I dump the cardboard box onto the kitchen bench and off-load the fish into the fridge. After knocking back a cold drink, I head outside again and grab the spare set of keys hanging on a hook in the shed.

I go the quick way this time. I cut through the trees past Gem's house and follow the river until I get to the jetty. Not surprisingly, the quad bike is where I left it.

I've wasted too much time already. There's something I need to do before Mick gets home so I drive back as fast as I can without killing myself.

I'm relieved when I hurtle around the bend and up the driveway. Barry comes tearing down the drive towards me. He looks particularly exhausted today, like he's just finished a chest session in the gym. There's no sign of Mick's pick-up so I park the quad bike in the shed and head quickly inside.

Barry's not helping. As soon as he smells the fish, he starts nudging me, starts pushing his way in and out between my legs. I'm trying to think about what needs to be done, but I can't concentrate.

I try talking to him first. I tell him he's a dog and that

he'll have to wait until I'm ready to feed him, but he seems to have no understanding at all of the lowly rank into which he was born. So I decide to lure him outside with the fish and then close the screen door on him.

He pushes his nose against the flywire and starts to sook. I ignore him and get to work. I grab a garbage bag from the cupboard underneath the sink, open the freezer door and start on the top row. I grab frozen dinners two at a time and toss them into the garbage bag on the floor. They clunk against each other like bricks, and the fridge beeps a warning about the open freezer door.

'Hey!'

I turn around and see a horrified Mick, standing in the living room with Barry by his side.

'What do you think you're doing?' he says.

'I'm throwing them out,' I say.

'Like hell, you are.'

I was hoping to get rid of them before Mick came home. He's angry now, but so am I. Without a word I turn my back on him. I grab two more frozen dinners and toss them into the garbage bag.

He's been playing dumb with me, and it feels like a betrayal. My head's spinning with all sorts of stuff, and I need some time to make sense of it. But I don't have time and it's too hard. I can't deal with everything right now. I won't.

I slam a Spaghetti Carbonara onto the floor and it hits the tiles with a *clack*. I turn back around and face Mick.

'How can you do this to yourself?' I say.

'Do what?' asks Mick.

I point to the frozen dinners on the floor.

'This,' I say.

Mick cocks his head and looks at me surprised. 'They were five bucks each.'

I think about everything I read in the pamphlets, all the bad stuff about leukaemia. I'm pretty sure none of them recommended a frozen-dinner diet.

'You're an adult, Mick. You're supposed to be intelligent. Look, I know you don't want me here and that's fine, I get that, but you have to look after yourself.'

'Hang on . . .' Mick takes a step back and takes me in. 'What makes you think I don't want you here?'

'Maybe it's got something to do with what you've been telling everyone. How I'm just like my father. How I've got his bad blood. Thanks for that, by the way.'

'Nate –'

'No, no, I appreciate it. It's nice to know you're –'

'Nate. Stop.'

All of a sudden Mick looks tired, and I feel kind of guilty. He makes a face and takes a deep breath.

'I'm sorry, Nate,' he says.

I close the freezer door to stop the beeping sound and move over to the kitchen bench. It's like the old days when I used to pop pills. The anger I was feeling before seems to have turned into something else.

'I did say that stuff,' says Mick. 'And you're right to be angry. But I said it before I met you, before I got to know you. You were just some kid in juvie then, a kid who bashed an old bloke.'

'Oh, that's okay, then.'

'No, it's not okay. I shouldn't have said it at all. You're nothing like your dad, Nate. You're like your mum. I can see her in you, you know, especially when you're with Henry.'

The tiny pause seems so much bigger than it is.

Mick smiles.

'It might not have been my idea, Nate,' he says. 'But I'm starting to think that getting custody of you might just be the best thing I've ever done.'

I didn't expect that from Mick. It feels warm, like an arm around my shoulder.

I'm not sure what to say so I look at the photo on the sideboard and see the two of them sitting on the jetty. It makes me smile, and I look at Mick slumped over on the other side of the kitchen bench. It's as if our conversation has drained him of energy. He points at the garbage bag on the floor.

'Is that really necessary?' he asks.

'Yeah,' I say. 'It is.'

'Okay, but how about we keep a couple of Lasagnes? You know, for emergencies.'

'No, Mick. For God's sake, Barry's been eating better than you. There's no nutritional value here at all. From now on we're eating healthy. We're juicing too.'

'Neither of us can cook, though, Nate.'

'I'm going to learn. And then I'll show you.'

Mick takes a few steps forward and has a look into the cardboard box. He pulls something out and holds it up.

'What's this?' he asks.

'It's called kale,' I say.

'What's kale?'

'I don't know. It's some sort of lettuce thing, apparently. It's ridiculously healthy, they reckon. You put it in salads, in juices as well.'

Mick puts the kale back, and for a few minutes there's silence.

'Do you want a hand with dinner?' he asks.

'Sure,' I say. 'You can cut the carrots, if you like. They're those long orange things with the green tops.'

# FOURTEEN

Although I've only just found out about
the leukaemia, it's hard not to think
about what's going on in Mick's body.
As I chop the tomatoes I think about
blood cells and bones and needles and
veins. I think about scans and x-rays
and MRIs. When I slice the avocado,
I see images of a bald-headed Mick in
a hospital room, hooked up to a machine
with chemo juice running through him.

I try to concentrate on preparing the
dinner but every now and then I catch a
glimpse of him doing an everyday thing and
I wonder how long it'll be until he starts to
struggle with things like that. I zone out and picture

the boat in the shed, its smooth golden wood lit by a shaft of evening light. I don't realise I'm staring into space until Mick pulls me up.

'You right?' he says.

'Huh?'

'You look weird,' says Mick.

'I'm fine,' I say.

I snap back to the kitchen and take a moment to work out where we're at. With the salad almost done, it's time to cook the fish so I look out through the window at the barbecue and see a gas bottle tucked in underneath it.

When the salad is done, I head out to the verandah with the bream. Barry follows me, and when I unwrap the fish, he starts to salivate and drool in a puddle by my feet.

'Forget it,' I say.

He looks up at me with pleading red eyes.

'No, Barry. You can look at me all you want, but I'm afraid that things are about to change around here. There's a new sheriff in town, all right? And you, my friend, are no longer running the show. You're a dog.'

I point to Barry to show him what I mean. 'You. Dog.'

Next I point to my own chest. 'Me. human.'

I keep going like that for a bit, back and forth a few times just to drill it in.

'Dog. Human. Dog. Human.'

I have a feeling it's going to take some time for Barry to catch on, so I fire up the barbie. A few minutes later Mick comes out in his board shorts and t-shirt carrying a beer and a glass of soda water. He sees me staring at the bottle in his hand.

'Sorry,' he says. 'I'd probably offer you one, but I don't

think the parole people would like it all that much. Do you mind if I . . . ?'

'Go ahead.'

I had a hard time of it when I first went into Croxley. I climbed the walls for a good two weeks coming off the stuff I'd been on. Slipping back into it would be easy, too easy, but that's one thing I promised myself I wouldn't do.

Mick hands me the glass of soda water. Floating amongst the cubes of ice is a twist of lime.

'Fancy,' I say.

Mick holds his brown bottle out and clinks my glass. 'Cheers, Nate.'

———

Laziness is Mick's worst enemy in the kitchen but when the two of us work together, we somehow manage to make 'simple' look half decent. In fact, when we serve up the fish and salad onto our plates, it looks remarkably similar to the pictures in the books. We're a little light on for salad dressing and flavour, but given it's our first attempt I'm quietly confident about what's to come on our culinary journey in the months ahead.

To be honest, I hadn't expected to like cooking all that much, but something about putting it all together from scratch has filled me with a sense of achievement. I take a mouthful of tender bream, mark my place in *Juicing for Life* and look up.

'You heard of chia seeds?' I ask.

Mick has a think. 'Maybe,' he says. 'Not sure.'

'They're amazing little things,' I say. 'Says here they're

an excellent source of omega three fatty acids, high in antioxidants, fibre, iron and calcium.'

'Yeah?'

'Yeah. It's like a superfood. People put them in their juices, on cereal too. What about acai bowls? You heard of them?'

Mick shrugs. He seems preoccupied with something else.

'What's the matter?' I say.

'Nothing,' he says.

'Do you feel sick?' I ask.

'No, Nate, I don't feel sick.'

'But if you did, you'd tell me, yeah?'

'Of course.'

'Well, what is it, then?'

Mick shifts his eyes to something next to me and I follow them down to the table setting between us, to the empty plate, the knife and fork, the napkin and the glass. I look back at Mick.

I know he's sick but I can't help it. He's holding on to something that's gone.

'You know she's not coming back, right?' I say.

'Yeah, I know,' he says. 'I knew when she left, when she packed her bags and went.'

'So, why don't you clear it away?'

'I don't know why. It's weird, isn't it?'

'Hell, yeah. It's creepy. And the house too. I take it all these things you've got, the way they're arranged . . . that was Malaya as well?'

'Yep.'

'Maybe you need to find someone else. How's Oyster

Bay off for older single women?'

'Cut it out, Nate.'

'No, I mean it. You should have someone nice. How long's it been, anyway?'

'How long's what been?'

'You know . . . sex?'

Mick looks away then forks some fish into his mouth and swallows.

'This bream's nice,' he says.

'I'm serious, Mick. How long? Obviously it's been a while.'

'Why do you say that?'

'Well, it's obvious.'

'Why?'

'You look desperate, like you're not getting any.'

'Okay, you can stop right there, Nate. Thank you for your concern, and I appreciate the cooking and all, but I don't think you need to get involved in my love life.'

'You haven't got a love life,' I say.

'Thank you, Nate. I am aware of that.'

Mick takes a deep breath and sighs. I'd rather not get involved in his non-existent love life to be honest and I don't want to hurt his feelings, but it's kind of funny seeing him squirm.

'It's good we can talk,' I say. 'Especially now. We're family, right?'

Finally, Mick manages a smile. 'We are, Nate.'

The two of us sit there and finish our dinner in silence. It's a good silence. It feels comfortable and easy.

————

After dinner, Mick ducks out to the car and returns with a white plastic bag.

'I got you something in town,' he says.

He puts the bag onto the table and I reach into it and retrieve a three-set of differently coloured Bonds underwear.

'Really?' I say.

'Well, you know. Do you want to buy them second-hand at the church store?'

There's something else in the bag. I dip my hand back in and pull out a small cardboard envelope with a SIM inside.

'I noticed you had a mobile,' says Mick. 'The reception's a bit hit and miss around here, but I thought it'd be a good idea. It's a back-up for the two-way if you're out in the boat.'

I go to thank him, but he holds up a hand. 'Speaking of boats . . . I was thinking we could go out on the river soon. You're up with the theory, I take it?'

'I'm all over it.'

'Good.'

Behind us there's a knock on the screen door. I turn my head and see Gem standing behind the tattered grey flywire.

'Something smells good,' she says.

I go to say something, but then I realise she might be here to see Mick. It feels like more than a few hours since I saw her last. Maybe it's all too good to be true.

'Hey, Gem,' Mick says. 'What's up?'

'Nothing much,' she replies.

I'd like nothing more than to get up and let Gem in, but Mick's too quick.

'What can I help you with?' he says. 'Everything okay?'

Gem walks inside. She looks my way. 'Everything's good, Mick. Actually, I'm here to see Nate.'

'Oh . . .' Mick's not sure about things. It's as if he's trying to rearrange what's in his head. 'Okay. Um. Sure.'

'Do you mind?' I ask.

'Of course not. Off you go, I'll clean up.'

It's so good to see Gem again. When I signed the papers back in Croxley, I never imagined finding someone like her. She's so different from any other girl I've met. She's got a thing about her that's hard to describe, a strange kind of wonderful that makes the world a better place.

'So, what did you whip up?' she says. 'Smelt fishy.'

'Bream and salad,' I say. 'Pretty good for a first go, too. And I liked it more than I thought. The cooking, I mean.'

Gem looks at me and smiles.

'What?' I say.

'You'd be a good catch, you know?'

'You think so?'

'Yeah. I mean, don't get me wrong, there's a stack you need to work on.'

'Like what?'

'Like clothes.'

'What's wrong with my clothes?'

'Nothing, but you need to get some more. You've been wearing the same things for days.'

'So?'

'So, there's this thing called hygiene, not sure if you've heard of it but it's been around for a while. And that sucking thing you do with your teeth, that needs to stop too.'

'I get food stuck,' I say.

'Well, it's annoying.'

I glance at Gem and roll my eyes. 'Must be hard being perfect,' I say.

Gem laughs. 'You've got no idea, Nate.'

I'm keen to see Gem's house, but apparently there's no way we're doing that. Instead she suggests a walk to the main jetty. She grabs my hand and leads me down the grassy section, past the workshop and into the trees. Halfway in, we turn right and walk along a track that runs into another one down by the river. It's wide enough to walk alongside each other so we amble along slowly.

To be honest, I've always found it awkward holding hands with girls. Whenever I've been pressured into a hand-holding situation, it never felt right. I always felt stressed about how to do it, whether I should go with the finger-link set-up or the traditional whole hand grip. But with Gem, I don't even have to think. It just happens, and suddenly we're walking hand in hand and it's like it's meant to be. There's no clumsy readjustment and no sweaty palms. The two of us fit, and it feels like we've been holding hands forever.

At a bend in the river, Gem lets go of my hand and walks side on for a bit.

'Movie update,' she says.

I can't believe she's actually going for my whole movie analogy scenario. Somehow it's paid off. In fact, I think it might be a thing now. Our thing.

'What, again?' I say.

'Yes, again.'

'Okay, then. Well, it's a personal thing, I reckon. I've been totally hooked from the start but, to be fair, you're probably not everyone's cup of tea.'

'Oh yeah? Go on.'

'I mean, all that sitting around in holiday shacks and pretending to be someone else . . . most people would find that odd. So you're obviously a foreign film or one of those indie art-house ones.'

Gem looks happy with that. 'Cool.'

'Well, yes and no. Put it this way, you won't be winning any major awards or strolling down many red carpets.'

Gem opens her mouth wide. She looks disappointed. 'Why not?'

'Because you're not that type of movie, Gem.'

'Oh, here we go.'

'No, it's a good thing.'

'Why is missing out on awards and the red carpet a good thing?'

'Because it means you're different. It means you're unique.'

'Why do I have to be unique?'

'It means you're not mainstream. It means people don't know what to do with you.'

'Maybe I want people to know what to do with me.'

'Why?'

'I don't know. Maybe just once I want to be something people can like. Maybe I want to walk down the red carpet. God, imagine that.'

Gem's eyes get all faraway and dreamy. I think about kissing her but the moment doesn't last.

'Wow,' she says. 'Imagine walking down a red carpet, actually walking on one for real. With all the camera lights flashing and everyone looking. I'd wear green tartan, I reckon. A dress. And you could wear a kilt.'

'Me? Really?'

'Yeah. It'd suit you. It's not a skirt.'

'No, I know. I just mean, you'd want me to walk next to you?'

'Why not? Of course, you'd have to stop that teeth-sucking thing.'

'Consider it stopped.'

'And you'd have to smell nice and do your hair.'

'No problem. I'd hate to make you look bad or anything.'

Gem turns around and walks along the track ahead of me. It sounds weird, but all of a sudden I feel like doing something stupid like climbing a tree.

Around the bend, a family of ducks have taken shelter in the reeds, and we walk closer to have a look at the duck-lings. Despite our easy pace, Gem seems to be struggling with her breathing. She sucks in air and when we approach a huge magnolia tree, she veers left towards the wooden bench seat tucked in against its smooth pale trunk.

'Do you mind?' she says.

'Not at all,' I say.

We sit down next to each other, and the mother duck leaps onto the bank and waddles up, looking for food. Gem bends forward, then she dips her head and breathes.

'Are you okay?' I ask.

'Yeah, I'm fine,' she says. 'I get asthma sometimes. It's nothing.'

'Have you got a puffer?'

'Nuh. I'll be good in a minute.'

'We could head back home, if you like.'

'I'm fine, Nate. Really.'

Gem's breathing improves after a few minutes and soon we're off along the track again. I go slowly without making it look obvious, stopping every now and then to look at something on the river.

When we get to the playground near the boat ramp, Gem heads for one of the black rubber swings. She sits down and grabs hold of the metal chains, and I push her high into the air. When she tells me to stop I walk slowly around so I can get a proper look at her.

She leans back in the swing and closes her eyes and lets the wind rush across her face. She doesn't see me when I sit on the bouncy hippo in front of her and thread my feet through the tiny metal stirrups. Her wisp of purple hair flutters back and forward as she swings. She puts her arms out to the side as if she's flying. She smiles and at that moment she's the most beautiful thing I've ever seen.

We have to wait until the swing is completely still before Gem gets off. I'd never heard of it before, but according to Gem it's a good luck thing – an unwritten but unbreakable rule that's known in all the serious playgrounds around the world. The swing takes forever to finally stop, but maybe a bit of good luck is worth the wait.

When Gem finally dismounts, the two us walk slowly past the boat ramp, past two men in brand-new overalls, launching their boat from a trailer. After they give it a nudge, it grinds off noisily into the water. One of the men tries to hold it steady with a rope line, while the other man rushes clumsily back to the driver's-side door of the four wheel drive.

Gem laughs. 'Geared-up amateurs,' she says quietly. 'Part-time anglers from the city.'

She talks to me as if I've been here for years, as if I'm a part of Oyster Bay. It seems ridiculous now to think I felt so lost when I arrived.

I remember standing on the landing that first evening and gazing out across the water into the crimson sky above. The sky felt so big that first night. It felt as if it stretched on forever. I remember feeling lost without Croxley's walls, without its rules and routines to tell me what to do. It's only been a few days and I still feel them every now and then. Sometimes I react to a light going on or off, or the sound of footsteps coming up behind me. But I don't feel lost anymore, not like I did on that very first night. And I know that's got something to do with Gem. There's so much to do now, so much I want to do, and the days don't seem to be long enough.

It's that strange time just before evening, and it's hazy on the river. My mum always loved this time of day because of the colours in the sky. She said it was the day giving itself up, surrendering to the night. She told me that looking at the evening sky was like a gift because it made the good things extra good and the bad things not so bad.

Even when my father came home drunk and angry, my mum always managed to find something to be thankful for. I feel myself smile remembering all of that, and when I look up at the orange streak splashed across the western sky I can't help but think my mum knew what she was talking about. Right now, with Gem, the good feels extra good.

I'm not paying much attention to what's going on around me as we walk along the jetty, but when Gem squeezes my hand I realise we're approaching a group of people. They're gathered against the side rail on our right, drinking coolers and beers. There are about seven, maybe eight all up, a mixture of boys and girls. Some of them are familiar, and then I spot Marty and Stevie sitting on the metal railing.

It's not too late to turn around so I whisper to Gem beside me. 'You okay?'

'Yeah.'

'We can go back, if you like.'

She shakes her head.

'Are you sure? We don't have to, Gem. We can turn around.'

'No, Nate. I want to see the sunset. I want to go to the end of the jetty. All the way to the end.'

We continue walking, hand in hand, and I keep my eyes peeled for any sudden movement within the group. There are a few other people around, anglers mostly and people walking off their dinners, but I'm mindful of the fading light. Soon enough we'll be the only ones on the jetty and, by the looks of it, Marty and Stevie have a few beers in them already.

The sky seems suddenly darker than it was before. I never liked the dark in Croxley. The dark was a time for payback, a time when things got done. I know this is different, it's a public place, after all, but it still puts me on edge.

As we approach the group, they begin to shift about and jostle for position. Marty and Stevie climb down off the rail and stand on the outskirts of the circle. I hear the sniggering first. I hear laughing and kissing noises. Gem and I keep walking, and we draw level with an awkward-looking boy at the front of the group whose face is pockmarked with acne. He steps aside, and for a few seconds it looks as if we might make it past them without any serious issues, but at the very last moment Marty and Stevie step out in front of us. I squeeze Gem's hand, and ball my other hand into a fist. The two of us try to walk around them, but they shift sideways and block our path.

'Give it a rest,' I say.

Marty's in front of me, one step and he'll be within reach.

'Did you hear that?' he says. 'Tough guy wants a rest. You two been at it, have you?'

Some of the group begin to laugh. I go to say something, but Gem cuts in first.

'Is that all you've got, Marty?' she says. 'That's the best you can do?'

'I've got more,' he says. 'Want me to tell your boyfriend all about it?'

'I've heard it all before, though. You're unoriginal, Marty. You're boring.'

'Yeah? You didn't seem to think so at Gus's party.'

Gem seems unfazed. 'Well, people change, Marty. They grow up. They get smarter. You should try it.'

One of the girls in the group laughs. It's the orange girl from the store. Her friend elbows her to stop.

Gem waves Marty aside. 'Excuse us. You're in the way.'

But they're not done. Stevie wants a go. He leans in, uncomfortably close to Gem. 'Where's Henry today?'

This time, Gem reacts. She straightens up and glares at him.

'Hope he's being careful,' says Stevie, smirking. 'Not

walking around on his own again, is he, the little space cadet? I'd hate him to get into strife or anything.'

I let go of Gem's hand and shift forward a little, ready to go. Doing nothing doesn't seem right. I'm an arm's-length from Stevie's face. I hate the way they treat Gem, but she seems to want to deal with them on her own. And that's fine. She's been handling their crap long before I arrived. But Henry's a different story. He's just a kid. And that sounds like a threat.

I look into Stevie's eyes before I speak. 'Go on. Open your mouth again and give me a reason.'

It's lightning fast. Stevie pushes my chest with two hands, and I stumble back, a little off balance. He rushes forward with his right arm cocked, but I tangle him up with my left leg. He crashes down on top of me and we scuffle on the ground for a bit. I'm not after a fight, but if it happens I don't mind it in close. It's where I do my best work.

'Hey!'

It's the orange girl again. She's shouting and pulling Stevie off me. As soon as he's up, I jump up too and turn to follow him. But the first thing I see is a little girl a few metres down the jetty. She's holding a chocolate ice-cream in her right hand and she's standing there alone. She looks frightened and confused, as if she's trying to make sense of what's going on. She must have snuck off for a second. All of a sudden her mother rushes over and scoops her up, then she retreats back down the jetty without a word.

It's over. It's like a balloon's gone *pop*.

I glance over at the girl who dragged Stevie off me, but she turns away and follows after the others.

Gem's beside me in a second. She looks startled.

'You okay?' she says.

'Yeah, I'm good.'

I look around and notice people staring. 'Do you want to go home?'

Gem's fingers brush against mine. 'Not home,' she says.

'Where then?'

She nods her head along the jetty and out towards the deep water.

'To the end,' she says. 'To the very end.'

# FIFTEEN

It's dark by the time we get back to
the boatshed. Barry's waiting on the
deck for us. When he sees us come
out through the trees, he bounds
over and starts licking – goes from
me to Gem as if he's not sure whose
legs taste better.

It's been a strange evening and, as
much as I'd like to set up the chairs and
sit for a while, I'm worried about Gem.
She seems preoccupied, nervous, and when
I offer to walk her home again, she ignores me
completely. I wonder if it's got something to do
with the aggro on the jetty. I wish we hadn't been
there. I wish it hadn't happened.

'Gem, did you hear me?'

'Yes, Nate. I heard you.'

'So . . .'

'So, I don't want to go home.'

I don't know what to say to that. Gem's acting kind of weird so I go for what's familiar. There are a few sour straps left over. I set up the chairs and grab the packet from inside.

When I'm sitting down next to Gem, watching her chew her way through a strap, I tell her I'm disappointed she's not a peeler. I tell her there are strict rules when it comes to eating a sour strap, something like staying on a swing until it stops moving. She doesn't buy it, though. I knew she wouldn't. She tells me that to fully appreciate a sour strap you have to eat all three flavours at once.

She's got a point, I suppose.

Every now and then, a twinkling ball of light dances along in front of us as a boat makes its way slowly up the river. When I first arrived in Oyster Bay, I never would have thought that sitting in a chair would be something you could refer to as a legitimate activity. I mean, it's just sitting. But I couldn't have been more wrong. Sitting in a chair, with the stars and the sky, with Gem beside me . . . it's the best kind of something there is.

Gem reaches out and puts her hand on mine.

'You okay?' she says.

'Yeah,' I say. 'I was just thinking about sitting.'

Gem smiles. 'Sitting?'

'I used to sit with Mum a lot,' I say. 'When the old man went out. She'd sit in this green velvet armchair, and I'd sit in front of her on one of those crappy vinyl footstools.

She'd get her guitar out, and I'd watch her play. I'd watch her fingers dance across the strings. She had beautiful fingers.'

'Did she teach you to play?' asks Gem.

'Yeah. I think I learnt most of what I know by just watching, though. And listening. I haven't played since she died.'

'Would you play for me?'

I turn my head and throw Gem a look.

'I can't.'

'Why not?' she says.

'I just can't.'

'You can, Nate. It's time. I think your mum would want you to play. I would.'

I grab the second-last sour strap from the packet and start to peel off a strip. 'Yellow,' I say. 'I always start with yellow.'

'Where is it?' says Gem quietly.

'I tried starting with blue one time, but it didn't feel right.'

Gem's not giving up. She reaches over and snatches the sour strap from my hand. 'Do you still have her guitar?' Her voice is louder this time.

'It's at the old flat,' I say. 'In Surrey Heights. The old man's still there, I think. I mean, I don't really know.'

Gem sits up straight in her chair and stares at me hard. 'Let's find out.'

'Excuse me?'

'If he still lives there,' she says. 'We could go get it. You and me. Together.'

I shake my head. 'It's not going to happen, Gem.'

She pauses, and in the silence I listen to the swarm of moths and bugs thwacking against the light bulb under the workshop awning.

I go to say something, but she cuts me off.

'Nate, I know what you're going to say, okay? You're going to say I'm being a hypocrite because my dad and I aren't cool either. And we're not, but at least I've put it to bed. You're laden, Nate.'

'Laden?'

'Yeah. You're carrying everything around with you. And it's weighing you down. You've got to let it go.'

I've lost count of the number of times I heard the same thing from the counsellors in Croxley, but no one has said it quite like Gem. It's different coming from her.

I'm not sold on laden, though.

'Laden's not even a word, Gem.'

'Yeah it is. Look it up and stop trying to change the subject.'

Gem sits quietly and waits for me to say something.

'So is that a yes?' she says finally.

'Is what a yes?'

She gets out of her chair and takes a few steps my way. She stands in front of me, and when she reaches for my hand I let her take it. She pulls me up so that we're standing close to each other.

'Your mum's guitar,' she says. 'I'm going to get it. Are you going to come with me?'

I feel the hem of her tartan skirt brush against my thighs, and I know I'll go wherever she asks me to.

'I might . . .'

'You might?'

'Yeah, I might . . . if you tell me where you've got your seahorse tattoo.'

Gem smiles, and all of a sudden I'm nervous. We're about to go next level, and I want it to be right.

'How about I show you?' she says.

The auto-timer gives out, and the light under the workshop awning blinks off. It feels like it's just me and Gem now.

The moon lights her up like an angel. I'm not nervous anymore. I'm not angry or frightened or scared. I've never really known a life without those things. They've been with me for a very long time. But standing here with Gem I feel free. I feel like I'm someone else, and that makes no sense because for the first time in my life, I actually feel like me.

Gem seems to know. She leans into me, and I kiss her lips. I feel her hands under my t-shirt, moving up my back. Her palms glide soft and gentle and settle between my shoulders.

She breaks from our kiss and nods her head towards the bed in the boatshed.

'What do you think?'

'I think it's a good idea,' I say.

It's like we can't bear to be apart, even for a second. We stumble sideways into the boatshed with our lips pressed together and then we get busy with buttons and zips. I'm hopeless with the weird leather ties on Gem's tartan skirt, but she doesn't care – she just laughs and lets me fumble.

Then we slip under the blankets, laughing and kissing like we were made just for each other.

# SIXTEEN

When I wake up, there's a girl in the bed
next to me and a familiar boy standing on
the deck outside.

'Are you tired?' says Henry.

I start to panic and look around
the room for my clothes. 'Ah, yeah,
mate. I'm really tired.'

'Is Gem tired too?' asks Henry.
'Karen's worried, you know.'

I give Gem a nudge with my elbow, and
she opens her eyes and sees me next to her.
'Shit.'

'You sweared, Gem,' I say.

'Yeah, sorry. Hell, what time is it?'

'Not sure,' I say. 'But Henry's here.'

'Oh God, really?'

Gem lifts her head off the pillow and looks out through the double doors. 'Good morning, mate.'

'You should go to bed earlier,' says Henry.

'You're right,' says Gem. 'I should. Can you give us a sec, please?'

'Where are your pyjamas?' says Henry.

'Ah, well, they're at home, I think.'

Henry's not budging. Barry joins him on the deck, and the two of them stand there gazing in. Somewhere nearby I hear a whistling noise, then the sound of footsteps and a familiar voice.

'Come on, Nate. It's time to get . . .'

All of a sudden Mick appears on the deck next to Barry. He freezes on the spot and the three of them stand in a line. I know full well that one of them is a dog, but I feel as if I need to address all three at once.

'It's not what you think, guys. We didn't, I mean, I wasn't . . . you know . . .' I look at Gem beside me, hiding under the blankets. 'Tell them, Gem.'

She starts to laugh.

'Cross my heart,' I say. 'I know it might not look good, but this is all totally above board.'

Strangely enough, none of the three seem to be moving. They just stand there gawking. Finally Gem stops laughing. She coughs into her hand, gets impatient.

'I know,' she says. 'How about you go and get Singlets, Mick? And while you're at it, grab Mum and bring her back for a squiz too. Or, hang on, here's another suggestion. Why don't the three of you bugger off so we can get dressed?'

Mick clears his throat. 'Oh, yeah, right . . . sorry.'

Mick puts his hand on Henry's shoulder, then he turns him around and steers him off along the jetty.

Once they're gone, I find my jeans on the floor, and after slipping them on I scoop up Gem's clothes and pass them to her lonely looking hand that's sticking out from underneath the blankets. I finishing dressing and when I'm done, I turn back around and Gem's sitting on the bed watching me with the blankets pulled up around her neck. I want to say something, but I'm not sure what.

'Gem, last night . . . It was . . .'

'Yeah.' She smiles. 'It was, wasn't it?'

———

I wouldn't mind a juice before we go, but I'm not sure if it's a good idea to push my luck with Mick. When I get to *Forever One*, Henry's got a yellow lifejacket on and he's checking the emergency gear in the back. I jump on board, and Mick calls me up to the front with a head tilt. When I get there, he slips out from the driver's seat and ushers me in.

'Do we need to talk?' he says.

For some reason, the question doesn't sound particularly nautical in its nature.

'About what?' I say.

'About stuff,' he says. 'Boy stuff and girl stuff. And about Gem.'

I'm pretty sure I'm about to get a lecture on birth control so I decide to get in first. I guess I deserve what's coming after our conversation about his love life the other day.

'I'm seventeen, Mick.'

'I know, and that's what worries me.'

I think about last night and smile.

'Look, last night wasn't what you think. But when it does happen, I'll make sure we're prepared. Everything's cool, Mick.'

Mick's struggling. He nods his head, but he's clearly not finished.

'Okay, but it's not just that. This is Gem we're talking about. She's special. I need to know that you realise that.'

'Of course I do, Mick. Her being special is the reason this is happening. Stop worrying, will you? Everything's good. In fact, it couldn't be better.'

Mick nods again. He seems a little calmer about it now.

I nod back. 'Another good talk, Mick. How are you feeling anyway?'

'I feel fantastic, as a matter of fact. I juiced this morning. Actually it's more of a smoothie.'

'No way?'

'Yes way. Banana, strawberry, blueberry, honey and oats. I've got some in the thermos for you. Now, how about we start her up?'

Barry's standing up front at the stern of the boat. He's wearing a white sailor hat with holes for his ears and *CAPTAIN* written across the front.

First up, Mick tests me on all the safety things Gem taught me, then we move on to the practical boating drills. Most of it's common sense, really, so it's not too difficult.

At the end of one of the drills, I bring the boat to idle and my mind starts to drift back to last night, to Gem. I think about lying there in the moonlight, staring at her face after she'd fallen asleep. I think about her seahorse tattoo and the way her fingers glided over my back like whispers across my skin. Nothing about what happened felt awkward or weird or rushed. It was easy with Gem, and it seemed to mean something every time we touched, every time we kissed.

It appears I'm not the only one who's drifting. Mick whacks my arm as *Forever One* gets dangerously close to the tangle of mangroves by the bank.

'Concentrate, mate,' he says. 'You're behind the wheel.'

After we've run through all the drills in the book, Henry and Mick invent a few scenarios so that I have to think on my feet, under pressure. We spend a good hour and a half drilling, and then Mick suggests we open the engine up and get her going to give me an idea of what she can do.

It's an amazing feeling being in a boat that's going flat out. I'd expected the ride to be rougher, but *Forever One* is designed for stability, even at speed, and, with a more powerful engine installed, Mick says she's a match for nearly any fishing boat on the market.

Henry loves it. He knows everything there is to know about the boat and the river. He's completely at home. Barry leans over the side of the boat. He closes his eyes and lets the wind rearrange his already rearranged face.

We do laps of the three islands. We go around each one, and on the way home Mick slows us down near the Franklin Bridge. We cruise slowly towards the bank and wave to a couple in a red kayak paddling by. Thirty metres from the bank, Mick cuts the engine and all of a sudden there's silence, glorious silence. Henry looks happy.

We head out from under the canopy and sit on the

bench seat on the port side of the boat.

Mick points to something about twenty metres away.

'You see those racks?' he says.

I follow his finger to what looks like a series of wooden shelves in the water. There are about ten in total, lined up in rows with spaces between them.

'I was wondering what they were,' I say. 'There's a few around, especially up the river a bit.'

'Well, this is ours. Grandpa Walt started it. Right here is where we farmed our oysters.'

'And how does it all work? I mean, where do the oysters come from?'

Mick looks at Henry who's being unusually quiet.

'Do you want to tell Nate how oysters work, Manolin?' he says.

'They start from spats,' says Henry.

But for some reason, his heart's not in it so Mick takes over.

'They're tiny little things in the water you can't see,' he says. 'They spawn in summer, between November and March. At low tide they attach themselves to those wooden racks over there. Some farmers start them off in a hatchery kind of set-up. Gives you more control over early growth, they reckon. I was about to install one in the work shed when the virus hit.'

Mick gets up and lifts the lid on the storage bench beside him. He retrieves the thermos and pours the dark-coloured smoothie into three plastic cups.

Henry stares into his cup and screws up his face. 'It's purple,' he says.

'That's the berries,' says Mick.

'It's got lumps and it smells.'

Mick downs a shot. The taste of it registers and he makes a face too.

'I call it Summer Surprise,' he says. 'Goodness in a cup.'

'I don't want goodness in a cup,' says Henry.

'Just try it, mate. It's good for you.'

'I don't want it.'

Henry hands his cup to me and goes off with Barry to drop a line off the other side of the boat.

I divide the smoothie up and share it with Mick.

My mum drank smoothies when I was little sometimes. When things got bad at home, she'd take me off to the Harvest Cafe where her friend Sinead worked. It was a kind of safe place, a haven, I suppose. Sinead had a nose ring and green-coloured hair and she made the best banana smoothies. It's funny, but the taste of bananas still brings back memories. Even the smell of them makes me feel strange.

I look over at Mick, at the way he's sitting hunched over. The thought that I might not have much time with him makes the uneasiness worse.

'Can I ask you something, Mick?' I say.

'Sure,' he says. 'Fire away.'

'How come you didn't come for us?'

Mick doesn't look in the least bit surprised by my question. It's like he's been expecting it. But something tells me the answer won't be easy to hear.

'It was tricky,' he says.

Tricky doesn't cut it. It doesn't seem like anywhere near enough. Not after what we endured.

'What's so tricky about helping your sister and your nephew?' I say.

'I did try, Nate, but I made it worse. I said some things to your mum. About your old man. When they were dating.'

'What did you say?'

'They weren't nice. I told her he was a loser, a dropkick and a drunk. I really went to town. She didn't listen, of course. She said she loved him and he loved her. I bloody begged her, Nate, pleaded with her, but she said I didn't understand.'

'Go on.'

'One night he hit her, and she came home with a swollen eye. I was that angry. I went looking for him and found him at the pub, laughing it up, pissed of course. Anyway, I walk right up to him, and he puts his arm around me, wants to buy me a beer like everything's fine. So I dropped him right there in the front bar. A week later, the two of them moved to the city. And six months later they had you.'

Henry grabs a fishing gaff, a long wooden pole with a hook on the end. He leans over the rail next to me and starts trailing it through the water.

I have a swig of my smoothie and all I can taste is banana.

'And so you just gave up, did you?'

'No. I tried to patch things up. I got her to come up for Christmas one year, when your grandpa was sick. That was the first time I saw you. You must have been three or four, I reckon.'

All of a sudden the red-and-green party hats make sense.

'And after that?' I say.

'I asked to come up to the city to see you, but she wouldn't let me. She told me I'd said too many things,

**151**

things I couldn't take back. It was pride, I suppose. Dumb, stupid pride. I saw you in that footy final, though.'

'What footy final?'

'Under elevens, I think it was. You were playing for the Bulldogs up forward. I don't remember who told me you were in it. I parked behind the church and snuck over. Got to see the last half.'

I reach back to a rainy day, to me with chicken legs and oversized shorts. I remember standing in a forward pocket for most of the game, standing next to a skinny boy with a headband and scanning the crowd for my father who never showed.

'We won,' I say.

'Yep. And you kicked that goal from the boundary.'

'And I didn't even mean it. Came off the side of my boot.'

The two of us smile, but there's nothing to smile about. Nothing happy, anyway.

'I'm sorry, Nate,' says Mick. 'Maybe I should've tried harder.'

'Yeah . . . I'm sorry too. About the funeral, I mean. You had every right to come. I was angry.'

All of a sudden the sun breaks through the clouds, and I feel it warm against my skin. Mick and I have come a long way since he picked me up that day at Croxley. We were strangers back then, and I suppose things could have gone a few different ways. But the two of us seem to have found something. We've found something in common besides my mum, and it makes me think we might not be so different after all.

'I've been thinking,' says Mick.

I look up. 'Yeah?'

'Yeah, well, me and Gunter – I mean Manolin. We've been thinking we could use some help with the boat. You interested?'

'Sure. I mean, yeah, that'd be great.'

'Good. This afternoon then.'

'This afternoon.'

The boat is Mick's pride and joy, so when I get to the workshop's entrance, I don't know what to do. I just stand there feeling useless for a bit. Mick looks up from a piece of golden wood and sees me.

'Are you going to help or not? Come on in and have a look at the plans, and we'll run you through what's what.'

When the three of us are gathered around the table, Mick straightens out the butcher's paper. He weighs each end down with a tool and turns to Henry beside him – Henry's wearing his horned Viking hat.

'Righto, Gunter, you may as well kick things off,' he says. 'Tell Nate what we're building.'

'We're building a Viking boat, Nate.'

Neither of them can see the weirdness in that, and when I ask Mick why, he just says, 'Why not?'

'It's a good boat,' Henry says.

'He's right,' says Mick. 'How do you think the Vikings managed to invade and conquer so many faraway lands?'

I take a moment and have a bit of a think.

'Because they were ferocious,' I say. 'Because they didn't take shit from anyone.'

'No,' says Mick. 'Actually, maybe, but mostly it was because they had superior vessels. Lightweight, manoeuvrable and fast.'

'So, you're thinking of invading somewhere, are you?'

Mick lets himself smile.

'Maybe,' he says. 'Might knock over Tassie when we're done.'

I smile back.

'See, the actual building side of things is simple,' says Mick. 'And that's what makes it special. They never worked from sketches or plans. The Viking dads taught their Viking kids how to build them by actually building them. Hands on, word of mouth. Isn't that right, Gunter?'

'That's right, Mick.'

Mick leaves the plans where they are, turns around and takes a few steps towards the boat. Henry and I follow him.

'See, you start with the keel,' he says, pointing. 'That's it there – that long T-shaped length of wood. You run it right along the bottom. Then you do the body, the strakes they're called. They're those long bits of wood. You overlap them and work your way up, one by one from the keel. I've decided to frame it up first to make things easier. The strakes are the hard part, though. You've got to sand them thinner at the stern and bow so they'll bend over the frame, and then you've got to connect them with metal rivets. To stop the leaks between strakes the Vikings used cow hair mixed with tar, but we're going to cheat a little bit and use a modern alternative. It sounds complicated, but it's not. It's actually quite simple.'

He's right. It doesn't sound simple. There were all sorts of words I've never heard before, and I'm a little worried the project might be over my head.

Mick seems to sense my concern. 'Look here,' he says.

I move up closer so I'm standing next to him.

'The hull is the body of the boat. And, basically, the keel is its spine,' he says, pointing again to the T-shaped length running along the base. 'I've flipped the boat upside down. It's easier to work that way.'

He points to the overlapping wooden sides next.

'They're the strakes,' he continues. 'The ribs, if you like, and you can see the metal rivets connecting them to the frame. Make sense now?'

I nod my head. 'Now that you say it like that, yeah.'

'Good,' says Mick. 'Now come with me.'

I follow him to the table, and he picks up a rectangular block with a strip of sandpaper attached to one side.

'We do everything by hand,' he says, passing me the sandpaper block. 'Just like the Vikings did. But if you want to help with the boat there's something you need to remember, something you need to remember every time you come in here. I want you to remember that it's a privilege. Working with wood, I mean. You need to be respectful. All these cuts of wood, all these pieces, were once living things. And they lived for a reason. They mattered.'

After a quick demonstration, I position myself the way Mick had been and start sanding the end of a strake, a length of wood about four metres long and a bit less than ten centimetres wide. Henry is already at work. Mick watches me for a bit, and nods his head. My technique isn't quite right, so he reaches out, grabs hold of my wrist and shows me again.

'Smooth,' he says. 'Long and sweeping, with the grain.'

He leaves me to it, and I sweep the sandpaper along the end of the strake. The music fades, then 'Stayin' Alive' by the Bee Gees starts up on the stereo. I look at Mick, standing at the table with his back to me. After a few bars something weird happens. Mick bends his knee and his hips begin to move from side to side. I watch him groove a little to the music and I feel myself smile. Soon enough the chorus kicks in and weird gets even weirder. I look down and see my right foot tapping on the floor.

# SEVENTEEN

Gem was right about my clothes. When I wake up the next morning, I'm definitely on the nose. As I drag my t-shirt over my head, it's clear I'm in desperate need of some more. But rather than come herself as I was expecting, Gem has sent an eight-year-old to help me with my fashion needs.

And there's another problem – Oyster Bay doesn't do regular clothes exactly. It caters entirely to the holiday crowd, which means a limited range of cheap and nasty beach-type apparel.

With my money being tight like it is, Gem's recommended her shop of choice, the only place really, the second-hand store at the church hall.

When I walk down the verandah steps, Henry's sitting on the quad bike ready to go. He seems to have gone to a bit of trouble with his wardrobe. The smile on his face tells me he's pretty pleased with himself.

'Very nice, Henry,' I say. 'Very, very smart. What do you call that shirt?'

'It's called a polo,' he says. 'It's not my best one.'

'It's not?'

'Nuh. My best is in the wash. It's a blue one with an alligator on it. You might see it this week. I wear it on Thursdays.'

---

The church hall is on the corner of the main road and the next street up from the shops. It's an old white building with a medium-sized bell tower and an arched double door at the front. Along either side of the building, a row of stained-glass windows are covered with heavy-duty wire screens to protect them from rock throwers and vandals.

It's easy to imagine a time when the God-fearing folk of Oyster Bay would've spilled through the doors every Sunday to listen to a crusty old priest in white robes. Still, it was only a matter of time before the Word of the Lord lost its shine. I mean, the bloke's got some clout, he's worked a few miracles, but not even God can go up against fishing and win. Not in Oyster Bay.

The last time I was in a church was the day of my mother's funeral. I don't remember much, to be honest. I don't remember who was there or what people said. All

I remember is the coffin and how small it looked.

And having a go at my uncle. I remember that.

As soon as I set foot inside, I smell the familiar combination of old people and moth balls. The smell of charity shops everywhere.

Off to our left, there's a lady standing at a desk. She's wearing a pastel mauve cardigan and matching slacks. She's sorting through clothes, attaching little white price tags to collars and hems.

'Hello, Henry,' she says.

Henry doesn't reply. He keeps walking towards the clothes racks further in so I smile at the lady as I go by. The menswear section is a lot better than I imagined. Don't get me wrong, there's some absolute trash, stuff you wouldn't ask your worst enemy to wear, but the range is more than decent. When I catch up to Henry, he's already plucked a few polo shirts off the racks.

'I got these, Nate. There's no alligator ones, but I found a man-on-a-horse one.'

'Nice, Henry. Do you think they'll fit?'

'They'll fit.'

I try to imagine us walking into town wearing matching polos.

'What about some t-shirts?' I say. 'I like t-shirts.'

'Okay.'

Henry strikes gold straight away. He's only just started on the t-shirts when I hear him call my name.

I turn around and he's holding up a classic – a brown Golden Breed number with an orange sun blazing across the chest.

'Yes, Henry. Yes.'

The two of us spend half an hour, maybe more, sorting through clothes and when we've had enough, we carry our bundles up to the desk. For his trouble, I let Henry choose two things for himself. He chooses a fishing jacket, and a felt hat for Gem. Vera, the lady in mauve, rings them up and puts them all into a bag.

When we're done, Henry and I head for Chester's.

I give Henry five dollars to spend and when he goes inside, I walk towards Singlets who's sitting in his usual spot.

He doesn't say anything when I walk up. I take that as a good sign and pull up a chair at the table next to him. The two of us sit there and stare at the lamp post for a bit. I'm the first to talk.

'Is that lean getting worse, do you reckon?'

'Maybe,' says Singlets. 'It's hard to tell.'

'Do you think they'll ever fix it?'

'Hope not. I wouldn't have anything to do then.'

Singlets turns his head and looks at me.

'I never told you the full story,' he says.

'What? About the lamp post?'

'Yeah,' he says. 'And it's the best part too.'

'Go on, then.'

'Well, it's about what happened after. After your mum walked head first into the post. Do you know what she did?'

'What?'

'She got straight back up and dusted herself off. Then she started walking again, singing, like nothing ever happened.'

I drag my eyes from the post and look at Singlets. 'Is that a metaphor? A little advice?'

'Take it how you like, Nate. I'm just telling you about your mum.'

I nod my head, sit back in the chair and stare at the lamp post for a bit. I'm not sure how to explain it exactly, but there's something kind of peaceful about its lean, something that makes me feel connected to Oyster Bay in some way. I'm not saying I'm a local, or anything, and maybe I never will be, but in a way I don't feel like a stranger anymore.

---

I was looking forward to seeing Gem, but she's not in today. Henry points to his Mars Bar and hands the five dollar note to fake-tan girl – the one who pulled Stevie off me. She's even more orange than usual. She looks like a Halloween outfit, like a pumpkin with eyes.

She slips the note into the till and gives Henry some change. If she's got anything to say about the night on the jetty, she doesn't let on.

'Doing some shopping, yeah?' she says.

I can't do 'yeahs' today so when Henry walks outside I nod and head for the meat fridge at the back of the store. I grab some chicken fillets and some steaks for tomorrow, then walk to the dairy section and pick up some parmesan and fetta. I spot the condoms on my way to the fruit section but can't bring myself to even go near them with fake-tan girl watching. Instead, I add two pears and some salad things to my shopping, then take them up to the front of the store and put them on the counter.

Orange girl puts her nail file down and starts to ring things up in silence. Once I've paid, I pick up the plastic bag and head for the door. But just as I get there, she stops me with a single word.

'Wait.'

I turn around. 'What?' I say.

'I'm sorry about the other night,' she says. 'About what happened with the boys, I mean. I feel bad.'

I stare at her for a few seconds. She seems genuine enough.

'Thanks,' I say. 'But it wasn't really you.'

'Not this time, it wasn't. But I haven't been very nice. I haven't been much of a friend to Gem.'

I nod my head and glance over my shoulder at Henry. He's leaning against the window, hands cupped around his eyes, looking in.

'Maybe you should talk to Gem,' I say. 'Tell her what you're telling me.'

'I know. I should. But I feel so bad. I've been such a mole.'

'Look, you're not telling the right person. I really think you need to tell this to Gem. I think she'd understand.'

'I can't. Not now.'

'What do you mean, not now?'

'I mean with her being sick and all. I just found out.'

'She's fine,' I say. 'It's only asthma.'

'Asthma?'

'Yeah.'

'What are you talking about?' says the girl. 'Gem hasn't got asthma. She's got leukaemia.'

I don't realise I've dropped the bag until the girl walks over and picks it up. She hands it to me, and I turn myself around and walk like a zombie out through the door.

Henry's wearing Gem's hat. He picks up the clothes bags and follows me across the gravel carpark. Maybe it's the change of light, the fact that I've stepped outside, but all of a sudden everything's blurry – the cars in the carpark, the lamp post, the streak of white clouds in the sky.

I don't even check for cars when I cross the road. I walk straight across, and Henry comes with me, going on about something I can't hear.

I don't know what to think on the way home. How can Gem have leukaemia? She would have told me if she did. She would have told me when we talked on Horseshoe Island. She would have told me when we were lying in bed looking out at the stars – if there was a time for telling me, then that would have been it.

I haven't got a clue what Henry says to me as we drive down the dirt road. An old scar opens up inside me and I feel something spill from the wound, feel it pour into me, hot and angry and wild. It's bad stuff – stuff I've tried to ignore for the past eighteen months – but I need it now. I need it inside me for when I get home and see Mick. He's known all along, all this time, and he didn't tell me.

I see Barry leap from the bougainvillea as we approach the house, but I don't even wait for the quad bike to pull up. As Henry veers right towards the shed, I jump from my seat and use the momentum to keep walking when I hit the ground. I bound up the verandah steps and burst into the house.

'You bastard,' I say.

Mick's at the kitchen sink. He knows what's coming before he turns around. 'Nate –'

'Don't you dare, Mick. Don't you fucking dare.'

'I'm sorry, Nate.'

'You lied to me.'

'I didn't lie.'

'Yes, you did. How could you keep that from me? We're talking about Gem.'

'I know. I'm sorry.'

It comes like a sledgehammer hearing Mick confirm it. I shift about on my feet, not sure what to do.

'She made me promise, Nate. She didn't want anyone to know.'

There's so much stuff swirling around in my head so I look away and stare at nothing on the wall. I go back over our time together, over all the moments we've shared, and I can't believe I missed so much. Even the things I noticed I got wrong, like the way she's always stopping to catch her breath. And I was so busy thinking about how her bruises made me feel that I didn't make the connection.

She's been good at pretending, I see that now, but I feel kind of stupid all the same. I think about the conversations we've had too. They don't feel the same anymore. If I'd known Gem was sick I would have heard her words differently. I would have listened to them differently, and they would have meant different things.

I look at Mick. He comes over and places his hands on my shoulders, and my eyes are blurry with tears.

'Is it bad?' I ask.

'Yeah, it's bad,' says Mick. 'She's done everything she could, everything – chemo, radiation, stem cells, all sorts of stuff – but it's too far gone. She's been through the wringer, mate. She's had enough.'

'Enough?'

Mick tries to smile, but it's the saddest smile I've ever seen. I feel my legs wobble a little so I put my other hand down onto the bench.

'What does that mean, Mick?'

'It means the treatment is over.'

'What? No treatment?'

'It's not our decision, Nate.'

I know full well it's not my decision, and I know that the two of us are only new, but doing nothing feels like surrender.

'Nate . . .'

I hardly hear Mick's voice, but I feel his arms. I feel them wrap around my shoulders and squeeze me tight.

# EIGHTEEN

When Gem's mum opens the door, I try to look happy but my smile doesn't seem to work. She's wearing a blue floral dress with bare feet and she looks tired and kind of wasted.

Funnily enough, she's close to what I imagined Gem's mum would be. Her hair is long and dark, and despite the baggy eyes and the frown lines, it's pretty clear they're related. She's a little shorter than Gem, with stronger features, and when I see her in front of me, for real, I have this stupid urge to thank her for the daughter she made.

'You must be Nate,' she says.

'Yeah,' I say. 'It's nice to meet you, Mrs . . .'

All of a sudden I realise I don't know Gem's surname.

'It's Chan,' she says. 'But please call me Karen. I've heard a lot about you, Nate.'

'Really?'

'Yeah, from Henry. Couldn't get a thing out of Gem. She must like you.'

'I heard that!'

Gem's voice comes from one of the rooms down the hall. Karen turns her head and throws her voice back to her daughter.

'You're supposed to be resting, young lady.'

'I'm rested, Mum,' shouts Gem. 'I'll be out in a minute, Nate. What colour tartan? Red or blue?'

'Red.'

It feels weird standing on the verandah with everything in my head. I haven't had a chance to process anything yet so nothing really makes sense. I've got questions galore – things I want to know – and not knowing makes me feel like I'm not really a part of things. Somehow, Karen seems to understand.

'It's hard,' she says.

I nod my head and manage to smile an awkward smile. I know I've just arrived in their lives, but the word 'hard' doesn't seem like it's enough. Algebra is hard and so is getting the steps right in triple jump, but leukaemia needs a different word.

'Hard?' I say.

'Yeah,' says Karen. 'It's really hard . . . for everyone.'

I don't know where to look. What to say.

'I'm her mum,' Karen says. 'Pretending I'm okay and

pretending I'm coping when I'm not is really hard.'

'Why do you do it, then?' I say. 'Pretend, I mean.'

'Because I have to – to get through the day. And because she asked me to be strong. I'm not doing a very good job, though.'

A banging noise inside the house brings a pause to our conversation. I glance at the front door then back at Karen.

'Do you want to come over for dinner?' I ask.

It's out of the blue, and Karen looks surprised. 'Me?'

'Yeah, you and Gem and Henry. Tonight. I'm cooking.'

'You are?'

'Yep. Steak and salad. Nothing fancy.'

Karen tosses the idea around in her head for a bit. Something tells me that she hasn't been invited out for a while.

'Okay, sure.'

She excuses herself for a second and comes back with a glass filled with clear liquid, ice cubes and slices of lemon. I'm pretty sure it's vodka. I'm also pretty sure it's not her first for the day.

Gem appears in the hallway dressed in a red tartan skirt, matching Doc Martens and a black long-sleeved top. As she waltzes towards us, she slaps on the felt hat Henry bought at the church hall.

'See ya, Mum.'

And just like that, we're off. Gem takes my hand. She leads me down the steps and through the trees. I thought I had it all ready, what I wanted to say, but seeing Gem again has messed everything up. I think about being next to her when she fell asleep. I think about how I just lay there, watching her breathe – soft and gentle like the shifting river outside. And I think about her seahorse tattoo, inked perfectly into the olive skin on the small of her back.

We walk through the trees, past the workshop, and head for the jetty. It's as if the two of us have the same idea. We don't bother to check any gear. Gem turns the key in the ignition and *Forever One* roars to life. We're away.

Despite her not telling me the truth, it's impossible to be angry with her. Especially knowing she's sick. But everything's changed. There's a whole new part of Gem I don't know.

She's chatty, and I do my best to be the same. But my heart's not in it and Gem seems to realise. We charge under bridges and tear past jetties, and when we get to Horseshoe Island she slows the boat about forty metres out from her favourite stretch of sand. She shuts down the engine and after tossing the anchor in, the two of us sit on one of the bench seats in the back. The rope line feeds out over the side of the boat, whirring madly until the anchor finds the riverbed.

Gem looks at me. 'This looks serious,' she says. 'Is it Mum? I kind of told you she drinks . . . Talk to me, Nate.'

I shake my head, open my hands in my lap and stare into my palms. I don't even know how to start.

'You should have told me, Gem,' I say.

Gem knows what I mean straight away. She bends over a little and makes a tiny sound likes she's wounded.

'I couldn't,' she says.

'Why not?'

'I wanted to. I really did.'

'Then why didn't you?'

'Because meeting you has changed everything. You make me feel good, Nate – normal. And I haven't felt normal in a long time.'

A green-and-yellow taxi ferry hums by and cuts its revs as it approaches the private jetty on the far side of the river.

'Why would telling me have changed that?' I say.

'It just would have. I didn't want leukaemia tagging along, Nate. I didn't want it to be there when you held my hand or when you kissed me. I wanted it to be just you and me. And the other night it was.'

Memories come rushing back.

'I would have liked a few more nights like that,' says Gem. 'But I suppose one night is better than nothing, right?'

I look at Gem, and I don't know what anything means.

'Can't we do it again?' I ask. My voice sounds small on the river. I don't even sound like me.

Gem smiles. 'I didn't think you'd want to.'

'Are you kidding?'

I've got so many things I want to ask, but I'm worried they're going to sound stupid and I hate that.

Gem reaches out but doesn't quite touch my hand. 'I'm sorry I didn't tell you, Nate.'

'I understand.'

'Really? Because it doesn't look like you do. Please tell me what you're thinking.'

'I'm not sure I know how to say it, Gem. And I'm not sure I have the right.'

'Just say it.'

I haven't got a clue what I'm going to say or where I'm going to end up so I just launch into it.

'Look, I know I wasn't here,' I say. 'I know I wasn't here to see all the stuff that's happened, all the treatment, all the pain you must have been through. I mean, I can't even imagine what that must have been like. It's just . . .'

I trail off. I don't know if I can say it.

'Just what?'

'Mick says you've stopped treatment. It feels like you've given up.'

This time Gem puts her hand on mine, and I see another bruise on the back of her hand.

'I haven't given up, Nate.'

'But there must be something they can do. Something's better than nothing.'

'That's true for most people. Most people our age respond really well to treatment. Everyone's different, of course, but around eighty percent of us go into remission after treatment. I wasn't one of them.'

Something goes off inside me and I feel a lump rise up in my throat.

'But you're not doing anything,' I say.

'They've tried everything already,' says Gem. 'I'm not going to get better, Nate. That's something I've known for a while. But you're wrong – I am doing something. I'm doing it right now, with you. I'm living.'

I look at Gem's face and try to force a smile.

'And it's okay,' she says. 'It's really okay. But it might not be for you. And I totally get that. I totally get it if you want to . . . you know . . .'

I look up, shocked. 'If I want to what?'

'If you want to call it quits. If you don't want to do us anymore.'

I'm not sure I understand what's happening. Everything's coming at me so fast.

'Let's face it, Nate, I'm not a long-term proposition. Even with the blood transfusions and the pain relief and the drugs, sooner or later I'm not going to be around. And it might be sooner, rather than later.'

'Don't say that, Gem.'

'It's true. And you may be all right with that for a while, but you have to think about what's coming. It's started already, and it's going to get ugly, really ugly.'

It's as if Gem's trying to set me free. She lets go of my hand, and I think about everything that's happened. I think about how I might feel when she's really sick, when I can see that she's in pain.

'I know,' I tell her.

'Really? Cause I'd rather we called it quits right now than have you feel sorry for me. I don't want your pity, Nate. And I want this to be the best time of my life. Because this is *my* movie. Remember? I know you thought we were at the beginning, but we're not. We're not even in the middle. We're coming to the end. So I need you to choose.'

I scramble through what life was like before Gem and what it's like now. The two don't even compare.

'I'm in, Gem.'

'You sure?'

'One hundred percent.'

'I was hoping you'd say that.'

Gem shuffles over, leans in and touches my face.

'Can I show you something?' she says.

Gem places my hand on her left forearm and pulls her sleeve all the way up to her shoulder. She turns her arm, and I see a small disc-like object under the skin on the inside of her bicep. She nods her head, and I touch it gently with two fingers. It's just one more thing I didn't see.

'What is it?' I ask.

'It's called a port-a-cath,' she says. 'It's a catheter for the blood transfusions and drugs and chemo when I had it. It goes straight to my heart.'

The port-a-cath is only small, the size of a twenty-cent coin, but seeing it and touching it brings everything home. It makes the leukaemia real, and all of a sudden I'm scared.

I don't know what to do so I kiss Gem softly on the lips, and when we pull away, she's blinking back tears.

I hold her hand, and she sits quietly for a bit as if she's trying to process things.

Somehow she manages a smile. And I burn that moment in my head. Forever.

'I want you to promise me something, Nate,' she says finally.

'Sure,' I say.

'I want you to promise you'll treat me like this, exactly like this, for as long as you can. And I want you to promise me that when we're together, you won't be sad. You can be sad when you're alone if you like, but when you're with me I want you to be happy. No gloomy dying stuff.'

I don't know if that's something I can do, but I tell myself, right then and there, that I'll try my best – that no matter how hard it gets, I won't let leukaemia be a part of what Gem and I have.

'Can you do that, Nate?' says Gem. 'Can you promise me happy?'

I look into Gem's eyes and all of a sudden it doesn't feel so hard.

'I promise, Gem,' I say. 'I promise you happy.'

# NINETEEN

It's not hard to understand why this is Gem's favourite spot. Although we're about forty metres out from her stretch of sand, it feels as if we're tucked away in a private nook. The small beach, if you can call it that, is set back into the island. It's a U-shaped oasis protected on either side by large outcrops of rocks. Unlike the smooth rocks on Blue Island, these ones are ankle rollers, jagged knee scrapers you'd think twice about before climbing.

It's funny, but after spending more time on the boat, I'm starting to appreciate the water like I never thought I would. The way it moves and the noises it makes – it feels peaceful and soothing in a strange lullaby kind of way.

'How'd you like to come for dinner tonight?' I say. 'I'm cooking. I've invited your mum and Henry too.'

'Are you sure about that?' says Gem. 'You don't know my mum, Nate.'

'I know. That's why I'm inviting her.'

'Suit yourself. What's on the menu?'

'I'm doing rib-eye fillet and a spinach salad with parmesan, pear and honeyed walnuts. I've texted Mick to go and get more steaks.'

'God, you're good. It's such a shame about the teeth-sucking thing. Still, at least you bought some new clothes.' Gem tips her hat.

'Do you reckon Henry's okay?' I ask. 'He seemed a bit stroppy today.'

'I think he's jealous,' says Gem.

'Jealous? Of who?'

'Of me. And you. He told me this afternoon that I had to get a different friend because you were his friend first. Buttons isn't well, either.'

'Who's Buttons?'

'He's Henry's snake. He's frothing at the mouth. Some respiratory thing, we think. Maybe you should spend some time with him.'

'No, thanks. I don't like snakes.'

'I mean with Henry, Nate.'

I smile. 'And what about us?'

'We don't have to spend every second together. Mum's right – I do have to rest. And anyway, I think it's good to do our own thing sometimes. It'll make the time we're together even better.'

Gem slides over towards the other end of the seat. She lies down on her back, puts her head in my lap and smiles.

'Movie update, please,' she says.

I look out across the water at Gem's beach.

'Well, I don't know who's writing the script but they're a cruel bastard, whoever they are. And that plot twist threw me. Absolutely blindsided, I was.'

'But you still want to watch, right?'

'Of course,' I say. 'I wouldn't miss it for the world.'

Gem looks peaceful with her eyes closed. She tilts her face to the sun and smiles as if she's grateful for its warmth. It's funny, but sometimes the two of us don't need to talk. It's like we've got this thing – a way of communicating without words. I know I'm not supposed to think about the end and I'm not religious either, but maybe when the end does come, it won't mean the end of us.

I know it sounds crazy – the idea of talking without words. It sounds crazy even to me, but if it means I get to be with Gem when she's gone, I'm up for being crazy every single day.

I walk Gem home and when we get there a grumpy Henry walks out through the front door in a pair of underpants.

'Are you ready?' I say.

He looks up, annoyed. 'For what?'

'For dinner,' I say. 'I thought you'd be dressed. You, me and Mick, we're cooking dinner for the girls tonight. I need you on the barbecue, mate. I thought Karen would have told you.'

Henry comes to life when I mention the barbecue. He

looks around in a panic and tries to work out what went wrong. 'She didn't tell me, Nate.'

Gem sighs and makes a drinking motion with her hand.

Henry takes off. He tears through the front door and into the house but stops a few metres down the hall. I know exactly what's on his mind.

'Maybe a polo, mate,' I say. 'Any one. They're all good.' He nods.

When Henry returns, he's jittery, buzzing with excitement. Seeing him like that makes me happy.

'Gem told me your snake's sick,' I say as we walk back to the house. 'What's wrong with him?'

'I don't know,' says Henry. 'Karen says the vet doesn't know about snakes. She said he has to ride it out on his own. Take pot luck. What does that mean, Nate?'

'Well, it means he'll have to try to get better by himself. Without medicine.'

'Like Gem, you mean.'

I'm trying not to think about that. I'm trying to stay in the now, in the present, so that I can enjoy every last bit of time with her. But when I hear what Henry says, I'm shocked. I find myself grabbing the remote control and fast-forwarding right to the end of the movie. I don't know why I do it. It's painful like you wouldn't believe, but I do it all the same. I fast-forward over the terrible things, over the frightening things, and when I hit play and the credits roll, there's someone waiting there after Gem's gone. He's standing on the landing outside the boatshed.

It's Henry. He's been there all along.

'I don't want Gem to die, Nate,' he says. 'It's not fair, is it?'

177

'No, mate, it's not. It's ... can I swear?'

'Yeah. I don't mind.'

'It's fucked, Henry. And I can't make any sense of it. But it's Gem's life so we have to do things the way she wants. And there's going to be a time soon when she's not around. So, you and me, we have to be tough guys.'

'Like Thor, you mean?'

'Well, probably even tougher than Thor. But we only have to be tough for Gem, when she's around. We don't have to be tough when it's just you and me. You can be whoever you want with me.'

Henry nods, then looks up into the trees, and just like that the conversation about Gem is over.

'He's the son of Odin,' he says.

'Who is?'

'Thor. Can we read a bit of the book before dinner?'

'Sure, mate.'

We've got an hour or so before dinner so we grab a few chairs from the boathouse and head for the landing.

A sleek white sailing boat drops its sail and motors past, then a flock of birds fly overhead in a perfect V formation and disappear behind the trees on the other side of the river.

Barry scoots down and, like always, he seems to know what's going on. He collapses between the chairs and gets comfortable as if he's there for the story as well. I lower myself into a chair beside him and open the book at the place where we left off.

'Do you remember where we were up to, Henry?' I say.

He looks out across the water as if the answer might be floating down the river.

'The young fishermen were being mean to Santiago,' he says.

'That's right,' I say.

'But he's smart, isn't he, Nate?'

'He is, mate.'

'And Manolin's the only one who's nice to him. He brings him coffee. That's because they're friends. Best friends, like us.'

'Yep.'

'Read it, Nate.'

I start to read and Henry and Barry settle in beside me.

---

I change into some new clothes I bought at the church, a white cotton shirt and a pair of grey shorts, and head for the house.

Mick's totally up for a few extra dinner guests, but he hasn't started preparing anything yet. I throw him a look when I walk in and give him the heads-up about Henry's mood.

'Thought we could use an extra chef tonight, Mick,' I say. 'This is Henry Lacoste from France. He comes highly recommended. Absolute gun on the barbecue, they reckon.'

'Is that so?' Mick walks over towards the fridge and lifts a spare apron from a hook on the wall. 'He better have this, then.'

I'm not sure Mick's fully thought through giving an eight-year-old boy an apron with a pair of plastic boobs on the front. But Henry doesn't seem to notice. He ties the apron on, and I open the fridge and grab all the stuff we need.

I open *Healthy and Hearty* and browse through the salad recipe I marked for tonight. I'm already up to speed with how to cook the steaks, so we're pretty much ready to go. Mick grabs a wooden chopping board and passes it to me. When I go to take it, he holds on to it for a bit and makes me look up.

'How'd it go?' he says quietly.

I think about Gem on the boat and I don't know what to say. I haven't got the words.

'Are you okay?' asks Mick.

'I don't know.'

'Let's talk later, hey?'

'Yeah.'

'Knock, knock!' The screen door is open so Gem and Karen let themselves in. Seeing them together, side by side, they look more like sisters really. Karen's wearing her floral dress and sandals, and Gem's stayed with the red tartan skirt, but instead of her usual long-sleeved tops or jackets she's opted for a white clingy t-shirt.

'Wow,' I say.

Karen pretends to blush. 'Thank you, Nate,' she says. 'It's nice of you to notice.'

Gem rolls her eyes, and I take her hand and pull her over to the mantelpiece.

When she kisses me, her eyes close. I breathe her in and she smells like ice cream, like vanilla. She pulls away, but our lips stick together and I feel myself tremble.

From the corner of my eye, I see Henry hovering uncomfortably close in his apron, and when Gem opens her eyes she cops an eyeful of rubber.

'Oh, classy,' she says. 'Really classy.'

Over at the table, Karen hands Mick the bottle of white wine she's brought. 'Be a darling, Mick,' she says.

He pours a couple of glasses and hands one to Karen. It's a beautiful night outside so I suggest we move the table onto the verandah so that we can eat our dinner while the sun goes down. I hadn't noticed anything different before but, when Mick and I take a side each, I realise there's no place set for Malaya anymore. I look up at Mick and nod approvingly.

'One step at a time,' he says.

Barry and I keep a close eye on Henry while we cook the steaks. The barbecue grill is sizzling hot and, despite my instructions to leave them alone, Henry wants to turn the cuts of meat every few seconds. They don't take long. In a few minutes we're done and Henry lifts each one carefully off the grill with the tongs and puts them onto a plate. When he takes them over to the table, we all cheer.

Once we're seated, Mick raises his drink. 'Do you want to do the first toast, Chef Lacoste?' he says.

'What's a toast?' Henry asks.

'Well, it's a kind of tradition, I suppose. It's when you make a point of acknowledging something or when you say thank you for something that's important.'

'That sounds hard,' says Henry.

'It's not hard. How about I do one and show you?'

Mick looks across the table at me. 'Here's to new beginnings,' he says.

We all clink our glasses, then Mick turns to Henry on his right. 'Your turn, now,' he says.

'Here's to Buttons,' says Henry.

Karen's next. 'To daughters,' she says.

I feel Gem's leg brush against mine under the table.

'To tartan,' I say. 'And to movies and red carpets.'

Gem's last to toast. She takes a moment to think and for the first time I see something in her eyes, something I've never seen before. She's scared.

'To life,' she says.

We clink our glasses again and start to dig in.

There's something nice about sitting around the table, talking and laughing and eating. There's something about sharing a meal that makes you want to share other stuff too, but Gem's not talking. I look at her every now and then, but she seems preoccupied. She speaks in small bursts and only contributes to the conversation when she has to. She hardly touches the food on her plate. She picks at the steak, but mostly she just pushes the food around with her fork.

When everyone's finished eating, she picks up a hessian bag from the ground next to her and after putting it on her lap, she retrieves some sheets of white paper and clears her throat with a cough.

'Can I have your attention, please, people?'

Everyone looks her way.

'I want to thank the boys for dinner,' she says. 'Especially Nate. Earlier today the two of us were talking about things, and it made me think about how hard this is for you all – knowing what's going to happen. Sometimes I try and remember what it was like when I wasn't sick, but it feels so long ago. All I can remember is being warm and feeling nice. I'm not sure if that's how you feel, but it's the only thing I remember. Now I feel like a cloud – a dark and depressing cloud that's hovering around and making everyone sad. I know you all love me and I love you too, but I don't want to be a cloud. I want to be the sun. When you think of me now and when you think of me when I'm gone, I want you to be happy. I want you to feel warm and nice.'

My eyes are blurry with un-cried tears. I can feel Henry fidgeting beside me so I reach a hand out and place it gently on his arm. Karen takes a gulp of her wine.

Gem coughs into her hand again and continues on.

'I know that's not as easy as it sounds,' she says. 'So I've written up a contract for each of you to sign.'

I look at Mick and he shrugs his shoulders.

'What kind of contract?' I ask.

'It's called a Happiness Agreement,' she says. 'I made it up, wrote it myself. And I don't want any arguments. Everyone has to sign one. For me. It's compulsory.'

Gem hands the papers to me so I take one and pass the rest on.

I wipe my eyes with my hand and start to read:

*I (insert name) promise that I won't be sad. Whenever I feel as if I want to cry or crack the sads, I'll think of Gem and how it was good to know her. I'll remember the good things I did with her, the fun things, and I'll remember how she laughed.*

*I won't be angry because she died and I won't feel guilty because I'm alive. I'll live every day the best I can and I'll appreciate the sun in the sky. I won't think of her as a memory or as something that has ended or gone. I'll take her with me every-where I go and I'll feel warm and nice because of her.*

*Signed . . . . . . . . . . . . . . . . . . . . . . . . . . . . . . . . . . . . . . . . . . . .*

I grab one of the pens on the table, write my name at the top of the page and sign it at the bottom. It feels easy writing my name on a piece of paper, but it's not. The thing is, dying doesn't come with a brochure or a set of instructions to tell you what to do. I wish it did. Maybe if I'd had something or someone after my mum died, maybe I might have done things differently.

I'm not blaming anyone. No one forced me into any-thing. It was me who did the things I did. But no one actually talks about dying. And maybe that's what makes it so difficult, so confusing when it comes around. I'm not saying that a Happiness Agreement will make it easy, but maybe it will make it a little less sad. It's classic Gem, but she's not done.

'And, Mum, while we're on the subject, I don't want to be buried,' she says.

Karen chokes on a mouthful of wine.

'Sweetheart. Do we have to do this now?'

'Mum, it's important,' says Gem. 'You never want to talk about it. And I know I always bang on about not doing the dying thing, but it's happening anyway. And this is something I have to say, now. And it's not like you're alone, Mum. Mick and Henry and Nate will help you through it.'

Gem glances across at Mick and smiles sadly.

'I don't want to be shoved in a box and buried,' she says. 'I want to be free.'

Karen makes a face. 'Free?'

'Yeah. I want to feel the sun. I want to float and drift.'

Karen's crying now. She tries to stop the tears, but they come anyway. They spill from her eyes and run down her cheeks.

Gem reaches out and puts her hand on hers. 'Please, Mum. I know this is hard, but I can't bear the idea of being in the ground. Please don't do that to me.'

Karen wipes her face with her forearm.

'So . . . what do you want then?' she asks.

'She wants a Viking funeral,' says Henry.

Karen stiffens in her chair.

I glance at Mick across the table and suddenly it all makes sense.

'That's why you're building the boat?' I say.

'I asked them to,' says Gem.

Karen's running on alcohol and sadness. She's a jumble of emotions.

'No way,' she says. 'You're not having a Viking funeral.'

'You don't even know what a Viking funeral is, Mum,' says Gem.

'I do,' says Henry proudly.

'And so do I,' says Karen. 'I watch Netflix, you know. I've seen *Vikings*. We are not burning you at sea.'

'You can't anyway,' says Gem, 'so relax. It's against the law.'

'Well, I'm not surprised,' says Karen.

'But I do want to be burned,' says Gem.

'I think you mean cremated,' says Karen.

'Whatever. And I want my ashes sprinkled into the river at Horseshoe Island. Nate knows where.'

Karen wipes her face with her free hand and throws the rest of her wine down her throat. She looks at Gem and all of a sudden her face softens and fills with love.

'Stubborn all the way,' she says. 'I wouldn't expect anything less.'

I wasn't sure what to make of Karen earlier. When we spoke on the verandah, it was clear she was struggling but she seemed kind of jokey at the same time. For some reason that surprised me. But I can't begin to understand how she must feel, knowing that each day that goes by is one day fewer with her daughter, one day closer to the end. Maybe jokey is Karen's way of doing things. I guess alcohol is too.

Gem wanting a Viking funeral doesn't surprise me at all. It's not your usual way to go out, but I guess it's no stranger than any other funeral. It must be hard for Karen to even think about that, but there's something beautiful about the idea of floating and drifting and being free.

There's something about it that feels like forever.

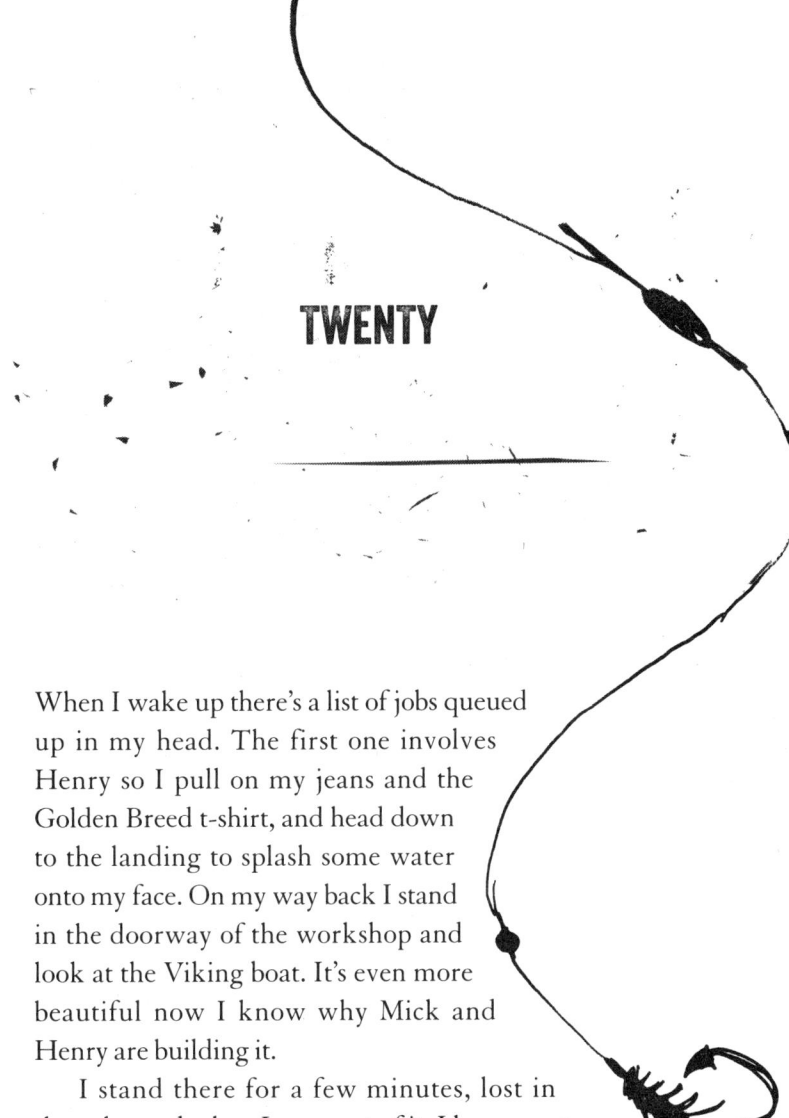

# TWENTY

When I wake up there's a list of jobs queued up in my head. The first one involves Henry so I pull on my jeans and the Golden Breed t-shirt, and head down to the landing to splash some water onto my face. On my way back I stand in the doorway of the workshop and look at the Viking boat. It's even more beautiful now I know why Mick and Henry are building it.

I stand there for a few minutes, lost in thought, and when I snap out of it, I hurry up to the house for breakfast.

I haven't got time to consult *Juicing for Life* so I grab a few items from the fruit bowl and the crisper, peel what I have to and toss everything into the NutriBullet. The result doesn't look all that great. It's kale heavy, green as pond scum, and when I throw it down my throat it tastes a bit like it too.

I call out to Mick, but I get no response so I leave the leftover smoothie in the fridge and write a short note:

*Mick,*
*Just because you've had a miraculous recovery doesn't mean we're going back to frozen dinners.*
*New smoothie concoction I'm calling 'Pond Scum' in the fridge. Really good for you. But like everything super healthy, it tastes like shit.*
*Going to see Frankie, the snake guy you told me about.*
*Talk later.*

When I get to Gem's place, Karen tells me there's a nurse with her in her room. While Henry gets ready, Karen steers me over to the far end of the porch. She's wearing a red-and-yellow dressing gown with black dragons on it. She looks serious.

'I want to talk to you, Nate,' she says.

'Sure,' I say.

Karen wraps the dressing gown around her, re-ties the cord around her waist and glances over her shoulder towards the front door.

'She's dying, Nate – do you realise that?'

I nod.

'She's having a blood transfusion as we speak. She pretends she's okay. With you, I mean. She pretends really hard. But she's not.'

'That's Gem,' I say.

'Yeah, I know. But she won't go to the hospital. She wants to stay here so she can see the water through her bedroom window.'

I turn my head and glance at the gleaming river through the trees.

'What's wrong with that?' I ask. 'You said it yourself, she's stubborn.'

'I'm not sure I can do it, Nate.'

'But the nurses come to you. Can't they care for her here? If it's not much different to the hospital . . . If they can make her comfortable . . .'

'I don't mean that, Nate. I mean I'm not sure I can watch it happen. Here. I'm not sure I can watch my daughter die.'

Karen's teary. I nod my head, and she wraps her arms around her torso as if she's cold. I think about hugging her, but I'm not sure we're at the hugging stage.

'I'm new here,' I say. 'I don't want to pretend I know what's right for Gem. I don't. Anyway, it doesn't matter what I think.'

'Actually, it does matter, Nate. You matter a lot because Gem's mad about you. I don't understand it at all, but I've never seen her happier than she is right now.'

'Yeah, well, I guess I turned up a little too late.'

'Maybe,' she says. 'Or maybe you turned up just at the right time. I don't know how she does it, but she's a tough cookie, Nate. She wasn't always this tough, but she found something from I don't know where. She's battled through some pretty hard things, some awful things, and she never once gave up. Never. And that's why she's okay with it, I suppose. I'm not saying she isn't scared, but this is her time, Nate, and she wants you in it.'

Karen's smile is broken. She turns the corners of her mouth upwards, she does everything right, but there's too much sadness in her eyes.

'It's not the end yet,' I say.

'I know,' she says. 'But can you just talk to her? Can you try and get her to think about the hospital? She'll listen to you.'

'It sounds like she's made up her mind,' I say.

'Just talk to her, Nate. For me?'

Henry pushes through the front door carrying a plastic storage box. He's wearing his blue alligator polo top. The box is medium-sized with small holes drilled into its lid.

'Ready,' he says.

'All right, then.'

I glance at Karen and see the desperation in her eyes.

'I'll talk to her,' I say. But I already know that if Gem wants something she's probably going to get it, no matter what. And I'm even more determined to do what I promised and make Gem as happy as I can.

I stop Henry to check out his portable snake container. Buttons is inside, coiled up under a pile of gum leaves and bark. But Henry's in a hurry. He ushers me down the verandah steps and towards the trees.

He's struggling with the plastic box. It's awkward carrying it alone so I reach a hand out and take an end.

'How is he, Henry?' I ask.

'Same,' he says. 'He's not eating his mice.'

Henry holds up a clear plastic bag with a frozen mouse inside. I groan and turn away.

'That sounds bad,' I say. 'Although I don't blame him to be honest.'

Henry looks worried.

'Do you think this person can fix him?' he says.

'I hope so. Mick reckons he's the guy. People call him the Snake Whisperer, apparently. What kind of snake is Buttons, anyway?'

'He's a carpet python.'

'And how long have you had him?'

'Two years. Karen still hates him. She said ever since I got him she's had to sleep with one eye open. He's shedding, you know. Do you want to hold him?'

'No, thanks.'

I've never been mad on snakes. I can't see all of Buttons, but I can see enough. He's black and green and he's trying to hide under the bark and the leaves. When I get a proper look at him through one of the holes in the top, I can see the creepy sheath of dead skin, peeling from his coiled body.

'You sure?' asks Henry.

'Yeah. I really am.'

When we get to the shed, Henry's keen to hold on to Buttons so I drive the quad bike to the end of the gravel road and park it in the usual place. After shutting it down, I shove the keys into my pocket and the two of us head for the bus stop opposite the shops.

We sit on the seat next to an old lady and what looks to be her grandson. There's graffiti on the bus-shelter glass behind them, fat black letters I can't read. The boy leans sideways a little and tries to get a look inside Henry's box. He's all buck-teeth and bed hair.

'What's in there?' he asks.

'It's a snake,' replies Henry.

'Why is he in a box?'

'He's sick.'

'What's wrong with him?' says the boy.

'I think he's got an infection,' says Henry.

'What kind of infection?'

'I don't know. We're going to the Snake Whisperer to find out.'

The boy runs his tongue across his top teeth. 'I've got a lizard,' he says.

'What type?' asks Henry.

'A bearded dragon. His name is Aragon. What's your snake's name?'

'Buttons,' says Henry.

'That's a stupid name,' says the boy.

Henry shifts away from the boy a little. 'It is not.'

'Well, a snake should have a snake name.'

'I like Buttons,' says Henry. 'I called him that because of his eyes.'

'You should call it Caligula.'

'Why?'

'Because it's snakey.'

Henry decides he's had enough. He gets up from the seat and sits on the other side of me so that he's no longer next to the boy. I look at Nan and notice a plastic hearing aid inserted into her ear. She's busy reading a magazine so I glance down at the boy. I know I'm twice his age and I know it's pathetic, but I can't help myself.

'You've got bed hair,' I say.

'I do not,' says the boy.

'Yeah, you do. You should really think about wearing

a cap with hair like that.'

The boy swivels on his seat and looks for his reflection in the glass shelter behind him. There's nothing to see except black letters so he swings back around and raises his voice.

'Nan, have I got bed hair?'

Nan looks up from her glossy magazine and smiles. 'What's that, Kevin?'

'Bed hair,' he says again. 'Have I got bed hair?'

'What's bed hair?'

It's perfect timing. All of a sudden an orange bus appears around the bend. It begins to slow as it approaches, and when it pulls up beside the bus stop its hydraulics splutter and hiss. The door swings open and Kevin charges up the steps, leaving his nan to fend for herself.

There are plenty of vacant spots, so after we swipe our cards Henry takes a window seat about halfway down. When I slide in after him, the bus takes off and the two of us settle in.

According to Google it's a twenty-minute ride and a short walk to the Snake Whisperer's place. Henry puts the box down on his lap and gazes out through the window.

'My dad's no good either,' he says.

It's as if he's talking to someone outside. But I know he's talking to me.

'How come?' I say.

'That's what Karen said. I heard her talking to someone on the phone. She said he's a selfish prick who doesn't give a stuff about his own son.'

Henry pokes a finger through one of the holes in the plastic box.

'You could be my dad,' he says.

The puff of air through my lips sounds like a laugh.

'Why not?' he says.

'Because I'm seventeen, Henry, and you've already got a dad. But I could be your best mate. That's even better.'

'Why is it better?' asks Henry.

'Well, best mates don't tell each other what to do. Best mates look after each other and make sure everything's all right.'

'Really?'

'Yeah. And once you're best mates, you can't not be best mates. It's something that's forever.'

'So, you're going to stay, then, in Oyster Bay?'

'Yep. I'm going to stay.'

We both pause to consider what I've just said.

Henry fidgets with the box and straightens it on his lap. 'You're just saying that. You're just saying that, like my dad did. You're just like him.'

I shake my head. 'I'm nothing like your dad, Henry.'

'Promise, then. Promise me you'll stay.'

'I promise, Henry.'

And I mean it.

We motor past a marine shop on our right. Its yard is filled with a variety of tinnies and boats, but we're moving further and further away from the river.

'Everything's bad,' says Henry. 'Everything's bad and everyone's sick.'

'Not everything's bad, Henry.'

'What's good, then?'

I think about my time in Oyster Bay and all the things that have happened. I think about how it must be for

Henry, how it must feel to see Gem sick, to have Karen freaking out, to have Marty and Stevie, and probably the kids at school, at you all the time.

'You're right,' I say. 'Everything must seem pretty bad right now. But not everyone's sick, Henry. Only Gem and Buttons are sick. And Buttons won't be sick for long, not after the Snake Whisperer gets his hands on him.'

Henry leans sideways and angles his head so that he can see inside the plastic box.

'Do you think Buttons is a good name for a snake?' he asks.

'It's a fantastic name,' I say.

'But it's not snakey.'

'There's no such thing as a snakey name, Henry.'

'What do you mean?'

'Well, like all animals, snakes have Latin names, but that's for things like species and genus. That's a science thing. When you've got a pet, you can call it anything you want.'

'Are there lizardy names?'

'No.'

'But Aragon sounds lizardy. It sounds really lizardy.'

'It's not. It's just an old name. It's no better than Buttons.'

'It sounds better.'

Henry's not buying it, so I reach into my pocket and pull out my phone. I type in *Aragon*.

'Here you go,' I say. 'Aragon's got nothing to do with lizards. In fact it's got nothing to do with reptiles at all. It's actually a landlocked region in north-eastern Spain. He may as well have called his lizard Madrid or Seville. Or Dubbo or Wagga Wagga.'

Henry's in a mood again. He turns his head away and looks out at the rolling green hills to our right.

Through the window, the mottled sun throws shadows across Henry's face, makes it look as if he's got some kind of skin condition. I watch him for a bit, and although he's sitting right beside me, his eyes let me know he's somewhere else.

In a way, he reminds me of myself. He reminds me of what I did in Croxley when things got too hard. I used to do the same thing. I used to carry myself off to the jetty and imagine myself lying in the sun all salty and warm. I wonder where Henry is.

All of a sudden Henry nudges my side, and the bus veers left and slows at a stop.

'Five Mile Creek,' he says. 'We're here.'

When we get off the bus, I check my phone for the directions. They seem simple enough. Frankie's place is no more than a kilometre from the bus stop, a short walk up Kilburn Street, a dirt road not far from where we are.

Once we're clear about which way to go, Henry agrees to let me help him carry Buttons. We cross the road and walk about five hundred metres back the way we came.

The smell becomes unbearable after some time in the sun. Despite Henry's reluctance, I convince him to get rid of the decomposing mouse he left in the box just in case Button's appetite miraculously returned. We stop for a moment by the side of the dirt road, and after Henry lifts the lid and tosses the tiny rodent into the scrub we pick up the box again and start walking.

A few minutes down the road, we arrive at a black letterbox – number twelve – and swing left up the driveway towards an A-framed cedar house with a triangular *Play School* window in the attic. There's a dirty white ute parked in the driveway with gardening gear stored in the tray.

We head for the front door of the house, but halfway there we hear voices coming from the shed at the back, so I tell Henry to follow me down the driveway past a pile of discarded car tyres and a rusted boat engine propped on a metal frame.

After placing the box on the ground, I take a few steps forward and knock on the weatherboard next to the open door. Henry hangs back with Buttons.

'Come in,' says a woman.

I walk into the shed and see a man with a ginger beard and work boots. He's wearing a red velvet dress and he's standing on a small wooden platform just off the ground. Kneeling in front of him is a woman with blue-framed glasses, holding the hem of the dress, plucking silver pins from a pin cushion strapped around her wrist.

'It's sold,' she says, without looking up.

I'm trying really hard not to stare, but a bloke in a red velvet dress isn't something you see every day. Not in Oyster Bay.

'You here about the kayak?' she asks.

'Ah, no,' I say.

'The jet ski, then?'

'Actually, we're here about a sick snake. Mick said he called.'

Finally the woman turns her head and looks at me. 'You must be Nate, then?'

'I am. And this is Henry.'

The woman smiles and sweeps a lock of silver hair back behind her ear. I know it sounds strange considering we've only just met, but there's something nice about the woman's face. I don't even know what that means, but there's something about her that puts me at ease.

'Buttons is outside,' I say.

'It's not Buttons anymore,' says Henry from the door.

I turn my head.

'It's not?'

'It's Vulcan,' says Henry.

'What happened to Buttons?'

'I changed it. He's Vulcan now.'

After piercing the hem with two more pins, the woman leans back a little to check her work.

'Can you spin around please, Jethro?' she says.

The man does as she asks and turns slowly on the platform. The woman seems happy with the new length so she raises herself up and gets to her feet.

'You can slip it off now,' she says. 'Just leave it on the hanger. Wednesday okay?'

The man nods his head, steps off the platform and walks towards the makeshift change area at the back of the shed. There's something about the way he walks, something about the dress and the boots together. He's awkward and elegant at the same time.

When he slides the curtain closed, I run my eyes around the room. It's more of a studio than a shed. There's a chunky wooden table in the middle of the room with a mismatch of differently shaped chairs tucked in under its sides. A large crystal chandelier hangs a metre above the table, its dusty crystals draped in abandoned spider webs. There's machinery and farm stuff on the left side of the studio – a ride-on mower, a circular saw, jerry cans and various tools, but on the right side I see a fancy sewing machine, a collection of silver scissors and spindles of thread. Stacked on the shelves above the work bench, rolls of material are sorted into groups according to colours and patterns.

I swing my head back to the woman in front of me dressed in denim overalls.

When Mick mentioned the snake whisperer I presumed it was a man – a rough and rugged Steve Irwin type.

'So you're Frankie?' I say.

'I am.'

'Right, sorry, I thought . . .'

'Yeah,' says Frankie. 'Sometimes it's best if you blokes don't think too much.'

Frankie seems to think she'll get more sense out of Henry so she walks to the door. I follow her out into the sunlight.

'Can you show me Vulcan?' she asks Henry.

Henry nods and Frankie kneels down and lifts the lid.

'Hello, Vulcan,' she says. 'Aren't you a handsome boy?'

She picks Vulcan up and pulls some dead skin from him. It's the first time I've seen him up close. As he wraps around Frankie's arm – a brilliant coil of green and black – he looks more like an accessory than a snake, something you might buy at one of those outdoor markets.

'Is he going to be all right?' asks Henry.

Frankie reaches her left hand out and tickles under Vulcan's jaw. He seems to like it. He opens his mouth and she peers inside.

'Stomatitis,' she says, holding Vulcan up a little higher. 'Mouth rot. Do you see that creamy saliva and that sore on the left side of his mouth?'

Henry crouches down a little.

'I see it,' he says.

'Classic signs,' says Frankie. 'But he's still coiling, which is good. If he was really crook he wouldn't be moving.'

'How did he get sick?' asks Henry.

'Could be the temperature you're running in his enclosure,' says Frankie. 'It could be an infection or a parasite or a virus, even some sort of trauma. All those things cause stress and affect the immune system. It makes a snake susceptible to infection. Just like a person, really. The good news is we got it early, before it spread, before he really got crook.'

The two of them walk off into the shed with Vulcan. Jethro has changed out of the dress into a short-sleeved shirt and work pants. He nods his head as he walks past.

'See you round,' he says.

I nod my head and smile goodbye as he walks away.

I look around the yard, now that I'm on my own. Everything feels different away from the river.

I feel different.

I'm fully aware that the bus ride took us inland, away from the Glamorgan River. Ever since we left it, I keep looking for it, searching for its colours between the trees.

The funny thing is, apart from those times in Croxley, I never thought about the water much. I never had a reason. Growing up in Surrey Heights, I only ever thought about what was around me and what I could see. I never thought to step outside the bricks and mortar or to dream about something bigger.

I suppose my father taught me that. He taught me not to expect too much. He taught me that I didn't deserve anything more than what I had and that to hope for more was a complete waste of time. So I stopped dreaming altogether. I shut myself down and I made my world small.

And it took a dying girl in a tartan skirt to show me how to live.

# TWENTY-ONE

Unfortunately Kevin, the bed-hair boy, and his nan happen to be on the bus on the way home. Henry and I settle into a seat a few rows back from the driver, and soon we're on the road back towards Oyster Bay.

It's weird now, reading *The Old Man and the Sea*. Whenever I head out to do something with Henry, I tuck the book into my back pocket, just in case. But the reading itself has become different for me. I used to read it to feel closer to my mum, but now that I'm reading it with Henry, out loud, sharing what I'd kept to myself for so long, it's as if I'm hearing the words differently. It's as if the words themselves have been set free. When they leave my mouth they seem bigger, they're shaped differently to how they look on the page. They conjure things and paint pictures. They make me feel and see and hear in ways I never did before. And maybe that's what stories are for. Maybe stories are for sharing. Maybe that's why people made them up and told them in the first place.

'How's Buttons?' Kevin sits behind us and peers through the gap between our seats.

'It's Vulcan,' says Henry.

'I thought he was Buttons,' says Kevin.

'I changed it,' says Henry. 'Anyway, he'll be fine. I've got ointment to put on his mouth.'

Kevin's done something to his hair since we last saw him. He's used some sort of product to change its shape, but it's got that half-wet half-dry look, like a cat that's just licked itself in front of a fire. He sees me staring and offers an explanation.

'It's moisturiser,' he says. 'I got it out of Nan's bag.'

I nod. I'm not sure if Kevin's hair is any better than it was before, but you've got to give him credit for trying.

'What's the book?' he says.

I hold it up so he can see the front cover.

'Is it about fishing?' he says.

'No,' says Henry.

'Why's it got a fish on the front, then? And a boat.'

'There's fishing in it,' says Henry, 'but it's not really about fishing.'

Kevin pushes forward and wedges his chin between the seats.

'That doesn't make sense,' he says.

Henry rolls his eyes then glances my way. 'Where are we up to?' he says.

'The old man's just said goodbye to Manolin,' I say. 'He's about to go fishing in the Gulf Stream.'

'I thought you said it wasn't about fishing,' says Kevin.

'There's fishing in it,' says Henry again.

'So it's about fishing then.'

'It's about life,' says Henry.

I turn my head and stare at Henry beside me. 'Life?'

'Yeah,' he says. 'Life.'

'How did you know that?'

'I just did. It's about good things and bad things.'

After Henry's unexpected philosophical take on *The Old Man and the Sea*, I'm having trouble moving on, but he nudges me with an elbow and points towards the book.

'Come on,' he says.

I drag my eyes away and open the book at the dog-eared page. I read about how the old man loved the sea and how he always called the sea '*la mar*' because the Spanish always thought of it as a woman.

Behind us, Kevin makes a huffing sound with his mouth. 'That's stupid,' he says. 'How can the sea be a woman?'

'Well . . . some languages are different to English,' I tell him. 'In Spanish, ordinary things are male or female. And I suppose the old man thought of the sea as a woman because he was in love with it, and because the sea can be unpredictable – that's kind of old-fashioned, I guess.'

It's hard to believe I'm sitting on a bus reading

Hemingway to two young boys.

'I still don't get it,' says Kevin.

'You should meet Karen,' says Henry. 'You'd get it then.'

'Who's Karen?'

Henry ignores him. He points to the book again so I lift it up and continue reading from where I left off. We're almost there, almost at the part of the story when the old man hooks the marlin, but the bus slows down and pulls into our stop.

Kevin wants to hear some more, but Nan wants to get home and have a cup of tea.

After the bus departs and the dust settles, Henry and I take one end each of the plastic box and head for the shops to grab something for dinner. I'm thinking chicken as we walk across the gravel carpark, maybe some sort of curry and rice.

'Nate.'

I look up and glance across at Henry beside me. 'Yeah?'

There's no Singlets out the front today, but I follow Henry's eyes to the group of people filing out of Chester's. It's the usual pack of morons – Marty and Stevie, and their mates.

'Hmmm.'

'What does that mean?' asks Henry.

'What does what mean?'

'Hmmm.'

'It means I'm thinking,' I say.

'What are you thinking about, Nate?'

'About what I'm going to do.'

'And what are you going to do?' asks Henry.

'I don't know yet.'

'Well, I'm thinking about a caramel slice,' says Henry, looking nervously at the group.

'Don't be scared of them, Henry,' I say. 'Just stay close to me.'

I decide I'll wait and see what happens, kind of play it by ear. As it turns out nothing happens, nothing except for the matching smirks on the faces as we walk by. Rather than leave Vulcan outside, we take him into the shop with us and place him on the ground just inside the door.

Orange girl's behind the counter again today.

'Can I leave my pet here?' Henry asks her.

The girl sees the box and her face lights up. 'Is that a puppy?' she says.

'No,' says Henry. 'It's way better than a puppy.'

'Oh my God, it's a kitten.'

Before we know what's happening, she ducks out from behind the counter and lifts the lid on the box.

Underneath the toxic orange of her skin, I'm guessing she's turned a ghostly white. She staggers back into a rack of bread and knocks the plastic box onto its side. A variety of different rolls spill from the shelves and patter the ground around her. A chunky-looking sourdough loaf hits the top of her head and leaves a dusty flour mark as a reminder.

Vulcan uncoils. He pokes his head out from under the scattering of bark and leaves to check what all the commotion is about. He starts to slither across the concrete floor towards the dairy section.

'Vulcan, no.' Henry goes after him, calling his name, but Vulcan doesn't respond. I wonder if he's not listening or if he might not be fully up to speed with his recent snakey name change.

It's like some comedy skit. Henry keeps calling as Vulcan spirals creepily across the floor and disappears under the fridge at the back.

I know he's not poisonous, but there's something about a slithering snake in a domestic environment that makes my skin crawl.

I walk down the aisle and join Henry who's standing in front of the drinks fridge. I look down.

'He sometimes goes under the fridge at home too,' he says. 'He likes the motor. It's warm.'

I nod my head. 'And how are we going to get him out?'

'A coathanger,' says Henry.

'Really?'

'Yeah. A wire one.'

I turn around and walk back to the front of the shop. A smaller girl with a Billabong cap is trying her best to calm orange girl down. 'Breathe, Mia, breathe.'

Despite everything I decide that now might be a good time for diplomacy.

'Sorry, Mia,' I say.

'A snake?' says the girl with the cap. 'You brought a snake into the shop?'

'It's only a carpet python,' I say. 'And he's crook.'

'It's a supermarket, you idiot.'

I look at the girl and take it on the chin. 'Sorry, I don't think we've met.'

'Kirsty,' says the girl.

'You're absolutely right, Kirsty, I wasn't thinking. I do that a lot.'

'Obviously.'

I shift my eyes to Mia who seems to be on top of her breathing again.

'You wouldn't have a coathanger, by any chance?'

Mia lifts her head and looks at me like I'm the idiot Kirsty said I was. 'What?'

'A coathanger,' I say. 'A metal one. For Vulcan.'

'Who's Vulcan?'

'The snake. Actually it used to be Buttons, but Henry changed it to Vulcan. Personally, I think he should have left it as it was. It's confusing. He didn't seem to respond just now.'

Mia places her palm on her chest, then turns around and walks through the door behind her. She lifts a coathanger off a hook then comes back and hands it to me.

'Just get rid of it,' she says with a shiver. 'And hurry up.'

It's tricky getting Vulcan out. While there were never any coathangers involved, it reminds me of all those mornings when my mum had to coax me out from under my doona to go to school. But the good news is Henry seems to have done it before. He leaves the metal loop at the end and unravels the coathanger to give it some length. He drops onto the ground and lies flat, and when I shine the light from my phone under the fridge, he slides the metal line in, hook first. I'm lying on my side and can't see what's going on.

'Can you see him?' I ask.

'Yeah, I see him.'

'And?'

'Well, he's coiled around the motor,' says Henry. 'We might need another coathanger.'

Every now and then customers stroll into the store.

Some walk straight out when they discover what's happening, but others don't seem to mind at all. In fact one man walks over and crouches down beside us. He's short and stout and he's decked out in fishing gear – waterproof pants, a khaki vest with lots of differently sized pockets and a pair of sleek modern sunglasses that hang from a chain around his neck. Something about his outfit, and the collection of brightly coloured lures pinned to his top, tells me he's all bluff.

'Classic snake behaviour,' he says. 'What type is it?'

Henry looks up.

'It's a carpet python,' he says. 'His name is Vulcan.'

'Good name,' says the man. 'It's . . .'

'Snakey?'

'Hell yeah, it's completely snakey. I had a green tree snake once.'

'What was its name?' asks Henry.

'It was Elvis.'

'Oh.'

'He used to do exactly the same thing as yours. Anywhere that was warm. The fridge motor, the car engine . . . used to curl up in front of the open fire some nights. He was a good snake, that one.'

'Vulcan's sick,' says Henry. 'He needs to go home.'

As the two of them chat, I get to my feet and head to the front of the store again. Mia grabs another coathanger, and soon I'm back with Henry, unravelling the metal wire the same way he did.

I drop to the floor, then slide into position on my stomach next to Henry and wait for further instruction. Apparently the fishing guy has a double degree in zoology and is an expert on snake wrangling as well.

'You won't get it out with those,' he says.

I turn my head and throw him a look.

'I'm just saying,' he adds. 'You've got your hooks too big. He's going to slide out. You've got to bend them over. Smaller.'

'Do you want to do it?' I say.

'No.'

'Well, how about keeping quiet, then?'

'I'm just trying to help.'

A car horn starts beeping outside. It's a long blast followed by two shorter ones, a weird Morse code kind of thing.

'Oops, that's me,' says the man. 'Gotta go.' And just like that he walks away.

I shine my torch under the fridge and Henry and I get to work. Turns out fishing man didn't have a clue. We're able to hook Vulcan without a problem and pull him out from under the fridge. While Mia and Kirsty take themselves off to the storeroom, Henry returns Vulcan to his box. Vulcan's still feeling curious so Henry pushes his head down with his hand, then follows quickly with the lid as if he's resetting a jack-in-the-box.

I grab a basket and race around the store gathering up the things I need for dinner. A few minutes later I'm standing at the counter. I smile at Mia leaning against the wall in the storeroom.

'Is it gone?' she says.

'Yeah,' I say. 'He's outside in his box.'

Mia steps through the door and looks around as if she doesn't believe me.

'I'm really sorry about that,' I say.

'I hate snakes,' she says. 'I really hate them.'

'Yeah, well, I'm not mad about them either.'

Mia clicks into gear and starts to ring things up. After a few items she's returned to her normal self.

'How's Gem?' she asks.

I look beneath the orange mask and wonder if she really means it. She seems genuine, but I don't know what to say. I mean, what can I say?

She's so-so.

She's average.

She's bad.

She's good.

She's good and bad.

She feels like shit.

She's going downhill.

She's dying.

I have no idea how Gem feels, to be honest. I have no idea at all, and that makes it impossible for me to speak for her. She puts on a brave face when she's around me – but I know she's far from okay. She acts as though dying doesn't scare her, as though she's somehow ready for it, and I'd get that if Gem was eighty years old. I'd be able to understand it, but how can a seventeen-year-old be ready for something like that?

'Nate?'

I look up at Mia in front of me. 'Huh?'

'How is she?' she says. 'How's Gem feeling?'

I tap my card.

'I don't know,' I say.

I'm angry when I step outside.

I'm angry at the world for giving me people I love and then taking them away. I'm angry at the cracks in the footpath and the chip packet on the ground, and I'm angry at the smirk I see on Stevie's face as I walk past.

Something starts to burn inside me and I tell myself to ignore it. I look at Henry beside me. He looks nervous.

We're nearly past the group when Marty takes a step back. But Stevie can't help himself. He makes a sad face with his mouth. 'How's your girlfriend?'

It's sudden, like a flick of a switch. I stop dead in my tracks and feel my hands clench tight around the shopping bags. I hear two voices, the yes and the no, competing in my head, then I feel a hot familiar rush surging through my veins. I feel my skin prickle, my muscles tense. I feel alive. And I like it. I like it a lot.

Henry tugs at my arm and tries to get me to move off, but I'm too far gone. I drop the bags and turn around. Marty is standing behind Stevie, smiling his stupid smile. I see a couple of guys in the group wince a little and step away.

But I don't wait for anything more. I run as fast as I can straight at Stevie. I run with my arms and my legs, with every part of my body. I don't know what I'm going to do when I get there, but I'm thinking that a decent head of speed will be an advantage.

It's only a short distance I've got to travel along the footpath, but while I'm on my way, the group breaks up until there's just Marty and Stevie standing together. Neither of them seem to think I'll see it through. Probably because I'm on probation. But I don't care.

I drop my shoulder and slam into Stevie's rib cage.

I hear something crack. I hear him heave, and the two of us go careering back onto the footpath.

Landing on top of him softens my fall, but Stevie shoves me off, and he's on me in a second.

We scuffle for a bit and a fist smashes hard into the side of my face. The pain is unbearable.

A little dazed, I raise my hands to take a swing, but someone steps in and drags Stevie off.

'That's enough.'

I look up and see Singlets with his arms clamped around his grandson, holding him back.

Stevie's wild. Even from the ground I can see the veins pulsing in his neck. 'This fucker started it,' he spits.

I catch a glimpse of Henry from the corner of my eye standing off to the side. He's shuffling from side to side. I can tell he's frightened.

'It's okay, Henry,' I try to say, but my mouth fills with blood.

I get up off the ground and spit a ball of red onto the footpath. Besides the cut in my mouth and the shooting pain in my jaw, I've come out pretty much unscathed.

Turns out Stevie's not so lucky. When Singlets lets him go, he can't straighten up. He's bent over, wheezing, his right arm folded across his ribs.

'What the hell happened here?' says Singlets.

'He went psycho,' says Stevie.

'He charged at us – just lost it for no reason,' says Marty.

Singlets looks at me. 'Is that right?' he says.

Blood begins to pool in my mouth again. I can taste it, warm and metallic.

'Which part?' I say.

Singlets frowns. 'Don't be a smart-arse, son.'

The small crowd has circled around us. Mia and Kirsty are whispering in the doorway of the shop. Singlets surveys the onlookers and picks out the boy from the jetty with the face full of pimples. He looks edgy. He seems a bit different to the others. He's a follower, a foot soldier with a nervous face, someone who might've been better if he'd been given the chance.

'Tell me what happened, Gus,' says Singlets. 'And tell me now.'

Gus has a think about which way to go. But I know what he's going to say before he does.

'He went nuts,' he says. 'He was walking along the footpath and he snapped for no reason. He's crazy. He should be locked up.'

I feel Singlet's gaze. He's waiting for an explanation.

'You got anything to add?' he asks finally.

'Will it make any difference?' I say.

'Well, you can talk to me or I can ring the local coppers, if you'd prefer.'

I glance over my shoulder at Henry, standing by himself.

'I had my reasons,' I say.

'Yeah? And what might they be?'

'Maybe you should ask your idiot grandson,' I say. 'Him and his piece-of-shit mate over there. Ask them what they've done, what they've been doing for years. Or even better, why don't you ask Henry. Or Gem.'

Singlets looks at Stevie, and I can see the disappointment in his eyes. He might not know the full story yet, but I'm pretty sure he knows a good chunk of it already.

'What've you done now?' he says.

Stevie looks at the ground. 'Nothin',' he says.

'Yeah? I should'a done something about you a long time ago. Get out of my sight. I'll deal with you later.'

He turns to look at the group standing on the verandah. 'All of you – get out of here.'

Singlets watches Stevie go, then he turns around and faces me.

'I thought you were smarter than this,' he says. 'I thought you might have learnt.'

I nod my head and come careering back. As weird as it may sound, I never feel like I'm there when the anger happens, when the damage is done. I'm there in the lead up, maybe, in the moments before when the decisions are made, but when the actual fighting starts, it's like I'm looking on at a version of me.

It was the same that night in the house. The same when Morry came home and caught us there. The drugs don't excuse a thing – nothing does. I'm ashamed of what I did that night, I always will be. I think that's why I've tucked it away, buried it. Why I can't remember it properly.

I'm buzzing, but at the same time there's a constant when it comes to violence. The thing is, it never feels good after – not even when the other person deserves it.

And now I'm worried I've blown it. I'm worried that a few seconds of anger, a few seconds of lost control has shattered everything that's important in my new life. I've made promises to people, and I've let them down.

Singlets shakes his head. 'You need to do something about that temper of yours,' he says. 'If you're going to hang around, I mean.' He nods his head to the road. 'Go on, off you go. I'll sort this out.'

I feel sick. I walk over to Henry, and he shifts away from me like he's scared.

# TWENTY-TWO

I pick up the shopping bags with my left
hand and grab one end of the plastic box.
The two of us walk in silence across
the carpark, and I can feel Henry
snatching looks at me as we go.

'So, obviously I could've handled
that better,' I say.

Henry doesn't reply.

'I mean, violence of any sort isn't on.
You know that, right?'

Henry nods.

'And it isn't cool under any circumstances.
You know that too, yeah?'

'Yeah. Can we have the caramel slice now?'

'Sure.'

When we get to the end of the carpark, we off-load Vulcan's box onto the grass. I sift through the shopping bags, dig out the caramel slice and sit on the wooden safety rail next to Henry. I press down on the chocolate coating a little too hard, and when it breaks in two a swirl of gooey caramel spills onto my thumb. I lick it off and pass the good half to Henry.

He doesn't rush into it like I thought he would. He holds it in his palm and stares at it for a bit.

'You did a bad thing,' he says. 'Again.'

'Yeah, I did.'

'They're going to send you away.'

I look over and swallow what's in my mouth.

'You and Mick are my only friends,' says Henry.

'You could be friends with Kevin,' I say. 'I know he's got funny hair, but he's from around here and he like reptiles too.'

'I don't want to be friends with Kevin,' says Henry. 'I want to be friends with you.'

'We're friends already.'

'We won't be if you go.'

'Of course we will. I told you before . . . best friends are always best friends.'

'You're just saying that.'

Henry takes a bite, then tosses the rest of his caramel slice in the bin. He slides off the wooden rail, picks up Vulcan and walks off towards the quad bike parked at the end of the gravel road.

I call out after him, but my phone starts to vibrate in my pocket. I pull it out and read the message. It's from Gem.

*What u doin' handsome?*

I don't tell her what's happened.

I tap a reply. *I think u have the wrong number*
*No, pretty sure it's right*
*Ok then, am caramel slicing with H*
*There's 2 deliveries to do. U in?*
*Really? You sure ur feeling ok?*
*Yes.*
*On my way.*

*xx*

Henry's cracked it. He takes off on the quad bike without me so I have no choice but to walk. When I get home the quad bike's parked in the shed. To my relief, there's no sign of anyone, not even Barry, but then I see Gem sitting on a deck chair on the landing.

I wave hello, and quickly take the shopping inside. In the bathroom, I clean up my face and rinse my mouth. I sit for a bit with a tea towel and ice pressed against my jaw.

After a few minutes, I look in the mirror and decide it's not too bad. Everyone will notice when it starts to swell up, but maybe I can get through the day without having to talk about it.

When I'm done, I hurry down to the jetty.

Gem's smiling. 'Hey,' she says.

I don't know how it's possible to miss someone when they're not even gone, when they're sitting right in front of you, smiling. I never had that feeling with my mum, I never had the chance. One minute she was there and the next she was gone.

But this is different. With Gem I know what's coming. Part of me still hopes for some kind of miracle, and I suppose that's normal, but deep down I know there's nothing anyone can do. People say that death is a part of life and that is true, but there's a lot more to it than that.

A whole lot more.

Gem reaches a hand up, and I help her out of the chair. She stands in front of me and pulls me in.

She kisses my lips, and I close my eyes and for one tiny moment I forget what happened today and I forget what's coming.

'I thought we were doing deliveries,' I say.

Gem smiles. 'I lied,' she says.

'Yeah?'

'Yeah. It was a ploy.'

'A ploy? No one says ploy anymore.'

'I do,' says Gem. 'I need to get out on the water again, get some air.'

I look at Gem and something in her face seems different.

'Are you sure you're okay?' I say.

'Yeah, Nate, I'm okay. I just need to breathe.'

I nod, and Gem lets go of my waist. The two of us gather up a few things from the boatshed and then back-track along the jetty. Gem lets me drive and soon we're cruising towards Coppins Bridge.

There are a few boats out today, taking advantage of the blue sky and calm water. A water skier glides by on one ski. When the speedboat towing her clears our bow, she swings wide in a magnificent arc and slices through the water.

I turn to Gem. 'You ever skied?'

'I tried once,' she says. 'Mick took us out. I got up. And then down.'

She doesn't need to ask if I've tried it. Maybe one day I will.

I head for Gem's favourite spot. It's nice to be in the driver's seat. After the session with Mick the other day, I feel as if I'm ready to go solo. I keep it slow and steady to be safe, and Gem lets me drive without instruction. She spends her time gazing out the window instead.

Something about the way she's looking at things tells me her thoughts aren't for sharing so I keep my mouth shut and let her enjoy whatever's going around in her head.

Soon enough, Franklin Bridge casts a shadow across the bow so I slow *Forever One* and cruise past the huge concrete pylons and out the other side. The pace seems strangely fitting.

As we approach Horseshoe Island and the sandy stretch of beach, I steer left, cut the engine and the momentum keeps us cruising forward for a bit. When we run out of steam, I follow Gem to the back deck. I unhitch the anchor and toss it overboard.

Once everything's set, we sit on the edge of the boat for a bit and gaze out at the sparkling blue of the Glamorgan River. A gentle breeze picks up from the north, and carries the smell of trees across the water – the smell of eucalyptus and pine.

After a while Gem gathers up the long padded cushions from the bench seats. She tosses them onto the deck floor and the two of us stretch out. It's warm in the sun. We lie down next to each other and my fingers search for Gem's hand and find it.

'Little things,' she says.

I turn my head, and Gem's looking at the sky.

'What do you mean?' I ask.

'I stubbed my toe on the coffee table this morning,' she says. 'Hurt like hell.'

'Sorry,' I say. 'I'm not getting it.'

Gem turns side on. 'How often do you reckon you stub your toe?'

'Hardly ever,' I say.

'That's right, hardly ever. So I'm probably never going to stub my toe again. I'm probably never going to cut my legs shaving again, or leave the oven on.'

'I'm not sure they're things you're actually going to miss, Gem.'

'But they're things, Nate. And that's the point. They're things I'll never do again.'

'Okay, I get that, but what do you reckon you'll miss the most? What good things?'

'I'll miss Mum and Henry, of course. But most of all I'm going to miss feeling things.'

'What do you mean?'

'I mean I'll miss feeling the things that make you feel alive. Like that feeling you get after you go for a swim. You know, when you come out of the water and you're all goose-bumped and tingling. I'll miss that.'

'Yeah.'

'I'll miss sitting in the sun and I'll miss looking at the stars. I'll miss kissing you, and I'll miss that feeling I get when I haven't seen you for a while and then I do.'

I reach my free hand up and place my palm gently on Gem's cheek. I kiss her softly and when I pull away her eyes are big and wide.

'I'll really miss you, Nate,' she says.

I could look at Gem forever – there's so much to see – but

my eyes are blurry with tears. I remember the promise I made about not being sad so I touch her lips with a tiny kiss, then raise myself up and get to my feet. I kick off my thongs and slip my t-shirt up over my head.

Gem sits up slowly. 'What are you doing?' she says.

'Well, it's the little things, Gem. You said so yourself.' I nod my head at the water. 'Come on.'

'What, now?'

'Why not?'

'I haven't got any bathers.'

'Neither have I.'

Gem gets to her feet next to me. She has a look around and seems unsure. 'Really?' she says.

I shrug. 'Yeah, why not?'

'Righto,' she says. 'You're on.'

Gem's totally up for it now. She strips off her clothes, tosses each item onto the seat, and stands in front of me in her red tartan bra and undies.

She's olive skin and dark brown eyes. And a wisp of purple hair. She's gorgeous.

She catches me staring so she slips into poses like she's in a fashion shoot. We carry on for a bit, snapping pretend photos and the two of us laugh. Then she grabs a metal ladder from the storage seat and hooks it over the side of the boat.

She looks at the water and chews her lip.

'I'll go first,' I say.

I pull off my jeans and put one foot on the top rung of the ladder. I'm about to climb down when Gem steps up onto the side of the boat. Before I know what's happening, she leaps into the air and pin drops into the water.

She disappears, and I dive off the ladder. When I hit the water I stretch myself out and torpedo through the cool towards her. Water fills my ears. It makes a *glug glug* sound, and I hear a muffled boat engine whizzing away somewhere in the distance.

The water is colder than I thought it would be, and below the surface it looks brown instead of blue.

I come up for air, swim over to Gem and we wrap each other up.

'What took you so long?' she says.

Our lips are wet and slippery, and it takes me back to the white house on Pine Tree Island, to the first time we kissed. Maybe the two of us really were made for each other.

When we climb back up the ladder, the warm sun goosebumps my skin and I tingle all over. Gem's chest is heaving, and when I move closer to her I can hear her wheezing, struggling for air. I return the padding to the bench seats and sit with her as she tries to catch her breath.

My phone begins to ring so I rummage through the pockets in my jeans and find it. It's Mick.

'Happy Hampers,' I say. 'Nate speaking.'

'Mate, where are you?' says Mick. He sounds stressed. I don't think Mick ever sounds stressed.

'Just off Horseshoe,' I say. 'Why? What's up?'

'It's Henry. He's taken off.'

I tap a button and put Mick on speaker.

'He's gone off in the tinnie,' he says. 'He's been gone for a while, I think. He left a note. Something about the Gulf Stream. Any idea what that means?'

'Actually, yeah, I do. It's from *The Old Man and the Sea*. I think he's gone out into the heads.'

'I need you to get him, Nate. Now. The winds picking up. He can't be out there in a tinnie.'

I look back up the river, at the little peaks whipping up in the breeze. 'We're on our way.'

'Okay . . . and, Nate?'

'Yeah?'

'I'm going next door to let Karen know. Keep me informed, all right? If you haven't found him in ten minutes, I'll grab a boat from somewhere.'

'Okay.'

I don't bother pulling on my jeans. I unhook the ladder, then haul up the anchor and stow it away. I hurry to the driver's seat and start the engine, then I swing *Forever One* back the way we came and push down hard on the throttle.

'Nate?'

Gem moves up next to me. She's wearing my t-shirt.

'Mick says Henry's headed out to sea,' I say.

'Why would he do that?' asks Gem, taking the wheel.

I step aside. 'He's mad at me.'

'Why?'

'He thinks I'm going to leave.'

Gem pauses for a moment. 'Are you?'

'I hope not,' I tell her.

Nothing's happening on the two-way when Gem turns it on so we charge towards the heads at full speed about twenty metres out from the right-hand bank. We fly under bridges, roar past jetties, sounding the horn to warn other vessels as we approach.

Soon enough we're back to more familiar territory.

After rounding a bend, I see flashes of Gem's house through the trees. I see Mick's boathouse and a wall of purple bougainvillea set back amongst the green. After a few more bends I can see the start of the Glamorgan River, the headland on either side, and the white-capped sea beyond.

Gem points to a built-in cupboard on my left. 'Binoculars,' she says.

I get them out and after some minor adjustments I put them to my eyes and start sweeping the distance for small boats. The view through the glasses isn't pretty. Mick's right – the sea beyond the headlands is rougher than I thought it would be.

Out in the open, without the protection of the hills, the white caps are more like small waves. I stand in my boxer shorts shivering. The canvas canopy starts to flap about in the wind.

Gem's incredible. Despite the chop, she keeps *Forever One* straight and steady, and we motor out past a few boats heading for the safety of the main jetty. Once we're clear of the congestion, Gem swings us out to the middle of the heads and I glass the open water around us.

Henry knows the river. He's been out on the water with Mick and Gem for years, but the currents that run through the heads are no place for an eight-year-old boy and a tinnie. Even I know that.

I start to get even more worried when we can't find him and wonder if I should call the water police. But then I see something in the chop – a tiny silver tinnie, buffeting up and down about two hundred metres away to our right.

I point to let Gem know, and text Mick.

*Found him.*

Gem steers towards Henry. She looks exhausted, so I squeeze her hand.

'I'll go,' I say. 'Sit down for a bit.'

She nods.

When we get closer, I head out onto the deck. We're about ten metres from the tinnie, and I see that Henry's wearing a life jacket. He drops his head and does his best to ignore me.

Barry's there too. He's not sure what's going on at first, but when he realises it's me he heads for the front of the boat. Despite the rough conditions, he puts his paws on the tip of the bow then lifts his front half up and sniffs the air. He looks like one of those elaborate figureheads they used to have on old sailing ships.

I'm not sure about the drift and our distance from Henry so I glance at Gem and she gives me the thumbs up.

'What are you doing, Manolin?' I call.

'Nothin',' he says.

'You must be doing something.'

'I'm going to Cuba.'

'Bit far, isn't it?'

'I don't care. I'm going to Cuba, and I'm going to be a fisherman. I'm going to catch marlin and drink beers and smoke cigars.'

I look at Henry in his little metal boat, and I smile. It might just be the best thing I've ever heard.

'You're not moving, though,' I say. 'The engine's off. Are you stalled?'

'We're having a rest,' he says.

'Uh huh. You got enough petrol to get to Cuba?'

Henry's got no anchor down so Gem keeps us steady, adjusting our position to suit the drift.

Henry looks at me like I'm an idiot. 'We're not going all the way in this,' he says.

'You're not?'

'We're going on a cargo ship. I'm going to be a deck hand. If you work on a cargo ship you don't have to pay.'

'You've got Barry there too, I see. Hello, Barry.'

Barry pricks his ears and barks.

'And is that Vulcan?'

'Yep.'

We're five metres from the tinnie now. The wind is picking up so I sit on the edge of the boat.

'I'll miss you if you go to Cuba,' I say.

'No, you won't.' Henry sneaks a look at Gem behind the wheel. 'You and Gem are going to leave me,' he says.

The wind is really whistling now. I glance over my shoulder at Gem and decide there's no way she'd be able to hear us.

'Gem's not leaving on purpose, Henry.'

'She's going to die.'

'Yes, mate, she is. But she loves you, and she'll be here as long as she can. Me too.'

Henry looks at me and makes a face. 'Why are you wearing underpants?'

I look down. 'Well . . . it's underpants day,' I say.

'It is not.'

'Yeah it is. Second Thursday of every month.'

'You just made that up.'

'No, I didn't. Look, Gem's got her undies on too.'

I wave Gem out to the deck, and she steps out from the cabin in my t-shirt.

'See?'

Barry's not handling the chop at the front of the tinnie. He gets down and steps clumsily back to Henry.

'Come on, Henry,' Gem calls out. 'Barry's not happy there. Let's go home, hey?'

Barry steadies himself. He presses between Henry's legs and gets a pat for his trouble.

'I'm cooking dinner tonight,' I say.

'What are you cooking?' asks Henry.

'Curry.'

'What kind?'

'Lamb. With jasmine rice and poppadums.'

'What's a poppadum?'

'It's a crispy wafer-type of thing you deep fry. I've never cooked them before so I might need some help. Someone who knows what they're doing.'

'I could help,' says Henry.

'Really?'

'Yeah. I'm good at deep frying. I can do chips.'

'Awesome,' Gem says. 'I'll get us in close.'

Gem's an expert behind the wheel. She shifts us slowly sideways. When we're a metre from the tinnie, Henry tosses me the rope line and I drag them in.

It's no trouble getting Henry and Vulcan off the tinnie, but Barry's weight is a problem. I haven't got any options so I decide that I'll have to jump onto the tinnie and get him.

It's not easy. Barry drops like a dead weight as soon as I lift him up. He starts carrying on, starts trembling and quivering like a Shih tzu with a top knot. I'm in no mood for it so I try to remind him of his glorious past.

'Harden up, Barry, for God's sake. Imagine if your mum and dad, if your grandfather and grandmother, saw you like this. They'd be embarrassed. Your lot used to fight bulls.'

But he's not budging.

'Get it together, Barry. I mean it.'

Henry appears at the side of the boat. 'Gem says to leave him there,' he calls.

'What? In the tinnie?'

'Yeah. He'll be right. She needs your help.'

As fast as I can, I tie the tinnie to the back of *Forever One* and follow Henry to the cabin.

Gem looks pale. I realise she's not coping with the pain and it comes as a shock. She tosses a white tablet into her mouth and swallows it down with some water.

She lifts herself up off the driver's seat and when her legs take her weight she clutches at her side. I rush forward to help her stand, but she waves me away. It's the first time I've seen her like that – hurting like that.

I want to make it better. I want to make it go away and stop, but all I do is smile.

She smiles back, exhausted. After a few deep breaths, she asks me to get us home, then she puts her arm around Henry's shoulders and steers him towards the back of the boat.

'Let's have a talk, mate,' she says.

## TWENTY-THREE

It's good to spend time in the workshop with Mick again. Although we haven't known each other very long, and I've got nothing to compare him to, he's shaping up as a pretty decent uncle, all things considered.

I'm pretty sure that Singlets has had a word. Mick raised an eyebrow when he saw the bruise on my face, but he seems to have decided to let things slide. The bruise is fading now, a kind of yellowy red.

*The Best of the Bee Gees* is playing on the stereo, and there's wood dust and laughter in the air. Henry's been better over the last week. Today he's wearing his Viking hat, and he's sanding strakes, sweeping the sandpaper along the golden wood in long fluid lines. Seeing him happy like that takes me back to the day out in the heads. It takes me back to Gem.

People talk all the time about 'special'. Commentators throw it around when someone kicks a ball into a net. Television judges heap praise on pimply singers and call them superstars. Don't get me wrong, I can appreciate talent when I see it but those sorts of words need to be saved for something more.

Special is swallowing a body full of pain. It's knowing you're dying and still caring about someone who's sad. It's about getting out of bed when it's the last thing you feel like doing, and it's about finding a smile when there's nothing to smile about.

'You okay?'

I come hurtling back to the workshop and see Mick in front of me, checking the bend in a piece of wood.

'I think so,' I say.

He nods his head like he's not convinced. 'Where were you just then?' he says.

'Where I always am,' I say.

'And where's that?'

'Hovering.'

'Hovering?'

'Yeah, I hover.' I tilt my head and look skyward. 'Up there. Thinking.'

'About what?'

'About all sorts of stuff. I think about Mum a lot, about what happened after. I think about Gem all the time. It's hard to get your head around. She's the one who's dying, but she seems to be the one who's handling it the best. How the hell does that work?'

'I don't know,' says Mick. 'And I've known her since she was small. Maybe it says something about her. But she's not invincible, Nate. I know she acts like she is.'

The two of us stand there for a bit, lost in our own thoughts.

'I imagine it's pretty amazing when you find the right one,' says Mick. 'I thought I'd hit the jackpot myself there for a bit.'

I look at Mick. 'You sound like you've given up,' I say.

'I have. I've hung up my . . . well, whatever it is you hang up when it comes to women. I'm hopeless.'

Henry joins us by the window. 'You're not hopeless, Mick,' he says.

Mick turns his head and smiles.

'Gunter's right,' I say. 'Of course, no one's perfect and I'm not saying there's not work to be done, but there's got to be a woman out there who'll see the potential in someone like you.'

'You reckon?'

'Course.'

'And where would a woman like that be, exactly? They don't grow on trees, you know. Not around here, anyway.'

I look at Mick and smile.

'You never know, Mick,' I say. 'You just never know.'

It's perfect timing. The Bee Gees start singing 'More than a Woman', and when the chorus kicks in, Henry and I start to sing along. We dance around the Viking boat, twirling every now and then just to make it interesting.

Mick leans on the edge of the table, straight-faced, and looks at the ground every time we pass by. When the song fades out, he shakes his head then pushes off the table and hitches up his board shorts a little.

'Are you two clowns finished?' he says.

'I'm not,' I say. 'Not yet. Come on, Mick. You need to keep an open mind. It's about getting yourself out there, about giving yourself the best possible chance to meet someone. The answer is simple.'

'It is?'

'Yep. It's called the internet.'

Mick rolls his eyes. 'Forget it.'

'Why?'

'Because that's not the way I want to meet someone. It's fabricated. And it's creepy. I'm an organic kind of guy.'

'Yeah? And how's that working out?'

'Oh nice. Thank you.'

'I'm just being honest, Mick. And it's only because you should have someone nice. You deserve it. It doesn't matter how you meet someone, but just imagine if you did. Someone awesome. Everyone's online now. That's how it's done.'

Mick takes a long deep organic breath and then lets it out. 'I'll think about it,' he says.

I don't let on, but I'm jumping for joy. I start to run through what Mick's profile will look like when I write it.

After a while, the bell begins to clang through the trees, and Henry takes off his Viking helmet and heads for home. Mick turns the stereo off for a bit, and the two of us put our heads down and get stuck into some serious work.

It's different without the music. I become aware of

sounds – the sweeping of sandpaper, the tapping of the mallet and the gentle creaking of the wood. It's as if the sounds themselves are part of the work, as if listening to the wood might be just as important as the construction itself.

As far as I can tell we're not all that far from finishing the boat. There are only four or five more strakes to attach to the frame and once that's done it's a matter of sealing the joins. I don't mind saying that the idea of finishing the boat makes me sad.

# TWENTY-FOUR

Curry and poppadums have become Mick and Henry's speciality. The sauce is simmering in a crockpot on the stove so I take the quad bike around to Gem's to pick her and Karen up. When I rumble up the driveway, there's a small white hatchback parked in front of the house with *North Shore Nursing* written across its side. It makes me feel uneasy.

Karen's sitting on the verandah steps with a glass of vodka in her hand. She's staring at the water through the trees.

I kill the engine and walk over. 'Are you okay?'

Karen's had a few too many. When she turns her

head my way, the rest of her takes a moment to catch up.

She lifts the glass to her lips and drinks.

'She's dying,' she snaps. 'How do you think I am?'

All of a sudden I'm a newcomer again. I'm a stranger who missed the early hard yards and has no right to be part of the final chapter.

Karen closes her eyes, then reaches a hand up and buries her face in her palm. 'Sorry,' she mouths.

'That's okay.' I look to the front door. 'Can I?'

'Yeah. The nurse is here. Knock first.'

I rap my knuckles on the wood beside the screen door and call down the hallway.

'Hey, Gem. It's me.'

'Come in,' she calls.

I close the screen door behind me and walk slowly down the hallway to Gem's room. There's a nurse wearing a blue uniform and comfortable shoes standing beside the bed. She drops a needle into a sharps container, turns my way and smiles.

'Hi,' she says. 'I'm Sal.'

'Hi, Sal. I'm Nate.'

'We're nearly done here,' says Sal, rolling the IV pole aside and taping a small dressing over the needle prick in Gem's port-a-cath. 'I'll get out of your way in a sec.'

She turns back to Gem who's propped up on pillows in her pyjamas and a singlet top.

'All done, sweetheart,' she says. 'How's the pain, one to ten?'

Gem whispers something, and Sal puts a hand on Gem's arm.

'It'll take a moment to kick in,' she says. 'But it'll knock it right down. You're doing great.'

Sal runs through Gem's medication and scribbles notes on the sheet of paper on the bedside table. She checks Gem's chest with a stethoscope, tells her she'll be back tomorrow, then she packs up her things and says goodbye.

When she's gone, Gem pushes herself back towards the bedhead and props herself up a little higher.

'I'm still in trouble with Sal,' she says. 'She can't believe I went swimming. She reckons I'm overdoing it.'

'Sorry.' I pull a face.

Gem grins. 'Don't worry. It was worth it. Can you sit for a bit? Before we go, I mean.'

'Yeah, course,' I say.

I sit down gently on the bed.

'I need to talk to you about Henry,' she says.

I wait a moment before asking. 'What about Henry?'

'I want to . . . I need to make sure he'll be okay,' she says. 'He loves you, Nate.'

I wasn't expecting that word. It sounds so big.

'Don't look so worried,' says Gem. 'Love is a good thing, especially when it's coming from Henry.'

I think about our time together and smile. 'Yeah.'

'Look after him, Nate.'

'You know I will, Gem.'

'Good, now tell me a joke.'

'A joke?'

'Yeah, a joke. It's something people do to make themselves feel better.'

'I don't want to.'

'You promised you wouldn't be sad, Nate.'

'I didn't promise I'd tell you jokes.'

'Tell me one. I feel like shit.'

'I don't know any.'

'You do so. Everyone knows at least one joke.'

I sift through the rubbish in my head and pluck a long-ago memory from my days at school.

'All right, then,' I say. 'Did you know I'm friends with twenty-five letters of the alphabet?'

'No,' says Gem. 'I had no idea.'

'It's true,' I say. 'I don't know Y.'

It's one of the lamest jokes that's ever been told and, as much as Gem tries to resist, her mouth breaks into a smile. Mine does the same, then the two of us look at each other and laugh.

We laugh in fits, trying as hard as we can not to. But the more we try, the worse it is. Soon we're practically rolling on the bed. We do that for a while until Gem begins to cough.

It takes a few minutes for the coughing to stop, for the pain to become bearable again, but when it does Gem manages another smile.

'It wasn't even funny,' she whispers.

'I know,' I say.

Gem wipes her face with a damp washer, then tosses it onto the bed beside her. She raises herself up so that the two pillows are under her shoulders. She looks at me and the laughter has gone from her face.

'How's the movie going?' she says, moving over to one side of the bed. I move closer to her with my back against the bedhead.

'Well, let's see . . . There's certainly a lot happening for a short film.'

'Isn't there just?' says Gem.

'There's plenty of tension,' I say. 'I think we all know what's going to happen, but the talented actress – she's the star – she keeps everyone guessing.'

'She's good, is she?'

I look at Gem and catch her eye.

'Incredible,' I say. 'I've never seen anything like her.'

'Yeah?'

'Yeah.'

'So, we're talking awards and stuff, then? Even though the movie's not mainstream?'

'Definitely. I think it transcends genres – it's that good. We're talking Academy Awards, red carpet, the lot.'

'So, she'll need a date, then?'

'Of course.'

'What if she's single?'

'I'm pretty sure she's taken.'

'She sounds pretty awesome, though. It'd have to be a special kind of bloke to steal her heart.'

'Oh, there's definitely a bloke,' I say. 'He's got issues, though. He's laden, apparently.'

'Really? With what?'

'Stuff.'

'Like, stuff he blames himself for even though it wasn't his fault? Stuff he really needs to let go of?'

'Yeah, maybe. But he's also got some anger issues.'

'He sounds like a lot of work.'

'He is, but he's trying. And he's a really good cook, apparently.'

'Rubbish.'

'Nah, he is. Self-taught. Does an amazing steak and salad.'

'And is he musical, at all?'

'Well . . . he was.'

Gem raises her eyebrows and throws me a smile.

'I think you mean he is.'

---

It's been hard to watch Gem slow down. She was never one to dart around the place, but since that day on the boat she's been a lot more careful and measured in the way she goes about things. Every now and then she has to sit and rest, catch her breath so that she's got enough strength for the next thing she has to do.

It takes a while to get organised, but once we're ready Gem loops her arm through mine and the two of us walk through the front door.

Karen's still waiting on the verandah with a bottle of wine in her hand. She seems better now – nowhere near sober but more in control.

After putting Gem's bag in the back, we squash three people into the two seats. I try to avoid as many pot holes as I can along the way and soon enough we're back at Mick's place.

When we motor up the driveway, Barry bounds across the grass towards us. Someone's tied a fancy red ribbon through his collar.

A few seconds later Mick comes through the front door and walks down the verandah steps. By the looks of him, he's put in considerable effort. He's showered and shaved, and he's wearing beige chinos and a white shirt. He looks good. Presentable.

Everything is set for dinner so after some small talk we dish up the curry. The five of us take our plates and drinks and sit around the table on the verandah. Mick and Henry have done a great job with the poppadums. They're crispy and crunchy, a perfect accompaniment to the tender chicken curry.

'Delicious,' says Karen. 'A beautiful sauce, Mick. What spices did you use?'

Mick freezes for a second, then he drops his eyes to his plate and tries to recall the spices I gave him to put in.

'Well, the usual stuff,' he says. 'A bit of chilli, of course, some garlic . . . er . . . coriander . . .'

'Cardamom?'

'Oh, yeah, cardamom for sure.'

'And that leafy thing in there? What's that?'

'That's your green leaf,' says Mick. 'Goes by the name of . . .'

Mick glances my way, and I mouth a silent word.

'Bay,' he says. 'It's your bay leaf. Not essential in a curry, but it just gives it that little extra tang.'

Karen smiles. 'Very nice,' she says. 'I never picked you for a chef, Mick. It was probably the aprons. But this is very nice, very nice indeed.'

Gem dips her spoon into her bowl and scoops up some sauce.

'Any chance of a lift tomorrow, Mick?' she says.

Mick looks a little surprised. 'Sure.' he says. 'What did you have in mind?'

'It's just me and Nate,' says Gem. 'We thought we might head into town. Have a look around. And before you ask . . . Yes, I'm fine.'

'No problem. I've got a couple of things I need to do anyway.'

Mick reaches for a poppadum and crunches it into his bowl. 'That reminds me . . .' he says to no one in particular. 'Singlets gave me a ring, just before.'

Thankfully, Henry's more interested in his food. When I turn my head to look at Mick, he's got me fair and square in his sights.

'He told me to tell you everything's sorted, Nate.'

A wave of relief washes over me.

'Good news?' he asks.

'Yeah,' I say. 'Really good.'

'I'm glad,' says Mick. 'Sounded kind of serious.'

I'm not sure how much Mick knows or how much he wants to be told so I keep things vague.

'It was,' I say. 'But it's all done now. Finished. It won't happen again.'

'Good.'

Henry lifts his head from his bowl and looks at Mick and Karen.

'Did you know Thursday was underpants day?' he says.

# TWENTY-FIVE

Gem looks amazing when she walks through her bedroom door in a green tartan skirt, black denim jacket and red Doc Martens. Just for a moment I forget she's even sick.

Henry's insisted on coming with us, so Mick's had to borrow Singlets four wheel drive. We pile into it, and Mick and Henry start talking about their trip to the museum.

Once we're out on the highway, I watch Gem looking out the window beside me. She's good today. There's colour in her cheeks and a smile on her face. She's excited to see where I grew up, excited to know a bit more about who I was before we knew each other existed. But the idea of going back terrifies me.

I can't explain why I still carry with me a tiny pinch of hope. I thought I'd let it go after Croxley, but I haven't. In Surrey Heights, there were moments that were tolerable, moments when my father made it seem as if he was actually a good dad and a decent husband. But those moments were mostly for show. He played those roles in front of others, big-noting himself at barbecues and gatherings. People even said we were lucky. I remember some woman telling my mum he was a laugh, telling her she'd struck gold and she wished she had someone just like him at home.

The problem was that guy never made it home. Not the barbecue bloke, anyway. He saved all the shit for us. As soon as he walked through the door and closed it behind him, you could feel the change in him – the shifting mood, the unpredictability.

And when the door did close, my mum and I were forced to change too. We dialled our senses up to high so we could detect the little warning signs. We worked as a team because, when it came to him, two was always better than one. And he hated that. He hated what my mum and I had, more than anything.

It's a two-hour trip all up. Gem tries her best to stay awake, but after we stop for a snack in town and head out to the western suburbs, she falls asleep on my shoulder.

We pass through Benton and then Gladesville, and things start to feel a little like home. We always used to say that west was best, and I loved the busy streets and the shops and cafes crammed in next to each other. My friends were there. My life. I wouldn't have imagined being anywhere else. But after tasting what Oyster Bay has on offer, I think I've changed my mind about what home means – what it means for me, anyway.

The houses begin to get smaller, and when we hit Surrey Heights everything seems to run out of space. It's residential and commercial, a combination of factories and small houses and flats and shops. Since I've been gone the council's planted trees to green things up. The trees are identical, and they stand to attention, like soldiers on parade.

Gem stirs when Mick pulls over at the local shops. It's a hot day and everything looks dry and grubby. She wipes her chin, then lifts her head up and gazes outside.

'We're here,' I say.

Mick turns around and leans over the seat. 'Are you sure you want to do this?'

'I'm sure,' I say.

But Mick's not just talking to me.

'You could come to the museum with us,' he says, looking at Gem. 'It'd involve a fair bit of walking, but we could get you a wheelchair, push you around if it gets too much.'

Gem doesn't look impressed. 'I'm going to forget you said that, Mick.'

She turns to me. 'Let's go.'

There's no getting out of it now. I'm committed.

I point to a familiar building, a green-painted corner store with *Harvest Cafe* written on the window.

'You thirsty?' I say, getting out of the car. Gem looks up, and when I reach my hand out she takes it.

We say goodbye to Mick and Henry, wave at them as they drive away, then walk to the cafe.

The outdoor seats are filled with people looking at their mobile phones.

'Mum used to bring me here,' I say.

There's a baby boy in a high chair sitting with his mum at a table outside. It's the same spot where my mum and I used to sit. I don't know how long we'd sit there, exactly, but sometimes it felt as if we were there for hours. Mum would read. She'd take a book from her bag, and I'd jump on the iPad and play games. But I always knew why we were there. We weren't there for smoothies. We were there to escape – to be free – and it felt good.

'My shout,' I say.

I lead Gem through the door and look around for Mum's friend Sinead, the lady with the nose ring and green hair. She doesn't seem to be around so I order our drinks takeaway – a banana smoothie for old time's sake and a mango one for Gem. When they're ready, we take them outside. I take a sip of banana and it goes straight to my head.

Our old apartment block is only a short walk away. We go slowly, really slowly, sipping our smoothies as we walk. I can feel Gem snatching looks at me.

'Are you okay?' she says.

'I think so,' I say. 'It feels weird being back. It's been more than two years, but part of me feels like I never left.'

We turn a corner into Ferguson Street and I see them – the grey walls of the apartment block. I've never told Gem what they looked like so I'm surprised when she looks my way.

'Is that it?' she says.

I nod. We stop opposite the block, on the other side of

the road, and sit on the waist-high brick fence.

'We used to play cricket up the driveway,' I say. 'See those wickets, painted on the bricks over there?'

Gem smiles.

'And see that tree on the side of the road? The one all smashed up in the middle?'

'Uh huh.'

'Nick Kotuziak hit it with his Commodore when he was doing burnouts.'

I can't look at our apartment at first. I skirt around it. I look up and down along the balcony rails, and then I slow things down and settle on the second floor. It's two apartments from the corner.

Gem puts her hand on mine. 'Laden,' she says.

I turn my head to her and smile. 'Yeah. I guess.'

'You'll know what to say, Nate,' says Gem. 'You'll know when you see him. But you have to remember who this is about. It's not about him. It's about you.'

Boy, she's good. I'd love to sit with Gem for a bit longer or ask her to come, but I know this is something I have to do by myself. I squeeze her arm, then hand her the smoothie and start walking across the road.

I thought I might see someone I know, but school's just gone back so there aren't any kids about. Apart from the traffic, it's weirdly quiet.

As I pass the letterboxes, I recognise Mr Nguyen. He's wearing a straw hat and he's pulling shopping brochures out of his letterbox.

I smile at him as I go past, but he doesn't know who I am. He's not expecting to see me, I guess. Or maybe I've changed.

I head for the stairs and go slowly up them. The shape of the metal railing feels familiar in my hand. I hear muffled sounds from apartments and smell cooking smells wafting through the open windows. Finally I get to the second floor. Down below, in the carpark, I spot Mr Ritchie from number five, washing his car. I walk along the balcony landing and stop in front of number twenty-two. There's the gold metal tapper in the middle of the door, and the heavy crack in the wood down low.

I stand there frozen, and just for a second I think about leaving. I even turn sideways and start to walk away. But then I see Gem. I see her through the branches of the crumpled street tree out front. She's still sitting on the fence.

She's right. I'm laden, and I don't want to feel like that anymore. I want to feel like I did when I sat with my mum outside the cafe, free of him. And I don't want that feeling to just come and go. I want that feeling to last forever.

I don't bother with the tapper. I rap my knuckles on the door – four, five times.

I hear him shout something inside. I hear footsteps and then the door opens.

'Holy shit.'

He's surprised all right.

'You're out?' he says.

'Yep.'

'How long you been out?'

'A while.'

'Jesus. Why didn't anyone tell me?'

'They did tell you,' I say.

'When?'

'It doesn't matter.'

It's awkward as hell. He wipes a hand down his singlet, then runs his fingers through his thinning hair. He steps to the side a little, gives me room to get past, so I walk through the door and inside.

There's a cigarette in the ashtray on the coffee table, a column of purple smoke spiralling up from its tip. The place smells like booze.

'Do you want to sit down?' he says.

'Nah, I'm right,' I say. 'I'm not staying.'

'So, what do you want, then?'

The question doesn't hurt as much as I thought it would. But I am tempted to tell him what I want. What I wanted. I'm tempted to tell him about all the things he didn't do.

But there'd be no point. My father hasn't got anything to give.

'I've come for Mum's guitar,' I say.

My father has a think, then nods his head to the spare room. I walk into the corridor and turn into the first doorway on the right. I see the black leather guitar case straight away. It's standing against the wall in the corner. I crouch down a little when I get there, and I reach a finger out and trace my mum's gold initials, the K and the C, branded into the black leather hide. I wonder if he's kept her stuff for a reason, or if he just can't be bothered to get rid of it.

It's funny, but I can't remember Mum playing the guitar much herself after I started learning. I wonder if she stopped so she could give it to me, so I could have it as my own. I pick it up and head back into the living room.

'Drink?' he says.

I shake my head, and he walks to the kitchenette.

I follow him with my eyes and wonder if the top-right hotplate is still the only one that's working. It used to drive my mum crazy.

My father cracks a beer, walks back around the kitchen bench and joins me in the living room. All of a sudden the apartment feels so small. I feel closed in and trapped. I feel like I did all those years ago when the three of us would pretend to be a family, when my mum and I would tip-toe around him, when we would try to steer clear and give him some space when there was no space to give.

I don't say goodbye. I just head for the door, for the blue sky outside and Gem.

'You think you're better than me?' my father says. 'Is that it?'

I stop just inside the door. I want to keep going, all the way to Gem, but something makes me stay. I turn around, and he's standing there all tangled up and mean. I try to stay calm, but my right hand makes a fist and the anger begins to boil inside me.

'You don't get it, do you?' I say.

'So you're smarter than me too, are ya?' he says.

I step forward so that I'm closer to him.

'You're pathetic,' I say.

'Yeah?'

My father retreats, takes a half step back. And laughs.

'Like father like son,' he says. 'I know you'd like to think otherwise, but we're the same, you and me, whether you like it or not.'

'I'm nothing like you,' I say.

'Is that so?'

He looks down at my right hand balled up into a fist.

'Go on,' he says. 'You know you want to.'

I can't explain what happens next. I'm older now, bigger, and I've dreamt of this moment so many times. I've dreamt of standing up to him, of doing to him what he did to Mum and paying him back for all the years of hurt. But for some reason, now that it's here, I can't do it. I don't want to do it. I just want to go.

I take one last look at my father. I look into his eyes, then I nod my head and turn around and walk through the door.

When I cross the road, Gem gets off the fence and steps towards me. She hugs me tight and looks at my face to check if I'm okay.

And I am. I really am.

'What are you doing next Friday evening, around eight?' I ask her.

'Nothing.'

'Can we do something?' I say.

'Are you asking me out?'

'I am. If you feel up to it, that is.'

'Oh, I'm up to it, all right. What should I wear?'

'Something nice.'

I lean in and kiss Gem's cheek. I take her hand, and we walk towards the bus stop.

I don't look back.

# TWENTY-SIX

I've never been on a proper date before so I don't really know what goes on. But I've got plans, and it's going to be epic.

There are a lot of things to do. Things to borrow and buy. I've been in touch with Carpet Court and talked to Pete, the manager. He was a little reluctant at first, given the unusual nature of my request, but when I mentioned Singlets' name, he had a sudden change of heart and promised to deliver what I wanted to Mick's place during the week. Now all that's left is the food.

Gem's not eating much at the moment so I've decided on snacks, things that'll tie in with what I've got planned. I take the quad bike for a spin and park at the end of the gravel road. I toss the keys into the letterbox and walk to the shops.

There are a few loud tourists about, milling around the shops. Singlets is there too, sitting in his usual spot. He looks up from his coffee when I sit down.

'See that?' he says. He points to the froth on the top of his coffee. 'I just hired a new bloke for the store. It's not easy replacing Gem, but this guy's hopeless. Can't do a love heart for shit.'

A couple walk by in matching boating gear.

Singlets stirs in some sugar with a spoon. 'Still, I s'pose it'd be kind of weird getting a love heart from a bloke.'

'Pretty normal these days,' I say. 'You'll have to get used to it. Anyway, it's only a coffee.'

'Yeah, you're right. He did some sort of leaf, instead.'

So far, neither of us have mentioned what happened with Stevie. I've been waiting for Singlets to bring it up, but maybe he's waiting for me to say something.

'Thanks,' I say. 'For sorting things out.'

'You're welcome,' says Singlets. 'I won't be doing it again.'

'Fair enough,' I say. 'You won't have to.'

'So you staying, then?'

I turn my head and gaze at the lamp post for a bit.

'Yeah,' I say. 'I am.'

———

Back at the house, the day feels empty without Gem. When I get back and finish organising things, Henry and I make milkshakes and sit on the landing for a bit with Barry, watching the boats cruise by.

After that, Henry has a dive. He puts all his gear on – his weight belt, his goggles and snorkel and flippers – then he turns himself around, with his back to the river, and crouches down on the edge of the landing. Barry and I watch him with interest, and I laugh when he rolls backwards like a pro into the water.

Later on, the pelican visits again. He splashes down about twenty metres from the jetty and paddles over to see what's going on.

'Did you know their bills can hold thirteen litres of water?' says Henry.

'No, mate,' I say. 'I didn't know that.'

'It's true. And they don't have a nose so they breathe through their mouths. And some of them only live for ten years, you know. That's not long, is it?'

'No, it's not.'

'It's better than a butterfly, though. Some butterflies only live for one day. Can you imagine that, Nate?'

'I can't.'

'You'd wake up and have breakfast and maybe go to the shops. You might go for a drive or have a swim and then you'd have lunch. You could muck around a bit in the afternoon and have a cup of tea, then it'd be dinner. After dinner you could watch TV or play computer games and then you'd be dead.'

'You're right, Henry. Sounds like a good life, though.'

'What would you do, Nate, if you could only live for a day?'

'Well, I'd want to be somewhere nice, near the water.

And I'd want to be around the people I liked, people who meant something to me. I'm not sure I'd actually want to do anything. Maybe just sit around in the sun and talk.'

'Like now, you mean?'

Sometimes, Henry says the biggest things. I look at him and smile, then I turn my head and gaze out across the water.

'Yeah, mate,' I say. 'Exactly like now.'

# TWENTY-SEVEN

When the evening comes it's still warm.

There's heat trapped in the earth.
I can feel it radiating up from the
ground as I walk across it. I can feel
it in the boatshed as I stroll past and
I can feel it in the wooden planks of
the jetty. I know it won't stay like that.
When the sun disappears behind the
hills, the night will suck the heat from
the earth and splash its milky cool across the
sleeping town.

I've worked hard for two hours, I've
checked and double-checked and everything looks
amazing.

Now I'm dressed and ready to go. I thank Mick

for his help and head off on the quad bike to Gem's. I'm conscious of how unwell she's becoming. Some days are good and some are bad. All I can do is hope she'll be up for what I have in mind. But just seeing her happy will be enough.

When I get there, she's sitting in a chair on the verandah with a blanket draped around her shoulders. I park the quad bike and walk through the shadows towards her.

She smiles when I get closer. She puts her hand over her mouth and laughs.

'You've got to be kidding,' she says.

'Don't you like it?' I say.

'I love it. I really love it. You look fantastic. But I never picked you as a kilt-wearing kind of guy.'

'I'm not, really. I mean, I wouldn't normally wear one, but I've got this crazy girlfriend who's kind of obsessed with tartan.'

Gem reaches a hand out, and I help her up. She's wearing a green tartan skirt and a fitted black shirt.

'Hello, crazy girlfriend,' I say.

'Hello.'

She stands on her toes, and when she kisses me she smells like strawberries. I glance at the house and wonder if I should say a quick hello to Karen and Henry, but Gem waves a hand and steers me down the verandah. Halfway home I stop the bike and slip it into neutral. I reach into my shirt pocket and pull out one of Mick's old bandanas.

'I have to blindfold you,' I say.

'Really? Kinky.'

'It's a surprise,' I say. 'And you can't take it off until I say. All right?'

'God, this is exciting.'

I take it easy the rest of the way home. I rumble along with one hand on the handlebars and one hand holding Gem. Fortunately, Mick's agreed to keep Barry inside so there's no sign of him when we pull up in the driveway. Gem's a little unsteady when I help her down from the bike so I wrap an arm around her shoulders and hold her still. After a bit, we head off down the slope towards the river. When we get to the deck in front of the boatshed, we stop.

'I think I've been here before,' says Gem.

I stand in front of Gem and turn her slightly to the left so that she'll have a good view of the jetty.

'Okay,' I say. 'You ready?'

'Totally,' says Gem.

'All right, then, here goes.'

I walk around so that I'm standing by her side, then I reach for the knot at the back of her head. I undo it and the bandana falls from her eyes.

Gem gasps.

'Red carpet,' she says.

'Forty metres to be exact,' I say. 'You reckon they didn't think I was weird?'

'And the little lantern lights as well.'

'Of course.'

It looks incredible. In the fading half-light, thirty-five fairy lanterns are twinkling along the length of the jetty. A perfect roll of red carpet, the same colour red they use at the Oscars, starts at the landing and runs all the way to the end of the jetty. It's the only date I've ever been on, but I know already I'll never have another one like it.

I grab the bandana and wipe the tears from Gem's cheeks.

'They're waiting,' I say.

Gem looks around as if there really are people nearby.

'Who?' she says.

'The paparazzi,' I say. 'There are cameras everywhere.'

'God, no, is my make-up running?'

'A little.'

'Shit.'

We start towards the jetty, but Gem stops me a few metres away.

'So, try not to talk too much,' she says.

'What do you mean?'

'Well, you're my date. They'll be interested in me. You don't actually need to speak.'

I laugh. 'Oh, okay. I'll just stand there and look stupid, will I?'

She nods. 'If you could.'

Gem loops her arm through mine and we walk to the start of the jetty. We stand there for a moment and look along the red carpet rolled all the way to the end. On the hand rails, the little paper lantern lights sway in the gentle breeze, lighting the way. Gem takes a step and I go with her.

The carpet's soft under our feet. We walk slowly, stopping every now and then so that Gem can pose and wave to the invisible cameras. But the pretending doesn't last long. She sees the day bed at the end of the jetty, the blankets and pillows and the platter of food, and when she looks at me her face is different.

'It's beautiful, Nate,' she says.

At the end of the jetty, I lift the back rest of the day bed so that it's on a comfortable angle for Gem. We kick off our shoes and, after I arrange the pillows just right, we stretch out side by side. We share some popcorn and chocolate and slurp Fanta through red-and-white straws.

Gem puts her glass down and looks up at the stars, glowing in the darkening sky.

'Which one is she again?' she says.

I shift closer to her and point to the lonely star, away from all the others.

'There,' I say.

I take Gem's hand and the two of us lie there and look up at my mum's star.

'Do you think she would have liked me?' says Gem.

'She would have loved you,' I say.

'Why?'

'Because you're good.'

'Good?'

'Inside, I mean. She would've loved you because you're good and because of what you've done to me.'

'And what have I done to you, Nate?'

'You've made me want to be better, Gem, and I didn't really want that until I met you. I never had a reason. I know I've got a way to go. I know I get angry when I'm pushed, but I'm trying. I'm trying really hard. And you've made me see things, Gem, you've made me appreciate things that no one else could. I didn't even know about the little things before I met you.'

Gem smiles.

'They're not even little, are they?' I say.

'No, Nate, they're not.'

I reach for a blanket and pull it up over Gem's legs. When I lie back down, she turns onto her side, facing me, and rests her cheek on a hand.

It's perfect with Gem. I have to keep reminding myself that we've only known each other for a short time. But I can't think like that because thinking like that makes me wonder, what if? What if we'd had longer? What if we'd had years? A decade? A lifetime, even?

I can't help it.

'We would've been so good,' I say.

Gem looks at me. 'I know. You would've got sick of the tartan, though.'

'Yeah, probably. How many kids did you want to have?'

'Three,' says Gem. 'Three or seven.'

'You'll probably have to cut down on your acting jobs,' I say.

'Why? Can't you look after them?'

'I can, but I'd like to have a job as well. Henry can babysit. He can teach them to swim when they're older. I'm not sure about that snake, though.'

'Yeah, he'll be a good uncle. And Mum and Mick'll love it. We should think about travelling first, though.'

'Sure. Where will we go?'

'We'll have to go to Scotland and China. Paris'd be good too and New York.'

'Let's go to Greece,' I say. 'See some islands – Santorini and Mykonos. Just you and me, Gem. We can ride mopeds and eat cheese and drink wine. We can go to bed late and sleep in.'

'We can stay in bed for days,' says Gem.

I drift off for a bit and think about the two of us lying next to each other, tangled in white sheets.

'When we're old we can spend all our time boating,' Gem says. 'We can sit on the landing, or right here on the jetty, and we can drink tea from a thermos and eat shortbreads. And we can read books during the day and look at the stars at night.'

It feels perfectly natural planning a future with Gem and imagining the two of us together.

Gem might be planning our retirement, but I'm still far away, under the sheets in Mykonos, the sea breeze drifting through an open window.

'Nate?'

I look up, dreamy with thoughts of her.

'Yeah?'

'I need to say goodbye.'

All of a sudden everything comes to a grinding, shuddering halt. I look away.

'No,' I say.

'Yes, Nate. I want to. I want to say goodbye to you while I can.'

'I can't, Gem.'

'You can. I want to say it properly before I can't. I've never wanted to think about goodbye, but it's the perfect moment. You and me and all of this – the red carpet, the lights, everything you've done – it's incredible. It's the perfect ending to my movie.'

'I'm not ready, Gem. It's too soon.'

I feel Gem's hand on my cheek, soft and warm. I feel it shift to my chin and lift it up. 'Look at me, Nate,' she says.

My eyes find her face and she smiles.

'It's not really goodbye, anyway,' she says. 'It's more like, see you round.'

'Like a rissole, you mean?'

'Yeah . . . actually, no. It's nothing like a rissole. But I promise that even after it happens I'll still be around. Life will go on, Nate, and you'll need to go with it because you've wasted too much time already, but don't think you're going to get rid of me that easy. When you're out on the river, I'll be there. When you're sitting in the sun or looking at the stars, when you're at the shops, whenever you see tartan . . . God, you'll probably get sick of me.'

'Gem . . .'

She shakes her head and puts a finger over my lips.

'Wherever you go, I'll be with you. I'll be there when it's good and when it's bad. I'll be there always . . . except for when you're kissing another girl, of course. Although in my opinion the chances of that happening are pretty remote, given your poor hygiene and the teeth-sucking thing . . .'

She grins, but her eyes are sad.

'Knowing you a little bit was better than not knowing you at all, Nate. And it's funny because it feels like I've known you all my life. It hasn't been easy for you, I get that. It'll be a double whammy with your mum and me, but you've never once made me feel as if I was too hard. You made me feel special, Nate, and no one's ever done that before. Not like you did.'

I shift a little closer and breathe her in.

'You are special, Gem,' I say.

'You're not bad yourself,' she says. 'Even if you've got a bit of work to do.'

'Must be hard being perfect.'

Gem smiles. And this time it's the most beautiful smile I've ever seen. 'You've got no idea,' she says.

I smile back, but something's not right.

Gem takes a breath and shudders. Her face twists in pain and I see something register in her eyes.

'Nate . . .'

Blood begins to trickle from her nose.

'Gem?'

I call for Mick. I turn my head and thunder his name back towards the house.

I hear the screen door slap against the frame, and I cradle Gem's head in my hands. I lean in and gently kiss her cheek.

'No, Gem,' I whisper. 'Not yet. Please not yet.'

But I don't think she hears me.

# TWENTY-EIGHT

That wasn't the end, but it was the beginning of it.

We're all there when Gem dies.

Karen holds her hand. She sits with the nurse beside Gem's bed and watches her go, while the rest of us are huddled in the hall.

I'm so glad it's not the hospital. I'm so glad Gem got her wish. The shiny floors and the smell of disinfectant would have turned me inside out.

It's hard to remember much about the night my mum died. Being alone like I was, I always find it hard to latch on to the bigger picture. I remember little things. I remember the doctor who spoke to me, the one who told me my mother was dead. He was bald, I remember, not a single hair on his head, but there were tufts of black hair sprouting from his ears. I remember wondering if he had a wife and, if he did, why she hadn't told him.

But dealing with death is different with people around, with people you know and love. And it's different on Gem's terms – with the windows open and the warm river breeze drifting in. I'm not saying it isn't agonisingly sad but, in a way, the crying of tears and the not knowing what to say, all those things make it human somehow.

Losing Gem feels like a shared thing, a kind of spreading of the load. I suppose there's comfort to be found in knowing that others around you are sad too.

It's something I never had when my mum took her last breath. The nurses were polite enough. One of them sat with me for half an hour, I reckon. I'm not sure if she wanted to, to be honest. While she was next to me she kept snatching looks at her watch, and I couldn't help wondering if she was thinking about her next break or what she was going to have for dinner or some other job she was supposed to be doing. There were others who sat with me too – a policewoman and someone from some government department – but nothing they were saying mattered. When I couldn't listen any longer I told them I had to go to the toilet and when I got there, to the signs in the corridor, I ran straight past. I ran out of the hospital, then I got angry and I stayed that way for a very long time.

But today, I don't want to run.

When we're told Gem's gone, Henry doesn't know

what to do. He's completely lost. He can't even speak. He just makes noises. Karen brings him Vulcan, and he seems calmer when the snake coils itself around his forearm.

After a while Mick comes over and the four of us bunch together.

I can't stop crying.

Everything's a blur, but I remember what Gem said. I'll take her with me everywhere I go. She'll never be gone and it's not really the end.

It's just different.

# TWENTY-NINE

It's as if Gem's had a hand in the weather.

It's sunshine and blue skies when we board *Forever One*. When Barry realises he's about to be left behind, he jumps on too and prances up to the front of the boat to assume his position on the bow.

I take the wheel now that I've got my licence, and Karen brings Gem up in the urn and places her on the dash like she asked us to. It's busier than usual on the river. As well as the fishing boats there are water skiers and speedboats, stand-up paddle boards, kayaks and canoes, but like always their numbers start to thin the further down the Glamorgan we go.

I'm not in a hurry to sprinkle Gem into the river so I cruise at an easy speed and enjoy the time I have left with her above water. Karen seems to be doing the same in the passenger seat beside me so I reach over and squeeze her hand.

'You okay?' I say.

She looks at me and smiles.

'Well . . . I'm a lot better than I thought I'd be, Nate. It's that bloody happiness contract, I reckon. I can't believe she got it framed and put it on the wall. Every time I walk past mine, I can't help smiling. Stubborn – right to the end. She's the best thing I ever did.'

It's a strange mix of emotions when I cut the engine and glide into the little cove near Gem's favourite stretch of beach. I'm filled with memories of her. The two of us swimming together in our undies. Delivering a hamper to her favourite house. And sitting on the white couch talking and kissing. I remember all the little things she loved.

Someone tugs at my arm. I turn around and see Mick standing beside me.

'You hovering again?' he says.

'Yeah.'

Mick nods his head to the back of the boat. 'It's time.'

Everyone's gathered on the deck, even Barry, who's tucked between Henry's legs. I walk over to Karen who's put on sunglasses and a floppy wide-brimmed hat. She's hugging the urn, holding it tight to her chest. Gem's made it clear how she wants things to go. I smile at Karen and take a piece of paper from my pocket and clear my throat.

I start to read.

*Hi, it's Gem,*

*First off, I want to remind you all about your contractual obligations.*

*So if you're not smiling, I want you to smile. I want you to hold the person's hand next to you and I want you to look up. It's sunny, right? I knew it would be.*

*I'm not going to bang on for long because it's not about me anymore. It's about all of you. But before I get sprinkled, I wanted to say thank you to each one of you for being a part of me. I would've liked more time. I would've liked to love you all more. I would've liked to have been well. But for some reason that wasn't the way it was supposed to be, and you can't argue with the way it's supposed to be.*

*I'm going to miss you all. And I'm going to miss the little things. But I'll never really be gone. I'll be everywhere. All you have to do is look.*

*See you around,*

*Gem*

I fold the piece of paper up and when I hand it to Karen she puts it in her pocket. She lifts the urn to her lips and kisses it, then she takes off its lid and sprinkles Gem's ashes into the sparkling blue water.

'Float and drift,' she says. 'You're free, my love.'

———

That afternoon is soft and warm. Henry and Barry join me on the landing.

We walk to the very edge, and Henry lifts a leather satchel from his shoulder. He dives a hand in and removes a glass jar. It's a jam jar with the old label removed and replaced with a brand-new white sticker. Written on the sticker in black texta is the name *Gem*. After unscrewing the lid, Henry reaches down to the river and scoops some water into the jar. He brings it up for a closer look and smiles then screws the lid back on. The two of us sit down in the chairs, and Henry puts the glass jar on the armrest next to him.

He looks out across the river. 'We're going to be Vikings tomorrow,' he says.

'We are, mate. Are you going to bring Gem when we launch it?'

'I'm going to take her everywhere.'

'Good man.'

The pelican's back. Barry sits up and watches it glide across the glassy water in front of us.

'Can you play us a song, Nate?' he says.

I look at the jam jar again, at Gem's name written on the white sticker. I throw her a smile, then I reach down and pick up my mum's guitar.

And play.

# ACKNOWLEDGEMENTS

First off, a special thank you to Laura Harris and Kristin Gill. It's been a few years now, and I'm forever grateful for your advice and for your continued support and friendship. To the wonderful Michelle Madden – the first person to mention the words 'love story' – thank you for knowing, and for making me see all the things I hadn't seen. *Promise Me Happy* is a better story because of you.

A lot of work goes into making a book and I am grateful to everyone at Penguin Random House who had a hand in that, especially Tina Gumnior, Dot Tonkin, Angela Duke and Windle. And the brilliant Marina Messiha – for her beautiful artwork. I loved it as soon as I saw it.

A big thank you to Rob Armstrong for his generosity and the stints at Hepburn View.

And to Daniella and Susie for Mornington.

I was born lucky, I reckon, in more ways than one, so to the two people who were there first – my parents, Margie and George Newton – thank you for showing me the way.

And lastly, to my four glorious girls who make me appreciate the little things every day.

You know how much.

———

Working on *Promise Me Happy* opened my eyes to many things I didn't know, especially on the subject of leukaemia and the amazing people who live with it day to day. I'd like to thank my friend Kate Page for her invaluable help and guidance, and Leukaemia Foundation for their enthusiasm for this project.

Leukaemia Foundation do amazing work with cancer patients and their families, so if you'd like to find out more about what they do, or if you'd like to become a blood or bone marrow donor, go to www.leukaemia.org.au for details.

# NOTE FROM THE AUTHOR

During a brief stint at uni, I worked part time as an orderly in a palliative care hospital. The hospital was divided into two sections and cared for patients with multiple sclerosis and patients with cancer.

I'll never forget my time there and the things I experienced. Amongst all the sadness and pain, in the middle of all the uncertainty and fear, there was also a lot of joy. There was hope and laughter too. It made me examine how I thought about life.

I've always been interested in people who are thought of as 'fringe dwellers' or 'outsiders'. I've always found them the most interesting people to write about. Perhaps that's got something to do with my own childhood. My father was an army officer so every year we had to move to different postings interstate or overseas. As you can imagine, it was a very restless sort of life, an unsettled and uncertain way to live, and by the time I was twelve I'd been to eight different schools. During that time, I never really felt as if I was a part of anything. I never felt as if I belonged.

So *Promise Me Happy* became a combination of those two things – that sense of being different, and my memories of joy in the face of sadness.

I'm not really sure, when we're talking about people, if 'different' is a word that has a place anymore. But if it means we're not all the same, then I reckon that's a good thing. Being different is something to be celebrated and, despite what some people might think, it's everything that's right with the world.

The fractured characters in *Promise Me Happy* – off-the-rails Nate and lonely Mick, stubborn Gem and wide-eyed Henry – are people you might meet every day without knowing the challenges they're facing. They live in a small country town, a place that harbours small ideas and intolerance, a place where masculinity is on the nose, where most of the young men don't know any better because they haven't been shown.

Initially the characters I threw together grated and butted heads. They were wary and guarded and unsure. But after a while something quite unexpected happened and the story found its heart. *Promise Me Happy* is a love story, and a story about family and what can happen when you find your people. It's a story about knowing and not knowing. It's about beginnings and ends, and about the little things in life we take for granted.

One of the things I love about writing is being surprised.

And *Promise Me Happy* was certainly full of surprises, full of right turns and left hooks. It ended up being a totally different story to what I had in mind when I started.

I hope you like it.

Robert Newton

**Full teachers' notes are available at:**
**penguin.com.au/teachers**

# Discover a
# new favourite

Visit **penguin.com.au/readmore**